Variation Seven

Mike Manolakes

Copyright 2014 Mike Manolakes

First Print Edition February 2016
Second Print Edition January 2017

ISBN 978-1-329-24618-8

For Rae, my past, present, and future.

Chapter 1

All of the windows of the diner exploded inward.

One moment Ruthie McDonald was standing, pouring coffee for one of her regular customers at booth six; the next, she was lying on the floor of the restaurant covered with broken glass. There was dust in the air, in her hair, and in her mouth, and she coughed to try to clear it from her air passages. It didn't help — every breath brought more of it into her lungs. She ached all over, but outside of a few scratches, she didn't seem to be bleeding anywhere. No sharp piece of glass had pierced her throat, no limbs ended in bloody stumps, so it seemed she was going to live.

Everything seemed deathly quiet, but as she rose to her knees and looked around, she realized that it couldn't be this quiet: everywhere was confusion. People looked like they were shouting and crying and screaming. Then she understood that the concussion had deafened her, and the unnatural quiet was due only to her inability to hear the chaos all around her.

Looking out of what was left of the window, all Ruthie could see was a great cloud of dust, with loose sheets of newspaper flying everywhere. Slowly awareness had begun to sink in — a bomb had exploded, somewhere nearby. Not in the diner itself, but maybe across the street, close enough to blow out all the windows and knock her to the floor. People were hurt, probably killed, but she was lucky, she had escaped with only a few scratches. She got to her feet, looking to see what she could do to help.

She noticed that the table at booth six was cleared of everything — a stack of newspapers had been blown all over the place by the blast, and even the coffee cups and silverware had ended up elsewhere. Then she remembered that her customer, the fair haired young man that his friend had called Miles, was gone. She didn't remember seeing him run past her, though he must have. And then she remembered his friend, the older man called Jack. Jack had gone across the street to buy another newspaper. The newsstand, once visible through the window, was completely obliterated.

There were people in the diner crouched under tables, sobbing and shaking, unable to place themselves at any further risk. Ruthie fought the urge to do the same and chose instead to do the opposite. She had to get outside and see if there was anything she could do to help. Carefully she made her way through the smashed glass and panicking customers within the diner and headed out the front door. Outside, dust and blowing papers were everywhere. Cars were stopped in the middle of the street, doors open, their occupants having left them to seek safety elsewhere. Ruthie could faintly hear, as if underwater, the sounds of sirens approaching. Good — her hearing was slowly returning.

Pieces of the newsstand were scattered everywhere. The bomb, if that's what it was, must have been close by the newsstand to destroy it completely. It might have even been in the newsstand. The nearest building was also heavily damaged, with much of the outer wall on the ground floor blown away. There was smoke in the air, and though she didn't see any open flames yet, something must be burning somewhere inside the building. Here and there were injured people, some moaning and limping away, some still and unmoving on the pavement. Those she couldn't tell if they were alive or dead. She wanted to help them all, but she needed to find Jack first. He had to have been near the newsstand when the bomb exploded, and must have been caught in the blast.

Why did she feel she must find him? She hardly knew him, and so many needed to be helped. But in her befuddled state, as she struggled to come to grips with the enormity of what had just happened, one thought seemed to override the rest: *he is my customer. I'm supposed to take care of my customers.*

Just fifteen minutes ago, it had seemed like a perfectly normal beginning to a typical day. Ruthie had just begun her shift at the diner, located on a busy corner in an eclectic Chicago neighborhood, where office buildings were squeezed between sushi bars and tattoo parlors. Ruthie knew most of her regular customers by sight. They knew her by name — it was on the name tag on her mint-green uniform top — but she generally didn't know theirs. Most of them wolfed down their eggs with a splash of coffee, then it was out the door to the office complex across the street. With luck, they'd remember to leave a reasonable tip behind.

But when Ruthie started her shift, she noted that table six, by the window, had her two most regular customers, and it was these two that were the exception to the rule. They never seemed to be in a hurry, but instead would sit in the booth for at least four hours, well into mid-morning, with a stack of newspapers in front of each of them. Ruthie would bring them a continuous supply of coffee and make small talk with the pair, who would always be friendly but never seemed to offer many clues as to why they were there, day after day.

The older man, who looked to be in his late forties, was balding with heavy eyebrows and a prominent nose. Ruthie had a good ear for accents, and his suggested New York. From his no-nonsense manner, she had the feeling he was a cop, although she'd never seen any sign of a badge or gun on him. The younger man looked to be about Ruthie's age, which was twenty-seven. He was fair-skinned with light brown hair and a neatly-trimmed mustache. Both his accent and manners suggested the South, though Ruthie couldn't place exactly where. But like his companion, he never volunteered any personal information about himself.

Each morning, the two men sat by the window, drinking coffee and reading newspapers. The newspapers, Ruthie could see, came from all over the country, and some from overseas. Occasionally one would stop and circle in red an item in a paper, or stop to show it to the other. But Ruthie would never be close enough to hear what they were saying about it, and if she walked to their booth to refill a coffee cup while they were discussing a news item, they stopped talking as soon as she was close enough to hear.

It all seemed very mysterious, and Ruthie couldn't help weaving stories in her mind about who the two men were, and what they were up to. Whatever it was, they seemed so serious and intent on their work, which Ruthie enjoyed imagining was something slightly illegal and probably dangerous. Maybe they were foreign spies, looking for coded messages buried on page 7 of the Des Moines Register. Ruthie hoped it was true, though it didn't seem very likely. Whoever they were, they were polite to her, tipped her well, and always had a smile and a friendly greeting for her when they saw her.

And during the eight hours of a mind-numbingly routine job, they were the most interesting part of her day, so Ruthie found she spent much of it observing them from across the room. She had long ago decided they were no more than professional colleagues, not really close friends, and certainly not a gay couple —

like herself, they were merely going through the daily routine of a job they had to do. She just had no idea what it could be.

She caught herself studying them again this morning, and then she noticed that one or both of them was conscious of being watched by her. So she decided to make her way to their booth to refill their coffees.

"Thank you, Ruthie," the younger man said, polite as always. The older man did not look up; he was circling an item on the financial page of the Boston Globe.

"Got enough papers today?" Ruthie asked innocently. Today's stack was at least twenty newspapers, no less than any other day.

The younger man paused to look at the stack, as if seeing it for the first time. "We could use a few more, I guess," he said with a straight face.

Ruthie didn't know if he was joking, but she decided to play along. Maybe they would say something that would reveal the point of this strange exercise. "There's a newsstand across the street. I'm sure there's a few over there you don't have yet."

At this the older man looked up and glanced out the window. A white van was pulling up to the newsstand, decorated with an oversized logo of the Chicago Sun-Times. The back door of the van opened and bundles of newspapers were being tossed out to the curb. "Next edition of the Sun-Times is here," he said. "Miles, mind if I...?"

"Go ahead, Jack." Miles and Jack. Finally she had names to go with the faces.

The older man — Jack — got up from the booth. "Excuse me," he said as he crossed Ruthie from behind, never making eye contact, and headed for the diner's front door.

"I was only kidding, you know," Ruthie said after Jack had left. "Really, it looks like you've got enough newspapers here for... whatever it is you do with them."

"That's all right," Miles said in his soft Southern drawl. "Jack gets a little obsessive about his papers. So do I, I guess. One or two more won't make any difference at all."

There was a pause in the conversation, and Ruthie said, "Your breakfast will be up in a minute," which was true. She wanted to ask what the papers were for, but she found she couldn't. What if they were doing something nefarious? Something not quite legal, not quite moral? Would proper polite Miles tell the truth about what they were doing, or would he tell a charming lie? Or would he suddenly turn cold and refuse to talk, thus ending the possibility of any more pleasant morning banter, not to mention a good tip? In any case, what they were doing was their own business, and Ruthie had no right to invade their privacy.

So she changed the subject. "Have you and Jack known each other long?"

"Ages," Miles said, and chuckled softly to himself. Ruthie laughed with him, not knowing how that could possibly be funny. Then, as if there should be no misunderstanding about in what sense they were together, he added, "We're not a couple, if that's what you're thinking. We just work together."

"Oh, no. I didn't mean to imply —" Embarrassed, Ruthie started pouring more coffee into Miles's cup, even though she had just refilled it two minutes earlier. She had to change the subject, so she went instead to the one question she had been previously avoided. "So what do you do with all those papers?"

Miles looked up at her, his pale blue eyes locked onto her own. For a moment, Ruthie thought he didn't know whether to tell her the truth, or concoct a fabulous lie.

She never knew what he was going to say, for at that moment all the windows of the diner exploded inward.

Chapter 2

He is my customer. I'm supposed to take care of my customers.

Rational or not, that thought led Ruthie to dash across the bomb-blasted street, around stopped cars and trucks, and search the debris where the newsstand once stood to find Jack.

It took a moment for Ruthie to get her bearings. Was this where the newsstand had been? There was very little here to suggest it, but she could see the nearby intersection, and she knew how far up the street the small blue and white structure had stood. Apart from the newspaper pages flying everywhere, no trace of the newsstand remained. But where was Jack? Then, in the midst of a pile of concrete rubble, she saw a figure lying motionless on the ground. The body was coated with a layer of white dust and ash, but Ruthie knew it must be Jack.

When she approached him, Ruthie found that Jack was pinned under a concrete slab that had fallen from the building facade. She had no medical training, but she didn't need any to realize at once that he wasn't going to survive. He was struggling to breathe, and blood was starting to trickle from his mouth as his eyes rolled back into his head. One hand was still clutching the late morning edition of the Sun-Times.

"Hang on," Ruthie pleaded, although she wasn't sure if she was speaking to Jack or herself. "Help will be here soon."

But she knew help would not be here soon enough. Any emergency personnel in the area were already occupied dealing with casualties that numbered at least in the dozens. Jack would be gone before they could get to him.

Ruthie couldn't move the concrete slab, and she knew that wouldn't even save him if she could. All she could do was cradle Jack's head in her lap as his life was slipping away. Tears came to her eyes as he dropped the newspaper. With his last effort, he tugged at the left sleeve of his jacket as he coughed up more blood.

Ruthie watched, confused, as Jack undid the cuff button on his shirt sleeve and pulled it back. There was something wrapped around his forearm. From a distance it would be invisible, but up close Ruthie could see that it was a fine mesh, about seven inches in length, that enclosed his arm. Within the strands of mesh, yellow and green lights were dimly glowing and flashing. It fit his arm so snugly, it was almost a second skin. Obviously Jack meant to show this thing to Ruthie, but he would not get the chance to tell her why. His body went limp; his breathing stopped.

At the instant of his death, the tiny lights in the mesh stopped glowing. A seam that had not been visible before down the length of the object popped open, and the entire thing dropped off his arm. It fell to the pavement beside them.

With the dead man's head still resting on her knees, Ruthie picked up the strange item. It felt light, almost weightless. She could not tell what it was made of. It was stiff like metal, but the strands were almost transparent, like some kind of synthetic. There was some sort of invisible hinge along one side, so the two halves functioned together like a bracelet. Wondering how it opened and closed, Ruthie put it around her own left arm and pressed it closed.

It was a gesture with little thought behind it. However, it was an action that would change the course of the rest of her life.

Once it was on her arm, the two halves of the thing snapped closed, with no trace of the seam remaining where it had opened. Green lights began madly running down the length of the object, flickering to life the instant it was on her arm. It fitted to her skin exactly, even though her arm must have been a good deal thinner than Jack's. But strangest of all was the sensation she felt with the thing on her arm, like an electric current, not painful but vaguely pleasant. She had the odd sensation that the object, the device, was exploring the nerve endings in her skin, getting to know the network of nerves in her arm and making connections with the rest of her nervous system.

She knew she ought to be frightened, but she wasn't. Somehow this seemed perfectly natural to have this thing attaching itself to her arm, to her nervous system. She was fascinated by this process, and stared intently at the procession of green lights dancing down her arm. Perhaps it was the succession of abrupt shocks — the explosion, the death of her customer — that numbed her to the idea of a strange object making itself at home on her arm. Maybe the item itself was doing something to calm her during the process of adopting a new host. Whatever the reason, Ruthie didn't fight it, but sat unmoving for almost a minute, watching and feeling the object attach itself to her.

"He's dead. isn't he?" a voice said behind her. Ruthie turned to see Miles. She had not heard him approach — suddenly he was just there. Miles's voice was thick with emotion and heavy with exhaustion; he sounded as if he had just run a marathon.

"Yes," Ruthie replied, and she let Miles help her lower Jack's head to the pavement. As Miles did so, he saw for the first time the mesh-like object on Ruthie's arm.

There was a note of panic in his voice. "Ruthie," he said, his voice barely under control. "You don't want that on you. Listen carefully. I need to tell you how to take it off."

"Why?" she said. "What is it? I don't mind having it on me..."

"Listen to me! If you keep that on you, your life as you know it is over!"

"Over?" Ruthie repeated. She was startled by his extreme reaction, and for the first time she wondered if she really had made a mistake in putting it on. "You mean it will kill me?"

"No, no, but nothing will be the same again. If you want to go back to the life you knew, you have to take it off. Pay attention, the unlock procedure is complicated. Do as I tell you, and we'll have it off in no time." As he spoke, he took Ruthie's ensheathed arm in both his hands. His jacket sleeve rode up a little on his left arm, and Ruthie could see that Miles also had the mesh around his own arm. The lights on his device were blinking in a pattern that perfectly synchronized with the lights on Ruthie's arm.

None of this was making any sense to Ruthie. "I don't understand. What is it? What does it do?"

"I'll tell you later," Miles said, but there was something in his voice that made Ruthie think that *later* meant *never*. He pointed at a location on the inside of her arm where a green light was blinking rapidly. "Press there four times, wait two seconds, then press it six times more. Then —"

Suddenly every light on her arm started pulsing red. What she could see of the thing on Miles's arm was doing the same. "Shit!" Miles said. "Not now!"

"What? What's happening?"

Miles started pressing on the blinking light on her arm himself, frantically. He continued for several seconds more, then stopped. "Damn. There's not enough time."

He let go of Ruthie's arm and took her hands in his. The two of them made a strange sight, kneeling on the sidewalk oblivious to the scene of destruction and rescue around them, not to mention the dead man at their side. "Listen to me," he said. His voice was calm, but there was a note of urgency in it as well. "There's going to be a reality wave. There's no time to explain it to you but it will be bad, worse for you because you're not fully integrated into the timeband yet. Just hold on and it will be over soon. Once it passes — well, we'll see what we've got to work with."

Ruthie couldn't follow any of this at all. "What are you talking about? Aren't we still trying to remove this from me?"

"No time. We'd never make it through the entire unlock procedure in time. For better or worse, you're one of us now."

One of whom? Ruthie wanted to ask, but suddenly an invisible hand reached into her gut, squeezed and twisted. Vision blurred, and she felt herself falling, even though she could still feel the solid pavement beneath her. There was a roaring and a ringing in her ears and a bitter taste in her mouth. She could feel Miles squeezing her hands, and she squeezed back. Now she was surrounded by a swirl of colors and a multitude of sounds, making it impossible to see or hear anything else. The colors persisted even when she closed her eyes. Her arm was itching and burning under the mesh-like object, and if Miles wasn't gripping her hands she'd probably try to rip it off of her, but instead she could do nothing except ride it out.

Several eternities later, or maybe just a few seconds, all the unpleasant sensations stopped. Ruthie found she was shaking uncontrollably, and tears were running down her face. "It's all right," Miles said to her. "It's over." He put his arms around her to comfort her, as one would a child. Ruthie was in no condition to refuse the gesture. She sobbed into his shoulder as she struggled to regain her composure and make sense of the situation.

Miles began speaking to her in a low, calm voice. "Ruthie, you made it. The reality wave has passed, and next time you have to go through one, you'll be better prepared. But listen to me. When you bring your head up and look around, you're going to see that everything is different. That's to be expected, but I don't want you to be shocked. People are staring at us already, and I don't want you to make a scene. Just act like everything's normal, and I'll explain everything as soon as I get a chance. Okay?"

"What do you mean?" she asked, but then she lifted her head from his shoulder and saw what he meant.

They were kneeling on the sidewalk, in the same position as they were before, and her green waitress uniform still showed the dust and ash from the bomb explosion. But everything around them was different. There was no sign of any explosion — no debris, no blasted buildings, no sirens from ambulances or police cars. Jack's body was not there. People were walking down the street as people do in every city, walking around them and giving them a puzzled look as they did so. At first glance it looked just as if would have if the explosion had never happened.

But as Ruthie studied the scene more closely, she realized that more had changed than just that. She thought this was still Lincoln Avenue in Chicago, but now she wasn't so sure. Most of the buildings didn't look familiar to her, but some of the older ones did. Across the street, where the diner should have stood, was a small grocery store. Other familiar businesses in the neighborhood were missing, replaced by ones she'd never heard of.

Puzzled, she stood up. Miles did so also, brushing bits of plaster out of her hair. The pedestrians on the street also had changed somehow. It took Ruthie a moment to figure out what it was, and then she realized that it was their clothing. There was an odd sameness to what people were wearing, not the typical colorful variety that one would expect in this neighborhood. The clothes were conservative, the colors muted, and the styles looked oddly similar, as if everyone shopped in the same store or had developed similar tastes.

This was reflected in the cars on the street, too. There seemed to be a lot more boxy compact cars on the street than usual. No SUVs, no sports cars, just one mundane style of car after another, with a very limited palette of colors, soft browns and greens and grays.

"I don't get it, Miles. What's happened?"

She saw that he was studying their surroundings, too, taking in all the differences just as she was. "I'm not sure. Keep looking, but try not to attract attention to yourself."

"Where are we? This isn't —"

"We're still in the same place," he insisted. "This is Chicago, Illinois, on November 7, 2007, just as before. But it's not your Chicago. I'll explain everything — oh, God."

He stopped and stared, and now Ruthie saw what he was staring at.

It was an American flag, flying from a flagpole outside a bank building. Ruthie could see the red and white stripes as it fluttered in the breeze. But when the wind caught it and unfurled it to its full length, she could see that was should have been a blue field in the upper left quadrant was instead black. It did not contain fifty white stars. In their place was a single white symbol, instantly recognizable and unmistakably abhorrent.

It was a Nazi swastika.

Chapter 3

Ruthie stared at the hateful symbol. Who would display openly such a desecration of the flag? While Ruthie never had any strong political leanings, she was brought up to believe that the flag was a sort of sacred object, and should always be treated with the utmost respect. A sudden fury rose in her at the sight of the symbol of fascism and genocide corrupting the Stars and Stripes.

"That's horrible," she said. "Who would —"

"Shh." Miles stopped her from continuing. "Don't let people hear you. No one here sees anything out of place about that flag. Act like everything's normal. Don't make a scene. That's not the only one."

He nodded in the direction of another flag, further down the street. Even at this distance she could see it also bore the same combination of patriotic and profane symbols.

"Let's just start walking," Miles suggested. "I'll explain as we go."

Ruthie didn't budge, totally confused by the latest in the strange sequence of events. "But my job — the diner —"

"Forget about it. We need to walk."

Ruthie started to panic. "You don't understand! My purse is in the diner — my driver's license, my credit cards. I'm supposed to be working now — I can't leave in the middle of my shift without letting Carol know first — *where did the diner go?*"

Miles shook his head. "Ruthie, you have to calm down. I know this doesn't make any sense, but I doubt if you'll ever see that diner again. Everything you knew is gone, and if you'll listen, I'll try to explain it to you. Come on, walk with me. We'll attract less attention if we're walking."

"Everything... is gone?" She felt dazed and completely disoriented, but forcing herself to be calm, she did as he asked and started walking.

"Everything. I'll try to explain."

There was something about Miles's voice that seemed to help. It was a soft, almost melodious voice with a trace of a pleasant

Southern accent. In the last fifteen minutes Ruthie had witnessed a succession of traumatic events: the bomb explosion, the death of a man with his head in her lap, the strange device attaching itself to her arm, and now the inexplicable disappearance of her workplace and most of the surrounding neighborhood. Yet when Miles spoke to her, it made the impossible seem almost rational, and the catastrophic seem almost routine.

"That awful sensation you experienced is something we call a reality wave," he began, talking in a low voice that Ruthie had to strain to hear. "It starts someplace back in the past and races forward to the future, erasing everything that happened and replacing it with a new series of events. The world you know is gone, Ruthie, wiped out of existence by the reality wave. You and I would never have known it happened except for the timebands. They kept you and I out of the timestream, so we were unchanged. We can still remember the previous history, but no one around us will, because it never happened to them."

"Timebands?" she repeated, looking at the fine mesh on her arm. It was barely visible; no lights were flashing within it now.

"It's what you put on when Jack died. We're Travelers, Ruthie. Time travelers."

Ruthie tried to wrap her mind around that concept. She always tried to keep an open mind about things like UFOs and aliens and such. She wasn't a big science fiction fan, but she always conceded that more things were possible than people generally knew about. But time travel? That was a lot to accept all at once. It would be more believable to simply admit she must be hallucinating, all this must be some kind of a delusion. But it all seemed too real — it didn't feel like a hallucination. And Miles seemed so earnest. She thought she could usually tell when someone was trying to deceive her, but Miles sounded like he really believed what he was saying. Could Miles be telling the truth?

"But the flag...?"

"It's the flag of this country, Ruthie. Something happened in the past — something happened *to* the past — and the U.S.A. isn't the same any more. I think the Nazis are in power. Maybe they have been since World War Two ended. I don't know for sure. We've got to learn more. Until we do, don't —"

He stopped talking because a police officer was approaching. He looked straight at the two of them and then walked directly toward them. To Ruthie, he looked exactly like a regular Chicago cop. Same uniform, including the distinctive checkerboard band around the hat. Her first thought was that maybe this officer could help her. Maybe he could do something to help her find her way back to the world she had somehow lost. But then Ruthie noticed a look of apprehension in Miles's face, and she understood. In a city where people display the Nazi swastika openly, maybe the police are not here to help you.

"Passbooks, please," the policeman said, stepping directly into their path and blocking any further forward progress. The name tag on his uniform shirt said *O'Shea*. The man's manner was businesslike and not threatening, but his right hand rested on the baton attached to his belt.

"Sorry?" Miles said.

"I need to see your passbooks," O'Shea said slowly, irritation creeping into his voice. "You're required to show me your passbooks."

Ruthie almost said that they didn't have any passbooks, but Miles interrupted. "Our passbooks are back at our place of employment, officer. We had to step out for a moment to run an errand. We'll be happy to go back to get them if you like."

Officer O'Shea didn't seem happy to hear that. "Law says you have your passbook on your person at all times. Show me some I.D."

Ruthie realized that all of her identification — driver's license, credit cards, and so on — was in her purse, back in the diner. But the diner didn't exist any more. She had no identification at all, no way to prove who she was.

Miles gave the officer a driver's license. O'Shea turned it over in his hand, back and forth. "What kind of a card is this, Mr. Terwilliger? I see it says Illinois Drivers License on it, but it doesn't look like anything issued by the state of Illinois."

Ruthie didn't see how it was any different from any other driver's license, but the policeman acted like he had never seen one like it before. Miles shrugged. "It's what they gave me."

O'Shea spoke into his radio, clipped to his shoulder belt. "O'Shea. I've got two to bring in on passbook violations. Twenty-four hundred block of North Lincoln Avenue. Come pick me up." Moments later, a Chicago police car, red lights flashing, pulled up to the curb. It would have looked exactly like a Chicago police car should, except for the flag with the swastika painted on the door.

"This isn't necessary, officer —" Miles began.

"I'm afraid it is, Mr. Terwilliger. We received a citizen's report a few minutes ago that a man and a woman were acting strangely on Lincoln Avenue. We encourage citizens to report suspicious activity to us as a matter of public safety — you know that. Now to have no passbooks on top of that, well, I'm afraid we need to take you in."

Ruthie looked helplessly at Miles, who did not seem as concerned as she thought he should. "Don't worry," he said to her. "It will be all right."

Officer O'Shea shook his head and chuckled sardonically as he opened the rear door of the cruiser. The rear of the police car was separated from the front by thick Plexiglas, and there were no door handles on the inside. Miles and Ruthie reluctantly got into the car, and the door shut behind them.

"What are we going to do?" Ruthie asked.

Miles held up his left arm, where the timeband was hidden under his jacket sleeve. "The timeband goes into sleep mode after a reality wave. It's a necessary safety measure — the timeband needs time to recalibrate before it can safely make any jumps. As soon as the timebands go active again, we'll jump pastward and our disappearance will just be a frustrating mystery for the police."

"Pastward?"

"Into the past. A hour will be enough — they'll never know what happened to us. That's what the timebands do. They allow us to move back or forth in time."

Ruthie was doubtful, but she decided to take his word for it. "How long until the timebands... recalibrate?"

"Not long. Maybe fifteen minutes. Until then, sit back and enjoy the ride."

Amazingly, Miles did seem like he was enjoying it. He didn't seem at all bothered to be under arrest in a twisted version of the city. But Ruthie, who had never been placed in the back of a police car for any reason in her life, was having difficulty keeping herself from giving in to sheer panic. "This is all like a bad dream," she said to herself. "Why aren't I waking up?"

Ruthie looked out the window as the police car made its way down streets she thought she knew well. Much about the city was the same. The el tracks still thundered overhead, and streets still had the same names. Some buildings, if they were old enough, were recognizable. But there were other differences that let her know this was not her Chicago. In this neighborhood there should be dozens of ethnic restaurants with cuisine from as many different countries. She didn't see any — every restaurant seemed blandly Americanized. And there were no fast food chains. How far can you travel in a major American city without seeing a McDonalds? There weren't any, nor Burger King, Wendy's, Subway, or KFC.

They passed a movie theater, and the names of the movies and actors on the marquee were not any that she'd ever heard of before. Billboards advertised products with brand names that were different than the ones she had grown up knowing. She noted also that all the billboards were in English, while in her Chicago it was not uncommon to see billboards in Spanish or occasionally Chinese.

One billboard was especially disturbing. It showed Uncle Sam in his traditional red, white, and blue costume, arm and arm with a blonde-haired German Valkyrie, her other arm holding a spear with a Nazi banner flying from the shaft. The caption, in large letters, simply read: *ENFORCE RACIAL PURITY*. What had become of her country?

They arrived at the police station, which looked more like a small fortress than any that Ruthie could remember seeing. Men with automatic rifles stood guard at the outer wall, and Ruthie and Miles were quickly led past them into a maze of corridors and cubicles. A heavily-armed female officer came to take Ruthie away, and Ruthie began to panic when she realized that they meant to separate her and Miles. Without Miles, she was lost in this madness, unable to help herself in any way. But the officer pulled roughly on her arm and led her quickly to another part of the maze.

In a daze, Ruthie did not resist as the female officer thoroughly patted her down in a search for weapons. At the end of the search, the officer spotted the nearly invisible mesh covering Ruthie's left forearm. "What's this?"

What could she say? "It's — it's nothing."

"It will have to come off." The officer tugged at the edge of it, but it was so tightly wrapped around her that she could not get even a finger under it.

Ruthie shrugged. "It doesn't come off. I couldn't get it off if I tried."

"I'm sure we'll be able to get it off," the officer said, a note of menace in her voice. Ruthie didn't think it was possible without removing her arm, and then she realized that maybe that was exactly what the officer had in mind. What kind of a place was this?

However, the officer did not send for the bone saw right away, and instead led Ruthie to the next desk, where she was fingerprinted, and then to another desk, where Ruthie was given a chair to sit in while the officer took her statement on computer. The computer, Ruthie noticed, would have been about twenty or thirty years out of date on her world: low-resolution boxy white letters glowing on a green background.

"Name?"

"Ruthie — Ruth McDonald."

The officer used two index fingers to type it in, then asked for her address. The computer beeped loudly when the address was typed in.

"Computer says you're not listed in the database at that address," the officer said crossly.

"That's where I live," Ruthie said. She didn't know what else to say.

"No, you don't. There aren't any errors in this database. If the computer says you don't live there, then you don't. So don't give me a false address. Want to try again?"

"I — I don't think I'm anywhere in your database," Ruthie said, desperately trying to think of something to say that would not get her into worse trouble. "I don't think you'd believe me if I tried to explain it to you."

The woman smiled crookedly. "Try me."

What did she have to lose? "I don't belong here. Something happened, and my world disappeared and this one was in its place. Everything's wrong here. There shouldn't be a Nazi emblem on the flag — it should still be red, white, and blue — people shouldn't have to carry passbooks —"

"Stop!" the officer commanded. Ruthie did. "Before you say another word, Miss McDonald, you should be aware that there are microphones everywhere in this building. And they are monitored not just by the Chicago P.D., but also by Party officials. So far you're only going to be charged with passbook violation, a minor offense. No more than six months in jail. Sedition is a far more serious crime, and it is punishable by death. You would be advised to keep your political opinions to yourself."

Ruthie trembled, becoming more aware of the magnitude of the situation. "I want to talk to a lawyer."

The officer laughed. "Fat chance. Now, back to the problem with your address... "

The interrogation lasted for another forty-five minutes. During that time, the officer not only could not find Ruthie's address in her computer, but she couldn't find her parents' address, the address of the place she worked, or her school records. The officer was so intent on hammering away at the "false" information that Ruthie was giving that she did not notice soft lights beginning to flicker in the mesh on Ruthie's arm.

Ruthie not only saw them, but she felt them. As the timeband came out of sleep mode, it attached itself more securely to Ruthie's nervous system. Now she could "feel" the timeband as an extension of her body, as if it was another body part capable of sensation and motion. She was sure that she could manipulate the controls in the microcircuitry of the timeband with just a thought, as easily as she could move the fingers on her hands. But she had no idea what these controls did, so she ignored them for now. Even if she could use them to move through time, she did not wish to risk being separated from Miles in both time and space.

She found herself worrying about what was happening to him, and not just because she needed his help in escaping from here. Miles had always been nice to her, and she hoped that pleasant, polite man was not receiving any rough treatment from the police here.

The officer on the computer looked hard at Ruthie. "Miss, this is your last chance. You need to tell me a true piece of information so I can find you in the database. Home address, work history — doesn't matter, just something that isn't a lie."

Ruthie spread her hands out before her. "Everything I've said is the truth."

The female officer shook her head sadly. "No, it isn't. I'm sorry, dear. There are procedures I need to follow in cases like

25

yours." She picked up the phone and punched in a single digit. "Frank, this is Allison at the receiving desk. I need a specialist team, right away." The officer hung up the phone and turned away from Ruthie, leaving her to wonder what a specialist team was.

It didn't take long to find out.

Moments later, two brawny uniformed police officers showed up. Both had shaved heads and tobacco-stained teeth, and except for the badges on their leather jackets and other police paraphernalia, they would have looked more at home in a biker bar than in a police station.

"Ruth McDonald, passbook violation," the officer, Allison, informed them. "Suspect is uncooperative."

"I'm not —" she protested, but one of the men grabbed hold of her elbow and pulled her to her feet.

"Let's go," he said, giving her little choice in the matter.

As they took her away, Allison repeated, "I'm sorry, dear."

Keeping a firm grip on her arm, the men whisked Ruthie through the maze of corridors and into an elevator. One of them pushed the button marked B for basement and the doors closed.

"What's the point spread on the Bears?" one asked the other.

"Underdogs by three. I think they can win, though."

"Hope so. I've got money on the game." The two men conversed as if Ruthie was not there, paying no attention at all to her plight.

The elevator doors opened. Unlike the bustle of the main floor, the basement level was quiet. A long row of file cabinets lined the dimly-lit, dank corridor. There was no sound of anyone working down here. The two men led Ruthie into a small storeroom with no other exit, then closed and locked the door behind them.

With an overwhelming sense of panic, Ruthie realized what a "specialist team" was in this nightmare of a police department. They were a couple of thugs, probably rapists, and their violent assault upon her would be nothing more than a routine part of their day.

"Receiving desk says you've been uncooperative," one of the men said. "After we're done here, you'll be in a more cooperative mood. He unzipped his leather jacket and took it off, folding it neatly before placing it on a nearby crate.

The other man grabbed Ruthie's arms from behind and held them immobile. "Scream if you like," he said into her ear. "No one will hear you down here." Ruthie didn't scream, but she did struggle in vain. The man had a firm grip on her arms, and she wasn't going to free herself that way.

The first man, his leather jacket now put away, walked over to where Ruthie was squirming to get free. He took a moment to look her up and down in a way that revolted Ruthie, then he reached out to unbutton the front of Ruthie's dress.

Ruthie pushed hard with her mind in a direction that she didn't know was possible, and suddenly she was alone in the room.

Chapter 4

What had happened? The two men were gone, and the door which they had locked was now open. But her arms still hurt from where she had struggled to get free of the man who held her, and the top two buttons of her dress were undone. Then the answer came to her. This was three minutes earlier. Three minutes and nineteen seconds earlier, she suddenly knew, using an ability to sense the exact time that she seemed to have now acquired.

Miles had said that the timebands allow them to move back or forward in time, and now Ruthie realized it was true. She had stepped back in time, back to a time when the room was empty, before she had been brought here against her will by two Chicago policemen.

While struggling to resist the assault, she had inadvertently used the timeband to push herself back through time. She wasn't sure how she had done it, but she imagined that with a little practice, she should be able to do it again. She did still have the sensation of the timeband being an extension of herself, subject to her mental commands. Also, it somehow gave her some extra senses. Just as she could normally sense things like temperature and pressure, she found now she could sense location in time and rate of time flow, as well as some other sensations she couldn't put a name to yet.

Down the hallway, there was the sound of the elevator door opening, followed by the sound of footsteps. For a moment she was afraid of being discovered down here by other workers in the police station. But then she realized who was coming. It would be herself and the two goons.

She visualized how this encounter could go: the two rapist-cops would be surprised to find a second Ruthie in the room waiting for them. In their confusion they would let the first one of her go, and the two of herself would run and make a break for it. But if she escaped, then she would never have a reason to go back in time to this moment — would she? And even if it were possible, would that mean that there would now be two of herself in this world?

Her speculation ended when the two men pulled a frightened young woman into the room. Ruthie had trouble recognizing her as herself: her dark hair still disheveled from the explosion, dirt and blood stains on her green uniform dress. None of the three entering the room seemed to be aware of Ruthie at all. The scene was replaying exactly as it had the first time, except this time Ruthie was watching it while it was happening to someone who might as well have been someone else.

When the cop moved to grab her other self's arms from behind, Ruthie shouted "No!" and charged at him. No one showed any sign of hearing her or seeing her. When she was just inches from herself and her attacker, an odd thing happened. In the blink of an eye, she was back in the grip of the man, exactly where she was before. She was the only Ruthie in the room, and she was about to be assaulted again.

"Scream if you like," he said again, just as he did before. "No one will hear you down here."

Again the other man removed his jacket and folded it up, then approached to unbutton her dress. Everything seemed to be replaying exactly as it did before, but was she free to change her actions? She decided to test this idea by spitting in his face.

This act proved two things: she did still have free will, able to choose a different set of actions, and also that now events were following a different sequence from that point on. Instead of unbuttoning her top button, as he did the last time, he socked her in the jaw.

His full strength wasn't behind the blow, but it still made Ruthie's head swim. Before she could recover her wits, the attacker had opened all her buttons down to her waist, and he was reaching up toward her breasts.

Her mind cried for this indignity to stop, and she realized that she could make it stop. All she had to do was make a little push with her mind, again in a direction she hadn't previously known was possible, and suddenly the man's hand stopped moving, inches short of his target. Both men were as still as statues.

This new situation confused Ruthie until she took stock of the information that her new senses were supplying her brain. Her location in time hadn't changed — in fact, it wasn't changing at all.

Time was no longer moving from one moment to the next. Ruthie now resided in a single moment of time, and the rate of time flow, her mind told her, was now virtually zero. This was a frozen moment in time, and only she was free to move in it.

With effort, she slipped out of the grip of the man holding her, who was powerless to stop her. She stepped aside and buttoned her dress back up. Rubbing her sore jaw, she looked at the two pathetic figures who thought they had her in their power. In sudden anger she delivered a mighty kick to the groin of the man whom she had spat on, then she repeated the action with the other man. Neither man reacted, neither moved at all. But she was sure they would be feeling it in the next moment in time, once she allowed it to happen for them.

Having gotten her revenge, her only thought now was to find Miles. She unlocked the door to the room, exited through it, and returned to the elevator. She pushed the button marked UP, but nothing happened. Of course it wouldn't — this was still a single moment in time, and the elevator would arrive a few seconds in the future, but not at this moment. So she looked for the stairwell and made her way up the stairs to the main floor.

It was odd to see the crowded main floor of the police station, so noisy and full of activity before, now deathly silent, its occupants as frozen as department store mannequins. No one took notice of Ruthie as she moved carefully around the cubicles, stepping around individuals frozen in mid-stride. She didn't know how she was going to find Miles, but she knew she had all the time in the world.

She found that walking in this timeless state was a strange experience. Air didn't move out of her way as easily as it did normally, and it felt more like walking underwater from the additional air resistance. She knew it would be quite difficult to run with the air feeling as thick as this. Also, she realized that sound wasn't totally absent. There was a low hum, almost below the threshold of her hearing, that was present everywhere. This must be the sound waves of the room's normal noise level, frozen in place, but detectable by her eardrums as she moved through them.

Even light itself seemed affected by the stoppage of time. If she looked down at her feet as she walked, she noticed that there was a slight but noticeable difference between where she saw her feet and where she knew them to be, as if there was a slight delay in the image reaching her eyes. As she thought about it, she wondered how she was even able to see — shouldn't the light waves reflected off objects be frozen in place, and unable to reach her eyes? She would have to ask Miles about that, once she found him.

She spent a long time searching the police station from top to bottom. She found other prisoners in other areas of the building, some showing the signs of the brutal treatment they had intended to subject Ruthie to. With each beaten or starved prisoner she found, she felt even more urgency to find Miles. Not that there was any point to hurrying — in this frozen moment of time, there was nothing further they could do to him. But she still felt she had to hurry, and hurry she did.

Eventually she found him, sitting in a holding cell in another wing of the building. The door was closed and locked, and through the small window she could see that he was alone in the cell, sitting on a bench. But now she needed to get the door open, and it took her a while to figure out how it opened, since there didn't seem to be any apparent keyhole. The lock, it seemed, was controlled remotely by a switch on a desk on the opposite side of the corridor. Or so she surmised — the little plastic label under the button said CELL UNLOCK — but when she pushed the button nothing happened. She was afraid of this; the mechanism that unlocked the door would take a second or two to activate, and that was another second that she was not allowing to happen as long as she had stopped the rate of time flow. She understood what she had to do: return to a normal time flow for a few brief seconds, long enough for the door to unlock for her to slip inside. Could she do it and not be spotted by the numerous individuals in the vicinity? She didn't know, but now that she knew what the timeband could do, she felt it didn't matter — she could protect herself from anything by simply stopping time, or hopping into the past or future.

Ruthie pushed the button again, just to make sure the signal would be sent, then she moved close to the cell door. In her mind, she touched the timeband control that affected the rate of time flow, and moved it back to its normal setting. Immediately sound and motion resumed around her, and there was a loud "click" from the door lock. She opened the cell door just wide enough to squeeze through, then closed it almost all the way behind her. She didn't want the door to lock behind her, but she hoped no one would notice from the outside that it was still slightly ajar.

"Hi, Miles," she said, feeling pleased with her accomplishment. "Miss me?" Now that her fright from the assault in the basement had passed, she felt nearly giddy in comparison.

Miles continued staring ahead. He did not react to Ruthie's presence.

Now what was the problem? This was as unexpected as when the two cops and her earlier self couldn't see her in the storeroom. Ruthie mentally scanned the timeband controls, trying to find there what the difficulty was. It was a strange sensation, getting data and readouts in her mind. She knew the timeband was trying to tell her what she needed to know, but Ruthie still could make little sense of the torrent of information being inputted into her brain.

One piece of information seemed relevant. *Second timeband within range. Synchronicity deviation: -22 min 11 sec.*

Ruthie wasn't sure what synchronicity deviation was, but she made a guess that Miles wouldn't be able to see her unless that number was zero. Twenty-two minutes was probably about the amount of time Ruthie had spent in this frozen moment of time, searching for Miles and trying to get into his holding cell, plus the three minutes and change that she had spent jumping backward to escape from the goons the first time. So she must still be over twenty-two minutes "out of synch" with Miles, and he wouldn't be aware of her until they were back in synch again.

She tried to recall exactly what she had done during her first moment of panic, when the skinhead cop had reached for her and she jumped backward in time. Now she deliberately tried to do the opposite and carefully move forward, keeping a mental eye on the amount of synchronicity deviation. A slight push with her mind, and suddenly the number was zero. She had moved twenty-two minutes and eleven seconds into the future.

"Ruthie!" Miles looked up in surprise. "How...?"

She pointed to the timeband on her own arm, which sparkled in the dim light of the cell. "It works," she said, still feeling the shock of realization. "I can really move through time. It's... amazing."

"It is," Miles agreed. "It certainly is."

"Now can we get out of here?" She pointed to the cell door. Luckily, in the last twenty-two minutes, no one had noticed it was still slightly ajar.

"Right away." Ruthie noticed that her timeband had suddenly activated, without mental command from her; rate of time flow was back to zero. "I've slaved your timeband to mine, and stopped time flow for both of us," Miles explained. "Now there's one thing we need to do before we get to a — my God, Ruthie, what happened?" He was staring at her jaw.

She touched it. It was still sore, and no doubt had a lovely bruise on it by now. "I'm fine. Nothing to worry about."

"But your face — did someone hit you?"

"Yeah. It seems that when they can't find a woman suspect in their computer, they assign two of Chicago's Finest to rape her. But they didn't — I mean, I learned how to use the timeband before they got that far. If I had learned faster, I could have avoided getting hit, too, I guess. But I'm fine. Can we get out of here, please?"

"Ruthie, I'm so sorry. By the time my timeband was out of sleep mode, I was already locked in this cell. Rather than use it to skip to a moment when the cell was open, I thought I would just wait for them to open the cell and escape then — I didn't imagine they would do anything like that to you..."

"It's okay," Ruthie said. "I'm not hurt. Let's get out of here."

"There's a safe place we can get to," Miles said, swinging the cell door open. Apparently he had stopped time just in time; a couple of officers had noticed the cell door was unlocked, and they were approaching it with guns drawn. But now they were as immobile as statues, and Miles led Ruthie quickly around them. "But we have to find something first."

"What?"

"Some historical document of this era, something we can use to plot the course of this variation." He began inspecting nearby desks and shelves. Ruthie watched him; she couldn't help him, since she didn't know exactly what he was looking for.

Miles fished a thick Chicago Tribune out of a waste basket. "This will do." He took a quick glance at the headline and lead article. Ruthie could see it didn't seem out of place. The headline read *HEAVY FIGHTING AROUND BAGHDAD,* which would have been a typical recent headline from the world she had left behind. Miles saw her looking at the headline and said, "Yes, but this fighting in Iraq seems to be between the combined German-American forces against the Chinese. I will need to study this further."

Newspaper under his arm, he led Ruthie to an open space in the middle of the room. "Ready to say good-bye to Nazi Chicago?"

"More than ready."

"Let's go." Suddenly they were no longer in the police station. They were on the edge of a forest, the ground covered with a carpet of fallen autumn leaves. There was no sign of civilization in any direction. Ruthie blinked in surprise, then checked a readout that her timeband showed her.

"Is this right? There's something in my head that's telling me this is the year 1504. Did we just go back in time that many centuries? Where are we?"

"Same place, the north side of Chicago, except Chicago hasn't been built yet. Lake Michigan is not far in that direction, and there's a little Indian village to the south. The timeband can move us in time, but we have to do the movement in space the old-fashioned way, which means we have a bit of a hike ahead of us if we want to get to the safehouse. This way." He pointed in the direction of the trees.

They walked for a while, and then Ruthie said, "So this thing on my arm is some sort of a time machine?"

"Right," Miles said. "No one knows exactly where they came from or who made them. All we know is that it happened in a timeline that doesn't exist any more. Twelve timebands were made — only twelve could be made. Apparently twelve timebands is all the indignity the space-time continuum will put up with; try to put any more in operation, and they all shut down. So you're wearing one of the only twelve timebands that exist anywhere in the past, present, or future."

"Only twelve people have these?"

"We'll be meeting some of the others very soon. The rest — well, you'll find out about them in due time."

"How do they work?"

"Don't ask me to explain the physics of it. If you're interested, I'll introduce you to someone who can give you a couple of hours on the subject — though I suspect she doesn't really understand it any better than we do. All I can tell you is that without a timeband, you're locked into the normal rate of time flow, and there's nothing you can do about it. The timeband frees you from that. It allows you to move at will back and forth along the timeline — you can stop time, speed it up, run it backwards if you like. Or jump directly to any point in time, with a safe range of about five and a half centuries."

Ruthie thought about this in silence for a few minutes. That did seem to explain most of what she had experienced in the police station. "After we were separated, and those goons tried to attack me, I moved back in time a few minutes. When I saw myself in the past, my past self couldn't see me, and neither could those two men. When I tried to free myself from them, all of a sudden there was only one of me again, and I was back in their grip. What happened?"

Miles nodded with understanding. "You doubled yourself. That's one of the things the timeline tries to avoid, if possible. Think of it this way: normally, you're in many moments along the timeline — you were there at all the different events in your life, stretching back to when you were born. An infinity of Ruthies, all at different moments in time. But your consciousness only resides in one of them — the Ruthie in the present moment. Go back to visit any previous Ruthie, and she's just replaying a moment that has already happened for you, and that moment won't change for her yet. She can't see the present you, because that you hasn't happened yet for her. When you went back and saw yourself, you were invisible to her, because when that event happened originally, the second you wasn't there yet.

"All that is logical, but because the timeline hates it when some Traveler doubles herself, there are a few other effects that come into play. Within a certain range, no other consciousness is aware of the future version of a doubled Traveler. Otherwise, you'd have the illogical scene of others seeing something that one person couldn't. So everyone else in the vicinity is forced to replay events exactly as they originally occurred, despite the presence of a Traveler from their future. Outside of that range, though, you can interact normally with the people you meet, and even change the way past events occurred.

"And if you get very close to yourself while doubled, the timeline won't allow both bodies to coexist. Your consciousness is shunted back into your earlier self, which becomes your only self in that moment. Actually, it's a handy way to fix mistakes that you've made, since you're free to change your actions the second time around. Does that explain what happened to you?"

"I guess so," she said. "It's all very confusing — past selves and future selves and so on. Wait — when I found you in the cell, you couldn't see me at first, not until I jumped further into the future. Was that the same problem?"

"Right. Because you had used your timeband to jump into the past and stop time, and I hadn't, we were no longer in synch. Travelers can only be aware of each other if they are synchronous. When you saw me in the cell, my consciousness was many minutes ahead in the future, and the me that you saw was a past copy of myself that was only replaying events the way they had already happened for me. We couldn't interact until we were both occupying the same moment."

"When synchronicity deviation became zero," she said uncertainly.

"You've been listening to your timeband!" Miles said. "Exactly. Just remember — there are a lot of past copies of yourself that you've left behind on the timeline, but there's only one you that has awareness, has consciousness, and that's the one inhabiting this moment. And there are no future copies of yourself — those haven't happened yet. You make your own future as you go."

"So we do have free will after all," Ruthie said.

"Of course. If we didn't, what would be the point?"

"No matter where you go, there you are."

"Huh?"

Ruthie smiled. "Just something I heard a character in a movie say once."

They walked in silence for a while, and then Miles said, "By the way, I don't think we've been properly introduced. Miles Terwilliger, at your service."

She laughed, realizing that it had been only a short time ago — though still centuries in the future — that she had been pouring coffee for Miles and Jack in the diner. "I'm Ruthie McDonald. I'm so very sorry about Jack."

"Thank you. He was a good friend." Miles was silent for a long moment. Then he said, "I'm the one who should be sorry for you. I lost one friend today. But whether you realize it or not, you've just lost everyone you've ever known — every friend, every family member — you won't see them again."

Ruthie already knew this was true, but a shiver still ran up her back as Miles said the words. "I guess that's true. I just lost my whole world. There's a few friends I'll miss, but that's about it. No family that I'm close to — I've been on my own in Chicago for the past few years. For a while I was trying to make it as an actress, but I guess that was never going to happen. I haven't seen my father in over twenty years, and the last time I talked to my mother on the phone, she was heading back to rehab because of the booze and the pills. That was a few months ago. No kids, no boyfriend, nothing to look forward to except another day waiting tables at the diner. So please don't feel sorry for me, Miles. Someone else might have been all broken up if your reality wave had erased their whole world, but for me, it may just be the lucky break I've been waiting for. Honestly."

"All right," Miles said. "Still, this has to be a big shock for you. Maybe it just hasn't sunk in yet."

"Maybe," Ruthie said, and then they were both silent again. Finally she said, "So what's your story?"

"I met Jack Bruno in 1938," Miles began. "That's when he recruited me to be a Traveler. It seemed like a good idea at the time. My world was going to hell. I was a pilot in the Confederate States Air Force, and I had just survived the firebombing of Atlanta. The country was on the brink of collapse, and the rest of the world seemed to be going up in flames, too. But then Jack shows up, and he says there's a way to fix this, so that it doesn't have to happen. So I joined up with him, and we did fix it, and we kept on fixing history ever since."

"Back up — you were in the Confederate States Air Force. The South didn't lose the Civil War?"

"No — the South won the War of Southern Independence," Miles said with patriotic pride. "Care for a little history lesson?"

"Go ahead. I was a history major in college."

"Really? That will come in handy. Anyway, in 1863 President Jefferson Davis replaced General Braxton Bragg as commander of the Army of Tennessee with James Longstreet prior to the Battle of Chattanooga, and Longstreet was able to defend the city and hold off Grant until the following spring. By that time spirits were so low in the North that the Republican Party didn't even renominate Lincoln. They nominated Salmon B. Chase instead, and he lost the presidential election to George McClellan. McClellan's first act as president was to negotiate a peace agreement with the Confederacy, and independence was ours."

"That's not the way it happened," Ruthie said, trying to remember her Civil War studies in college.

"Right — because a reality wave changed all that. In the new version, Bragg stayed in command at Chattanooga, and lost the battle. Grant went on to become Lincoln's general-in-chief, and Sherman tore through Georgia. His victories lifted Northern morale, and Lincoln was elected to a second term. The war continued until the South was defeated, and my nation — the Confederate States of America — ceased to exist only four years after it was formed."

"Tell me about the reality waves," Ruthie asked.

"Well, being a Traveler means we have the ability to go back and change the past. But the timeline is a very resilient thing. Try to make a minor change, and the timeline manages to correct it. Eventually history is back on the same track that it had been. Some of the names of the major players might be different, and a few details might be altered, but the general flow of big events is unchanged. It's hard to change history, unless you know exactly where and when to make the change.

"Some events in history are so pivotal, though, that if you change them, the entire course of future events has to be different. That's what sets off the reality wave. When that happens, the old sequence is entirely erased, and a new sequence of events takes its place. We Travelers have a few seconds of warning when a reality wave is coming — that's why our timebands started pulsing red. But at that point, there's nothing to be done but to ride it out. The timebands keep up unaffected by the reality wave, so after it's passed, we're the only ones who remember how history used to be."

Ruthie thought about this, and then said, "So that wave today — someone changed the past, so that the Nazis won World War Two?"

"Could be. We'll figure it out at the safehouse. That's why I brought the newspaper. The others that we'll meet there will also be bringing in documents from their eras — that's the protocol in the event of a reality wave. As soon as we're able, each of us is to gather historical documents and meet back at the safehouse. Then we'll compare notes and try to determine what to do next."

"But who changed the past and started the reality wave?"

Miles took in a long breath, let it out, and said, "Remember I said there could be only twelve timebands, and twelve Travelers? Unfortunately, only seven of us are working together. The other five are working against us."

"But... why?"

"It all started with two men called Carlos and Caesar. I doubt those are really their names, but that's what we call them today. The two greatest time travelers ever, they explored up and down the timeline and did the first research on reality waves. They began mapping out the Variations — different historical patterns that the timeline tends to correct itself to follow, no matter how much you try to change history. They discovered that there's really only a small number of these Variations that are possible, probably less than twenty. Then sometime a few subjective decades ago, Carlos and Caesar had a falling-out. They disagreed over something, and each man began collecting the remaining timebands and assembling his own team of assistants.

"Carlos is the founder of our team. Its goal is to establish the timeline called Variation Seven. Carlos teaches us that Variation Seven is the only Variation that gives humanity a chance of survival. In all other Variations, we wipe ourselves out through nuclear war, or disease, or famine, or ecological disaster, or some combination of them all. That's why it's vital to adjust historical events so that Variation Seven prevails. Unfortunately, Caesar's team is trying to undo everything we do. For some perverted reason, his team wants to prevent Variation Seven from happening, and doom mankind. That's the reason why they caused today's reality wave, and they also set off the bomb that killed Jack."

"Jack was killed by rival time travelers?" Ruthie asked.

"I'm almost sure of it. As soon as the explosion happened, I froze time and searched the area for any sign of who did it, but I never found them. Then I jumped ahead to be in synch with Jack, but by that time he was already gone, and you had the timeband. You see, the reason Jack and I were in that diner, day after day, was because we knew that Ron Klausson worked in the office building across the street."

"Who?"

"You wouldn't have heard of him in 2007. But within fifteen years, he is the founder of the greatest political movement of the twenty-first century. He becomes that century's Gandhi, its Martin Luther King. He is able to articulate a philosophy that ends the religious strife that has divided people in countries all over the world. If he dies, years before his influential work is published, the course of future events changes. We expected that Caesar might send agents into your era to try to eliminate Klausson, and we hoped to prevent this. But we didn't anticipate a car bomb. Also, it seems to be an attack that was coordinated with another timeline distortion farther pastward, since the reality wave that we encountered must have had its origins many decades earlier."

Ruthie tried to follow it all; it was all too much to digest at once. "And the newspapers?" she asked at last.

"Huh? Oh, that's how Jack and I tried to track Traveler movements. Small changes in history might not set off a reality wave, but they might be noticeable to one of us if we're watching for them. So we tried to read as many newspapers as we can, looking for details that weren't consistent with what should have been the current version of history. If we found something, we might be able to locate the Traveler that was causing the change."

"I always thought Jack was a cop."

Miles smiled. "He was a cop, in the 1960's before he became a Traveler. Walked a beat in Brooklyn. Never quite lost that gruff policeman attitude." He was silent for a long moment. "I'm going to miss him."

They continued to walk through the forest silently, the only sound being the dead leaves crunching beneath their feet. Ruthie found it hard to believe that this quiet forest would one day become a great city — she still half expected that any moment, she'd be waking up from this dream. How could she accept that everything she knew was gone, and in the course of a morning she had gone from being a waitress to a time traveler?

"What's going to happen to me?" she finally asked.

"We'll find out when we get to the safehouse," Miles said. "That will be up to the rest of the group. I'm only one vote. They may ask you to join us. They may not."

And if they don't, Ruthie thought, what then?

They arrived at a large palisade of logs, each sixteen feet tall, constructed in an area cleared of trees. The huge wall was constructed so that no outsider could get a look at what was on the other side. Miles stepped up to the only doorway, which incongruously had a stainless steel plate set into the roughhewn wood. The plate had a set of numerical buttons on it. "Keeps the neighbors out," he explained. Miles punched in a six-digit code, and the door swung inward.

Once they walked through the door, it was like walking into another century. Inside was a well-trimmed lawn, with a beautiful garden and manicured shrubbery. There was a tennis court, and beyond that Ruthie thought she saw a swimming pool. But the feature that most caught her eye was the house, a huge two-story house that looked as modern as would be found in an American suburb in her day. The only thing that seemed to be missing was the attached three-car garage.

"We're here," Miles declared. "Welcome to Wrigley Field."

Chapter 5

It was called Wrigley Field, Ruthie learned, because centuries in the future, this location would be the corner of Clark and Addison Streets in Chicago, and here the beloved Cubs would play their years of futility in their "friendly confines". In this remote era, though, the team had built its safehouse, where they could meet in secrecy and safety. Any reality waves touched off by the other side would not be likely to affect them here.

"Won't some future archeologist be surprised to dig up this place?" Ruthie asked, as they made their way up the walkway to the house.

"Won't happen. In the year 1566, this entire compound burns to the ground. All traces of the comforts of civilization are destroyed. I know; I watched the place burn. Helped set the fire, too. Come on in, there's people I want you to meet."

There were three of them waiting in the great common room that served as the group's central meeting place. This was a large, comfortable room, with a high ceiling that went all the way up to a skylight in the roof, admitting generous amounts of bright sunshine during the day. A great staircase led up to the second floor, with a balcony that stretched all the way around the upper portion of the common room. There were quite a few couches and overstuffed armchairs in the room, with a wide, low cherrywood table at the room's exact center. All three occupants of the room reacted with surprise when Miles walked in with an unfamiliar woman.

"Sarah, Ben, Jason, this is Ruthie McDonald," Miles said immediately. "Jack's dead."

As Miles began relating the events of the day to the group, Ruthie settled into a comfortable sofa and sipped on a cup of hot tea they had offered her. She soon surmised that the woman called Sarah was the *de facto* leader of the group. She was older than the rest, in her fifties at least, with short-cropped steel-gray hair. While the others remained silent through Miles's explanation, she interrupted several times with pertinent questions.

While Miles told his story and Sarah interrupted with questions, another man sat quietly taking notes into a large notebook. This slightly-built black man with glasses was Ben, and Ruthie would later learn he was the group's historical expert. Ben would have the primary responsibility to put together the clues the team brought back and figure out what had happened to cause the reality wave.

Jason, the other man, was on his feet during Miles's story, pacing like a panther. He was a tall, wiry man with wavy brown hair and a short beard. He also said little, but he seemed far from calm. Ruthie would learn that Jason led the team's special missions, when they needed to take extraordinary actions to try to fix the timeline. Whether the job required a burglary, a demolition, or an assassination, Jason had the necessary skills. The only thing he couldn't do, it seemed, was relax.

Halfway through the tale, the last member of the team checked in: Denise, a small, athletic Asian woman, with a wide, winning smile and broad dark eyes. She had an armload of books and papers that she had brought back from the year 2091. So Miles had to start again from the beginning, going back to the explosion outside the diner and the death of Jack.

When Miles had at last reached the end, Sarah said, "Well, I think under the circumstances, you did the only thing you could do. We're glad you could make it back safely, and we're all sorry about Jack. Ruthie, please make yourself at home here. We haven't had a newcomer visit us in a long time, so pardon us if we're less than perfect hosts. But the group has a lot of work to do now, so we're going to be rather busy in the next few days."

"Sarah," Miles began, "I rather hoped that we would consider Ruthie for permanent inclusion in our group."

"We'll have to see about that," Sarah said. "No offense, Ruthie, but we don't know you yet. We don't know if you'll be an asset to our team or a liability. You see, each of us is on the team because we were specially chosen for our skills and abilities. You received a timeband by chance, a random accident. The timebands are too valuable to be given out that way. There can be only six of us, you know, and we have the responsibility to protect the entire future history of humanity."

"I thought there was another," Ruthie said. "Miles said something about someone named Carlos?"

Sarah nodded. "Carlos is our founder and our mentor, but he doesn't stay here. Carlos has his own researches to conduct, and he prefers working apart from us." Something in Sarah's manner made Ruthie suspect that Sarah wasn't telling the whole truth. Glancing around at the others in the room confirmed her suspicions. It was something about the way they all looked away and pretended not to be listening any more. All of them, even Miles, knew something about Carlos that they preferred that Ruthie didn't know yet.

Ruthie wanted to tell Sarah, *I have skills and abilities, too,* but she decided that sounded a little too self-serving. Besides, she wasn't entirely sure she wanted to join this unusual group. Instead, she said, "What becomes of me if you decide you don't want me here?"

"Obviously you can't go back home again," Sarah stated. "That world doesn't exist any more, and probably never will again. So we'll take you to any point in history you prefer, set you up with an new identity — we're rather good at that. Give you enough money to get you started in your new life; that's not a problem for us. Then we unlock the timeband from your arm, and you never see us again. If that's what you prefer, we'll do it as soon as we are able."

"I don't know," Ruthie said. It was tempting; there were many historical eras to which she had often wished she could escape. But she had had a fleeting taste of the power of the timeband, and she wasn't ready to give that up. "Let me think about it. I might still like to join you, and prove to you that I can be an asset to your group."

Sarah looked at her skeptically. Denise broke in, "Sarah, I think Ruthie probably needs a chance to freshen up and get into some clean clothes. Come with me."

Sarah agreed, and Denise led Ruthie down a corridor into a wing of guest rooms. "One thing this place has plenty of is spare rooms," Denise told Ruthie. "At most we only have six people living here, and yet the place was built with twelve bedrooms."

"Why?"

"Optimism," Denise explained. "There are twelve timebands, and Sarah has always hoped for the day when we would all be on the same side, and not warring with each other."

Denise opened the door to a rather good-sized spare bedroom, with an adjoining bathroom. Ruthie noted with surprise the presence of both electric lights and running water.

"Yeah, this place has its own generators," Denise explained, seeing Ruthie's reaction. "And we've got a water tower out back that we pump Lake Michigan water into. So feel free to take a shower, but go easy on the hot water. I've got some clothes you can fit into, and I'll be happy to share until we can take a shopping trip into the future for you."

Ruthie stood in front of the mirror that was hung over the dresser and looked at herself in dismay. She was still wearing her dirty, blood-stained uniform from her job at a diner that didn't even exist anymore. "This is all so confusing. You're all time-travelers, and it's your job to fix history when it goes off the track?"

"Something like that. It could be your job, too, if you want it. I know Sarah's not convinced, but we'll put in a good word for you."

"Sarah doesn't like me, does she?"

Denise laughed. "Don't let that hard-nosed act fool you. She's just looking out for the safety of the team, but once she gets to know you, she'll be the most loyal friend you've ever had. I think you'll fit in fine with us. If Miles is vouching for you, you must be okay. Get yourself cleaned up, and then come out and have lunch with us. Unfortunately it's Ben's turn to cook, but I promise it won't be too bad."

Following Denise's advice, Ruthie took a shower, guiltily using up far too much of the hot water. But it felt good to relax under the shower spray after the frightening events of the morning. When she got out, she found that Denise had laid out a change of clothes for her. It included a denim work shirt and a pair of jeans, the same casual clothing that most of the others seemed to favor here. Ruthie got dressed and went out to join the others.

She found the five of them gathered around a large dining table, with books and newspapers scattered across it. Miles and Ben were having a loud and excited discussion, with the others listening in and adding their own comments. There were the fixings for sandwiches on the sideboard, as well as bowls of salad and a pitcher of lemonade.

"Hi, Ruthie," Miles called when he saw her. "Grab some food and join us. Ben and I think we've pieced together what happened to the history we thought we knew."

Sarah shot Miles a look, and Ruthie thought that Sarah didn't approve of their discoveries being shared with her yet. But no one seemed deterred by it, and Ben launched into an explanation. "You see, we think it goes all the way back to December 7, 1941."

"Pearl Harbor," Ruthie said, putting roast beef between bread for a sandwich.

"Right, but now history has changed so that somehow the United States had some warning an attack was on its way. The U.S. carrier fleet intercepts the Japanese carriers, and there is a massive battle at sea which ends in an American victory. The Japanese fleet is turned back, and their planes never reach Oahu. There is no attack on Pearl Harbor."

"And that leads to the Nazis taking over America?" Ruthie asked.

"Unfortunately, yes," Miles said. "The next day, Adolf Hitler is so angered by the fiasco in the Pacific — the Japanese had planned their attack without consulting him — that he breaks off Germany's alliance with Japan and insists to the world that he had nothing to do with the Japanese war plans. As a result, the U.S. declares war on Japan, but Congress passes new neutrality measures to keep America out of the war in Europe. Britain and Russia are left to fight the Nazis without American help, and by 1944, both have fallen to Nazi Germany. Hitler is the master of all of Europe."

"The United States and Japan fight a long, inconsequential war in the Pacific that ends in armistice in 1947," Ben continued. "Neither side has won a clear victory, but both nations are war-weary and drained of resources. But only a few months after the armistice, Germany launches a surprise attack against the United States. German scientists had successfully developed a super-weapon that no other country had yet: the atomic bomb. First New York, then Washington are incinerated by German V-5 rockets with fission bomb payloads. Unable to defend itself, the United States reluctantly capitulates to German demands for surrender."

"The Chicago we saw had been living under Nazi rule for almost six decades," Miles told Ruthie. "The U.S. Constitution had been superseded by orders of occupation dictated by Hitler himself, who ruled America until his death in 1972. The United States became a semiautonomous country whose leaders were hand-picked by their German masters and elected in a mockery of free elections. By the early twenty-first century, the U.S. is one part of a Greater German Reich that includes almost half the Earth's land mass and about a third of its population."

"Variation Three," Ben said unhappily. "We spent all this time trying to figure out a way to move from Variation Six to Variation Seven, and now we're knocked all the way back to Three. It's so discouraging."

"Wow. You figured all this out while I was taking a shower?" Ruthie asked.

Miles nodded. "It helped that one of the books Denise brought back was a history textbook. We skimmed through the section on the 1940's and picked out the highlights."

"What we're not sure of yet is whether the reality wave started in 1941," Ben said, "or if the real damage to the timeline occurred much earlier, and only became noticeable then."

"What I don't get," interjected Jason, "is the bomb attack on Ron Klausson in 2007. Sure, kill Klausson and the world never gets to Variation Seven. It's stuck in Variation Five or Six for another couple of centuries or more. But why plan a major assassination in the early twenty-first century when you know you're also going to touch off a reality wave over sixty years earlier, which will wipe out the later attack? It doesn't make any sense."

Nobody had a good response to that. "I don't get it either," Ben said. "What did the bomb in 2007 accomplish?"

Only Ruthie spoke. "It killed Jack," she said quietly.

Chapter 6

The next morning the team held a memorial service for Jack. Ruthie felt awkward attending, since she had hardly known the man before he died in her arms. But she knew that, as a guest of the team, it would have been even more awkward not to attend.

The service was held on a small terrace in the compound's garden. The morning was crisp and cool — the automatic calendar in Ruthie's head, as provided by the timeband, told her that it was November in this year, as well — and the five surviving team members and Ruthie stood in a circle, remembering their fallen comrade.

"Jack liked playing the tough guy," Miles began. His voice was thick with emotion. "Those of us who knew him well knew that was just an act. He was a sentimental old soul who couldn't stand to see a dog mistreated, much less a human being. He fought for justice all his life, first as a police officer in Brooklyn, then on a much more global scale as a Traveler. He was my inspiration as well as my partner. The team will miss his wisdom and guidance, but he will always be a part of it. His mission continues, and those of us who remain will carry out that work in his name."

He was quiet again, looking drained from the emotional effort. Ben put a comforting hand on his shoulder.

The others also had their own memories of Jack to relate. Each spoke briefly, relating incidents from the past which revealed Jack's humor or courage or noble spirit. Sarah was the last team member to speak, adding a few brief words about Jack's dedication to the cause they served. Then, as the circle was about to break up, Ruthie surprised everyone, including herself, by offering to say something about Jack.

"I didn't know Jack very well," Ruthie said. "I knew how he liked his eggs, and that he preferred his coffee black, no sugars. Oh, and that he tipped well. Better than Miles." The group laughed at this. Ruthie continued, "I wish I had known him better when he was alive. Most of what I know about Jack, I learned after his death.

I know he was a good man, doing something important. I know he gave me his timeband."

Ruthie's voice began to falter; she wasn't sure if she should say what else she wanted to say, but she decided to plunge ahead anyway. "I'll never know for sure, but it seemed to me that he wanted me to have the timeband, and to continue to use it as he had. I know that won't be my decision; it will be yours, and you'll decide what's best for the team and the mission. But I wanted to let you know that I've decided that I want to keep the timeband, if you'll let me. I want to honor Jack by continuing what he dedicated his life to, and use the timeband to save the world from centuries of misery and oppression. I'm asking you to let me do this."

No one spoke. After a few long, uncomfortable moments, Ruthie turned and walked back toward the house. Before she had reached the front door, Miles was racing up the walkway after her.

"Wait, Ruthie, we just voted," he said, out of breath. "You're in."

That afternoon, Sarah called Ruthie into her office. This was a small room, windowless, with a large oaken desk and three tall bookshelves filled with books. Sarah was seated behind the desk, and the only other chair in the room was occupied by Denise. Ruthie stood, uncomfortably, in front of the table as Sarah spoke to her.

"Before we make this official, I want you to know exactly what you're signing on for. By agreeing you be part of our team, you are accepting a responsibility of almost unimaginable proportions. The timeband is no toy. It is perhaps the most powerful device ever created, capable of reshaping the lives of billions. With a timeband on your arm you could be the world's greatest thief, an unstoppable assassin, a spy without equal. If you join our team, you will be put through rigorous training. You need to be operating at peak mental and physical ability, or you cannot be part of the team. Denise will be the lead instructor, but the other team members will also be your instructors. Any one of them can fail you if you do not meet their expectations during training, and then we will remove your timeband and expel you from the team. Do you understand?"

Ruthie swallowed hard and nodded. She looked to Denise, who had been friendly to her the day before when they first met.

Denise's face was blank; she was giving no sign of encouragement to Ruthie.

"Ruthie," Sarah continued, "we are a small, tight-knit community. We trust each other with our lives, and we depend on each other to watch our backs. The five of us need to know that we can trust you without question. We need your loyalty and your absolute obedience in the field. I am team leader, and you need to accept my authority, or the authority of whichever senior member I designate on field assignments. If orders are questioned, lives could be lost. Understood?"

Ruthie nodded again. "I understand."

"I doubt if you do, fully. I doubt if you truly realize that your old life has ended and a new life begins today. Ruthie, if you make it through your training and become a full-fledged member of our team, you will be asked to do things that may be unimaginable to you. You will be placed in crucial moments in the past or future and have to act to change the course of history. Some of these tasks may be difficult and grueling, and some may challenge your core values. But they have to be undertaken if we are to achieve our goal of establishing Variation Seven, for the good of all humanity."

Ruthie looked Sarah in the eye. "You're trying to scare me. And I have to admit it's working. But I'm not changing my mind. I've never achieved anything great with my life before. Suddenly I have an opportunity to do something important, something significant. I know what lies ahead of me will be hard. I expect that. I welcome it. I want to prove to myself that I'm worthy of the timeband on my arm. Sarah, I want to be part of your team."

There was a long, uncomfortable silence. Finally Sarah said, "Very well. I hope you do not regret your decision. Denise, she's all yours."

Ruthie's training began that afternoon. Denise led Ruthie to the back wing of the safehouse, an area that was used mainly for storage. She opened the door to a room that was absolutely empty of everything except two mats on the floor. "Welcome to my classroom."

Denise invited Ruthie to sit on one of the mats, cross-legged. Then she closed the door, shutting out all light. Ruthie was sitting in almost total blackness. She heard Denise settle onto the mat across from her.

"Okay. What kind of training can we do here?" Ruthie asked.

"Very essential first steps. You know that control of the timeband is entirely mental. It requires only a thought to give the timeband a command. Also, the timeband is inputting data directly into your brain, having attached itself onto your neural network. But until you've trained your mind properly, you can't make sense of all the information the timeband is trying to tell you, nor can you command the timeband with precision."

"I did all right yesterday, in the Chicago police station."

"That's right, but I'm afraid that was probably pure luck. Nine times out of ten you probably wouldn't be able to do it again. We're going to spend some sessions in deep meditation, so you can focus your attention on the new connections your brain has made with the timeband, and learn how to command it accurately every time."

"Are you a Zen master?" Ruthie asked.

"No. Actually I'm a theoretical physicist. I'm the closest thing we have to an expert on time travel. Compared to the people who designed the timebands — if they even were people like us — I'm barely in kindergarten, but I keep trying to learn what I can. And I've learned enough to be your driver's ed instructor when it comes to operating the timeband."

"Okay," Ruthie said. She wasn't sure that her earlier success with the timeband had been entirely due to luck. Though she didn't know exactly what she did to command the timeband, it did respond to her wishes well enough, especially when she ordered it to save her from the two cops that were assaulting her. But she intended to be completely cooperative when it came to her training, so she was ready to do whatever Denise had in mind for her. "What do I do now?"

"Relax. Clear your mind. Try not to think about anything in particular. The timeband is trying to find a way to communicate with you. Let it. Listen to what it's saying, and allow it to organize the messages in your brain."

Denise stopped talking, and Ruthie sat in the darkness and silence and allowed herself to become aware of the new presence in her mind. With her usual senses muted, Ruthie felt herself overwhelmed by a flood of images and information coming directly from the timeband on her arm. Some of it was in the form of quantities, units of time that ranged from fractions of a second to centuries. She could also sense the flow of time itself, and she could feel that this rate was not a constant, but a variable that could be changed by the application of her will. There was more, much more that she could sense. She could feel a connection to Denise's timeband, the only other timeband currently within range, and somehow Ruthie knew that she could send mental commands to that timeband as well, if Denise permitted it. But this was only the tip of the iceberg — most of the new data that she was receiving made no sense at all to her, and Ruthie suddenly felt lost, drowning in a mental sea of information filling all the parts of her consciousness…

She felt pressure on her shoulders, and she became aware that she was being shaken gently. "It's all right, Ruthie," Denise was saying. "Stay with us."

"I'm all right," Ruthie said, though she knew that wasn't entirely accurate. "It's just too much… too fast…"

"You're having the expected reaction to your new awareness," Denise said calmly. "You need to get used to the fact that you now have two brains. Your natural one inside your skull, and an artificial one wrapped around your left arm. The brain of the timeband is a highly specialized one, but it's also operating in the four dimensions of space-time, while your own brain is only wired for three. The two brains need to learn to communicate with each other, and you need to help them do just that."

"Okay," Ruthie said. As long as Denise kept talking, the babble of timeband data could be pushed to the back of her mind and safely ignored for now. "How do I do that?"

"Let's start with something easy. When are we? Give me the year, date, and time."

The answer came quickly to Ruthie. "It's 1504. November nineteenth. Two-thirty-two in the afternoon. Oh, and twelve seconds."

"Exactly right. That's one piece of information the timeband is always giving you. Now take a moment to find that data stream in your mind. Grab hold of it, bring it front and center. Make it big and bold in your mind and light it up with red neon."

Ruthie closed her eyes and tried to do just that. Now that the room was dark and silent again, the jumble of information became overpowering again, and it threatened to overwhelm her.

But Ruthie could still perceive the timeband telling her that it was November 19, 1504, and the clock was still ticking off the seconds past 2:32: *twenty-three, twenty-four, twenty-five...* She focused all of her awareness on that clock, letting the information expand in her mind and even imagining it glowing candy-apple red.

Ruthie kept her concentration focused on the clock-calendar data stream for several minutes until Denise spoke again. "You still have the time data? Good. Don't let go of it, but now we'll add a second stream. Look for where the timeband is telling you the rate of time flow. It's trying to tell you that time is flowing at normal rate, one minute for each subjective minute that passes..."

Slowly, Denise kept calling Ruthie's attention to various streams of data that the timeband was inputting into her brain. The session stretched out for several hours, but by the time they finally quit for the day, Ruthie had been able to identify and call easily to mind more than a dozen indicators that she was receiving from the timeband. What had once been a chaotic jumble in her brain was beginning to make sense. Her mind was starting to impose an ordered system of organization to the timeband data.

"You did good today," Denise told her. "Take tonight off, and see me at one o'clock tomorrow for our next session. But before that, in the morning, you're going to have your first lessons from Jason."

There was something in Denise's voice that Ruthie thought sounded ominous. She had a feeling that Jason's lessons were not going to be enjoyable.

When the pounding on her door started, the glowing red numbers in Ruthie's head told her it was exactly three minutes past four in the morning. Ruthie's first two thoughts upon achieving wakefulness were to congratulate herself on being able to summon up the exact time so quickly, and to wonder who the hell was pounding on her door at four-oh-three in the morning.

She had just pulled herself up to a sitting position in bed when the door burst open. Standing there was the silhouetted form of a tall, thin man. It took Ruthie a moment to recognize him as Jason.

"Jason? What —"

"Ruthie McDonald, you have sixty seconds from the moment I close this door to dress yourself and put on a pair of running shoes. After sixty seconds, I come in and drag you out whether you are dressed or not."

Ruthie began to protest, but Jason threw the door closed again. She had no doubt, from the tone of Jason's voice, that Jason would do exactly as he had promised at the exact moment that he had stated. As she stripped off her pajamas and found clothing in her dresser drawer, she noted that the clock in her head had automatically switched to a countdown mode and was ticking off the seconds left to her.

By the time she was down to five seconds left, she had thrown on a T-shirt and jeans over bra and panties, and was finding a pair of running shoes in the closet of the room she had been assigned. The door burst open again as she finished tying the laces of one shoe.

"Give me a second! I'm almost done!" she exclaimed.

"I gave you sixty seconds. Time to start your training." Ruthie looked up to see that Jason was dressed in a green sweatshirt and running pants. He was also wearing a thin leather belt with a knife and sheath on it, and tucked into a shoulder holster was a firearm.

"What kind of training has to start at four in the morning?" Ruthie asked. She glanced at the curtained window; it was still very dark outside.

"Physical training," Jason said. "And combat training."

Her shoes tied, Ruthie followed Jason out of the room, annoyed that she hadn't been allowed to brush her teeth, fix her hair, or do anything else that she would normally take care of upon rising in the morning.

The big house was dark and silent at this hour. Jason led Ruthie downstairs and out the rear door, into the cool crisp air of the safehouse grounds. Ruthie wished she was wearing a jacket, but Jason didn't seem to mind the cold, and she knew he wouldn't let her go back for one. "I knew you'd be teaching me this morning, but I didn't expect our session would start this early," she said.

"Life's full of surprises. Get used to it." He touched a control on the back gate of the palisade, which swung open. "See if you can keep up." He took off running into the woods. Ruthie thought he looked more like a jungle cat than human in the way he accelerated.

For a moment Ruthie considered turning around and going back to bed. That, she decided, would not be a good idea if she wanted to keep the timeband. So she started running after the figure that she could now barely see sprinting through the forest.

Ruthie had always kept herself in excellent physical shape. A high school athlete in track, softball, and volleyball, she had continued to work out at the gym in the years since then. This was primarily because she thought it would help her get acting jobs if she kept the extra pounds off, but also because she enjoyed the time she spent exercising; it was a pleasant break in her otherwise dull routine.

But this was no leisurely jog in a gymnasium. Jason was setting a fast pace, and Ruthie had to push herself to go even faster to catch up with him. After several minutes of hard running over uneven terrain, Ruthie finally was able to pull up even with Jason and match him stride for stride.

"Is this going to help me use the timeband?" Ruthie asked him, gasping for breath between almost every word.

"Denise will teach you to use the timeband. I'm going to find out if you can survive when missions become dangerous."

"Dangerous?"

"Don't kid yourself. Lots of ways to get yourself killed, doing what we do. The lives of your teammates might depend on how fit you are, or if you can handle yourself in a fight."

Ruthie thought about telling Jason about the two track medals she had won in high school, and the five-week course in stage combat she had finished last year, but she decided that Jason would not be impressed by either.

They had reached the edge of the forest, and Ruthie saw the shoreline of Lake Michigan, reflecting the rosy color of the approaching dawn. Ruthie had seen the lake from this vantage point many times before, but never without the presence of tall buildings, busy streets, and a multitude of people around. Jason steered them to run northward along the pebbly shore a few yards from the water's edge.

"I still don't see why we have to be up before dawn to do this. I'm freezing."

"My choice. I like running this early. Next time wear something with long sleeves. How do the shoes fit?"

"Not bad. I'll probably have blisters the rest of the day because they're not broken in, but the fit is about right. How did you happen to have shoes my size?"

"Thank Miles for that. He's our scrounger. I sent him out yesterday to bring back twentieth-century running shoes for you, and he made a good guess as to your foot size."

"Oh." Ruthie realized that if Miles had gone back to her own time to find her running shoes, he must have returned to a Chicago that was still under Nazi control. He had risked his life and freedom for a pair of shoes. She would remember to thank him.

Jason kept the pace up for another twenty minutes, and finally Ruthie could take no more. Her body was aching from her neck to her feet, and her lungs burned from gasping for air. She pulled up to a stop, and Jason reluctantly did the same.

"Five minute break," he said, "and then we run back to the safehouse."

"Thanks," she said, sitting down unceremoniously on the ground,

She looked at Jason with disgust. He hardly looked tired at all. He looked ready to run some more, at least a marathon or two.

"I hate you," Ruthie said. She had meant it as a joke, a comment on how he hardly looked tired at all after their run. But as soon as she said the words, she regretted it. She barely knew this man. In time, she might have reason to hate him — so far he had been nothing but cruel and sadistic toward her — but she didn't really know him, and she had no way to know if this first impression was a true one.

Jason seemed to realize this, too. "You don't know me well enough to hate me yet. But give it time. You will, soon enough."

"Why?" Ruthie asked.

Jason said nothing in reply. He kept jogging in place, unwilling to allow himself to relax for even a moment.

"What's the hardware for?" Ruthie asked, and she pointed at his knife and gun.

"To keep us safe." Jason looked annoyed at what obviously thought was a stupid question.

"Are we in danger here?"

"Miss, in case you haven't realized, this is still the wilderness. We built those high wooden walls to keep dangerous things out. There's wild animals out here, and people, too. Most of the Indians in this region are peaceful, but maybe not all of them." He pronounced the word *Indians* more like *Injuns*, and there wasn't a hint of political correctness in his voice.

"Now you tell me."

"That's not all. There's a whole other team out there, hoping to ambush us and take our timebands. I don't mean to let that happen."

"Oh. Are you always armed?"

Jason nodded. "Are you ready to go back now?"

Ruthie got to her feet. She was more than ready.

When they returned to the team's safehouse, Ruthie expected that she'd be allowed to take a shower, get dressed, and have a leisurely breakfast before the next training session. But Jason directed her to go at once to the basement, where he had set up one end of it as a dojo, the floor covered with padded mats. "Have you studied any martial arts?" he asked.

Ruthie shook her head. "You have, I suppose."

"Only jujitsu, karate, aikido, savate, Sambo, kalaripayattu, Bartitsu, and bare-knuckle brawling. Probably two or three others as well. I'm not going to try to teach you all of them. Just a crash course in staying alive." He removed his knife belt and shoulder holster and placed them in a locker on the wall, then did the same with his shoes. Ruthie took off her shoes as well.

There was a large circle painted on the floor mat, and Jason directed Ruthie to stand in the center of it with him. He bowed to her, and Ruthie copied the motion back to him. "All right, come at me."

"What?"

"After that run you're probably ready to sock me in the jaw, so go ahead. You want to beat the crap out of me, go ahead and do it."

Ruthie had to admit to herself that it probably would feel good to pay Jason back a little for all the pain he had just put her through, so she launched herself at him and made ready to punch him.

She wasn't exactly sure what happened next. There was the sensation of her feet leaving the ground, the room spinning around her, and suddenly she was flat on her back. One of Jason's arms was pressed against her throat, and the other was holding both of her wrists pinned to the mat. Her right leg was trapped under Jason's knee, and most of his weight was on it.

"Ouch," she managed to say. She tried to wriggle out from under him, but she was completely immobilized. "Let me up?"

Slowly Jason released her and let her get back to her feet. Even with the padded mat, she was sore in all the places that had impacted the floor. "What was that supposed to be? Jujitsu, aikido, or kalari-whatever?"

"A little combination of my own. Let me show you again more slowly."

Before Ruthie could decline the invitation, Jason had again grabbed her wrists and swept her feet out from under her. He might have done the maneuver more slowly this time, but Ruthie couldn't detect any difference. The result was exactly the same, and once more Ruthie found herself pinned to the floor, unable to escape.

As Ruthie lay on the floor helpless, she came to a scary conclusion. Jason wasn't just trying to train her to defend herself. This was a sick individual, someone who found pleasure in hurting others, probably women especially. Here was a bully who had been given the opportunity to indulge his sadistic tendencies under the cover of a legitimate physical training program. Did the others know what kind of a man Jason was? Sarah had said that Ruthie had to obey her instructors without question — did she know she was turning Ruthie over to a monster? All of a sudden, Ruthie became very fearful for her own safety.

"Get... off... me!" Ruthie grunted, trying to put as much authority into each syllable as she could. It was an empty threat; she was completely in his power, and he knew it. If Jason did not choose to allow Ruthie to get off the mat, there was nothing she could do about it. She wondered if the power of the timeband could save her, as it did in the basement of the Chicago police station. Could she escape Jason by fleeing into another time, or would the timeband take both of them along? Ruthie decided it was time to find out. She tried to command the timeband to move her through time, maybe an hour or two, anything to get away from Jason.

Nothing happened.

But moments later, much to her relief, Jason stood up and even offered his hand to help her up. "You've got spirit, I'll grant you that," he said. "You haven't a hope of beating me in a fight, and yet you're ordering me around as if I should be scared of you."

"Yeah, well, I don't like feeling helpless like that."

"Good. Pay attention to the lessons I'm teaching you, and you'll never have to feel helpless again. Now let's starting running through some basics…"

Several hours later, Ruthie reported to Denise for her next lessons with the timeband. She felt bruised and battered from Jason's tutelage, but by the end of the lesson he had taught her a few useful self-defense tactics. After a shower and a late breakfast, Ruthie had to conclude that there might be quite a few valuable things she might learn from Jason about martial arts and self-defense. But she still didn't know what to make of him as a person.

Denise met Ruthie in the large, grassy area between the rear of the house and the large wooden walls, an area the residents called 'the back yard'. "You were working out with Jason this morning, I understand," Denise began. "How do you feel?"

"Like I've been through a car wreck or two. Denise, I'm not sure if I can do this."

"What do you mean?"

"I don't mind the workout. I've had to do worse from high school coaches and personal trainers. But Jason — I don't know. He's… scary, I guess. He scares me."

"Yeah, he comes on like that with everyone. He can be very intense."

"That's putting it mildly. Denise, should I be worried when I'm with him? Alone, I mean? I'm concerned about my own safety."

Denise didn't answer right away. Ruthie looked at the woman and thought she saw a trace of sadness, like some old wound, in her dark eyes. "You'll be fine with him," she said at last. "I promise you that."

"Are you sure? There were moments when I thought he was enjoying making me hurt. I know there are men who like hurting women…"

"You'll be fine," Denise insisted, and her tone suggested that further discussion would be futile. "Let's start today's lesson."

Ruthie knew that Denise wanted the subject of Jason dropped, and so she did not question Denise further about him. But there was one thing she was sure of. There had been something once between Denise and Jason. Some kind of unhappiness, the memory of which was still lurking below the surface. Ruthie didn't know the nature of the pain that Denise still felt, but she knew Denise was unable to hide it.

Denise began by reviewing the previous day's lesson. She asked Ruthie to summon up each of the data streams that the timeband was providing her, and Ruthie was able to do so with only a few minor errors. "Good," Denise said. "Whenever you've got a few minutes to spare, run through each of these readouts. Get so you can find and utilize each stream of data whenever you need it, instantly. Someday that skill might save your life. Now, are you ready to Travel?"

She pronounced the word *Travel* like it ought to be capitalized, and Ruthie understood this was how the team referred to moving through time. "Yes, I guess so."

"Good. Now, do you see the input that indicates that my timeband is within your range of control?"

Ruthie searched the various streams of information in her head. This was one of the ones that they had practiced finding the day before, and Ruthie found it within a few seconds. "I have it."

"What is our synchronicity deviation?"

"Zero," Ruthie reported.

"Naturally. If it wasn't, we couldn't speak to each other. One of us would be in the other's past, not her present. Now, what's my timeband's status?"

Ruthie was confused for a moment by the question, but she examined the readout for Denise's timeband and found a datum that seemed relevant. "Independent?"

"That's right. That means that I'm controlling my timeband right now, and you're controlling your own. Now see if you can push back along that info stream, and change the status from *Independent* to *Linked*."

"I don't know how to do that..."

"Doesn't matter. The timeband is trying to teach you how to do it. Let it. Concentrate on my timeband's status, and think about it changing to Linked. The timeband will help you do it."

It seemed like an impossibility to Ruthie. The brain wasn't a muscle — she couldn't push with it like she could with her arms or hands. But she knew that Denise knew what she was talking about, so she tried to do exactly as Denise had commanded. Push back along the info stream... change the status to Linked... All of a sudden it was like something had clicked in her head. The status of Denise's timeband, according the data being channeled into her brain, was now Linked.

Denise knew it at once. "Very good! You did it."

"What did I do?"

"Your timeband is now controlling mine. Whatever command you give it will be obeyed by both timebands. When you Travel, I'll be Traveling with you. You experienced this already, I believe. When Miles brought you back to 1504?"

Ruthie nodded. Miles had brought her back over five centuries, and Ruthie didn't have to do anything; she was just along for the ride. But this time, Ruthie was in control. She would be bringing Denise along if she Traveled. Denise would be in the passenger seat, but Ruthie would be driving.

"Now what?"

"Now I want you to take us back exactly five years. Today's date — November 20, but in the year 1499. The same time of day. It's before the safehouse was built, so we won't cross the paths of any team members. Do you understand? November 20, 1499, same time of day."

"Denise, I don't know how to do that," Ruthie admitted.

"You need to let the timeband teach you. Concentrate on the calendar stream — focus on changing the year from 1504 to 1499. Impose your will on the timeband, and it will respond. Go ahead, I'll be right with you."

"All right, I'll try." Ruthie focused her attention on the red numbers in her head that read *1504* and tried to imagine them changing into *1499*. She tried to remember what it had felt like when she had jumped back a few minutes to escape from the Chicago cops that had been assaulting her. But replicating what she had done then was not something easily done. No matter how hard she tried, the number stubbornly refused to change.

"Nothing's happening!" Ruthie cried in frustration.

"Patience. This takes time. It took time for me, when I first got the timeband. Relax — it will happen."

Then, suddenly, it was like a doorknob that she had been groping for in the dark found its way into her hand, and she gave it a mental twist and the numbers started changing. She tried to focus her adjustment onto the year alone, but she found that she couldn't master that kind of precision yet. All the date and time readouts were changing, not just the year, but the month, date, hour, and minute as well. In a panic, she ordered them to stop changing.

Ruthie opened her eyes wide in surprise and shock. It was totally dark, bitterly cold, and she was soaking wet. *"Denise!"*

"I'm here, Ruthie," came the calm voice of her friend. "You overshot a little." There was a flash of lightning in the distance, and from its light Ruthie could see the silhouette of the other woman, still a few paces away from her.

Ruthie checked the calendar in her head. The readout had changed to *May 11, 1388, 4:38 a.m.* "Oh, my God. It's the year 1388?"

"It is. Not a problem. Let me get us out of this rainstorm." Ruthie noticed that something changed in her head. The status of Denise's timeband, she realized, had changed from *Linked* to *Master*. Seconds later, the two women were standing in bright sunshine in a grassy clearing near a forest. There was no sign of the safehouse. Now the timeband was telling Ruthie that the date was May 13, 1388, and it was 1:19 in the afternoon.

"That's better," Denise said. Both women's hair, skin, and clothing were still very wet from the thunderstorm, but Ruthie could feel herself already starting to dry in the bright sun. "I took control of your timeband to jump us ahead a couple of days. No sense standing in foul weather if you don't have to."

"You could have brought us back to 1504."

"No. You'll do that. It may take some time, but you'll learn how to control your timeband with precision. I have faith in you, Ruthie."

Ruthie wished she had the same faith in herself. "What you just did — taking control of my timeband. Miles did that, too. Couldn't that be dangerous? The others who oppose your team — couldn't they take control of your timeband and use it against you?"

Denise shook her head. "You have to allow the other Traveler to control your timeband. Unless you give permission, other timebands are automatically blocked from taking control of your timeband. Otherwise, you'd be vulnerable to any rogue Traveler in synch with you who came in range. Your timeband still has the default permissions that Jack set. The other members of our team can take control, but no one else. In a later lesson, I'll teach you how to alter those permissions."

Ruthie thought about that. Jason, she realized, had permission to take control of Ruthie's timeband whenever he wanted and could lock her out. During the morning workout, when he had Ruthie pinned to the mat, he probably was also preventing her from using her timeband. Ruthie was sure that as soon as she was able, she'd change the permissions on her timeband and deny Jason the ability to take control.

"We're really in 1388?" Ruthie asked.

"Absolutely. Right now, over in Europe, the Crusades are still going on. Christopher Columbus hasn't made it to America yet — hasn't even been born, actually. Get used to it. If you're going to be one of us, you'll be visiting a lot of different eras. With the timeband, you can go to any year you want. But now I want you to take control of both timebands again, and concentrate on returning us to 1504. It's my turn to make dinner, and I don't want the team mad at me if their meal is late."

Ruthie found the mental readout for the status of Denise's timeband, gave a little push, and it quickly switched over from *Master* to *Linked*. That was easy, she thought. Maybe she was getting the hang of it. She turned her attention to the date, and gave a mental push in that direction, imagining the numbers changing back to November 20, 1504.

In her mind, the numbers spun out of control. She urgently forced them to stop, and was immediately disoriented by what she saw around her. The trees and grass were gone — she was on solid pavement, and all around her was noise and tall buildings and people and — *cars!*

"Move!" Denise cried, pushing her hard.

Ruthie stumbled quickly toward the curb just as a black sedan roared past, missing both women by inches.

The date in her head was August 14, 1923. In the blink of an eye, they had jumped from the fourteenth to the twentieth century.

"I'm sorry!" Ruthie cried, shaken from nearly being hit by a car. "I tried to get us to 1504, but I overshot, again. I'm going to get us killed!"

"No, you're not. Relax. Everyone has trouble controlling their timebands at first. You'll get good at it. I promise you."

As Ruthie calmed down, she looked around her. They were standing on a Chicago sidewalk — Clark Street, by the looks of it. It was 8:09 in the morning, and many people were hurrying on their way to work. Some people were looking at Denise and Ruthie strangely, but no one stopped to question or confront them. "We just popped into the middle of the street," Ruthie said. "I'd think people would be frightened of us, but no one's doing anything except giving us weird looks."

"That's because of the way we're dressed." Both women were wearing light jackets, blue jeans, and sneakers, just as women in the early twenty-first century might, but not the typical attire for 1920's Chicago, and their clothing was still damp from a storm over five centuries in the past. "No one noticed us arrive. The human brain doesn't react to time anomalies. Unless someone was staring right at us, no one would pay any attention to us arriving or leaving. Are you all right?"

Ruthie realized that she was still shaking with fright. "No. Give me a moment, then I'll try again."

"That's all right. I think you've had enough for one day. I'll drive us home."

When Denise took control of both timebands again, Ruthie was both grateful and sorry. She wanted so badly to succeed at this. She wanted, more than she had ever wanted anything before, to fit in on this team and become a time traveler. But it was hard, harder than she thought it would be. What if she never mastered the timeband? Would they take it away from her? And if they did, where would she go? Her home was gone — it had never existed.

A moment later, they were back in the back yard of the safehouse. It was November 20, 1504, again, just minutes after they had left. "Come in and let's get into some dry clothes," Denise said. "Lesson's over for the day. We'll try again tomorrow."

Chapter 7

After the training session with Denise ended, Ruthie returned to her bedroom, exchanged her wet clothes for a dry pair of pajamas, and lay down on her bed for a nap. She was quite upset about how badly her training was going. Between being nearly beaten up by Jason and going astray in time with Denise, it seemed to Ruthie that it was only a matter of time before she washed out of the program. How long would it be before Sarah demanded her timeband, and the team took her to some strange era and stranded her there? Would it be soon, or would the team continue to force Ruthie to endure one nightmare after another until she called it quits herself?

Ruthie lay on her bed and worried herself to sleep. She was awakened by knocking on her door — not pounding like this morning, but polite and gentle rapping instead.

"Ruthie?" She recognized Sarah's voice. "It's dinnertime. Come down and join us, please."

Fully dressed now and feeling refreshed, Ruthie came down the large staircase and entered the spacious dining room. The team had started eating without her; there was a large serving dish of something that smelled wonderful in the center of the table. There were two available seats; Ruthie took the one between Sarah and Ben. The other unoccupied place at the table was for Miles, who was absent. Ruthie didn't pick that seat because it would have seated her next to Jason, and she wanted to stay well away from him for now.

"Give me your plate, Ruthie, and I'll fill it for you," Denise said, scooping out a large helping of something thick and brown over noodles with the serving spoon. "Hope you like beef stroganoff."

"I do," Ruthie said, realizing how hungry she was. "Where's Miles?"

"Miles is on assignment," Sarah told her. "He'll be back in two or three days."

"Oh." Ruthie realized that it was Miles she most wanted to talk to. She had always found his honest, confident face reassuring, even before she knew he was a time traveler, and she needed reassurance now.

Much of the rest of the meal proceeded in silence. No one bothered to ask Ruthie how her training was going. It seemed clear to Ruthie that all of them already knew; perhaps they had been talking about her before she came down to dinner. Sarah ate her meal in stony silence, and Ruthie could not even guess what the team leader might be contemplating. Jason wolfed down his food quickly, not making eye contact with any of his teammates. Ben and Denise, on the other hand, were carrying on a private conversation between them, mostly in low, whispered voices. They seemed very friendly with each other, and Ruthie guessed for the first time that they must be a couple. All in all, Ruthie found herself eating dinner with four individuals who were still largely strangers to her. She had little in common with them except for the timeband on her arm, and she was having a hard time feeling comfortable with any of them.

When the meal ended, Ben stood up to help clear the table. "Come by the library in an hour," he said to Ruthie. "Your training with me starts tonight."

"What training would that be?" Ruthie wondered aloud. She was quite sure that it wouldn't be combat training with the slightly-built, bookish-looking man.

"We'll be studying history. Or histories, to be more precise."

After the disastrous sessions with Jason and Denise, Ruthie found she was looking forward to learning history with Ben. History had been one of her majors in college, before she had switched to theater, and she thought she still remembered quite a bit from her survey courses in American and European history. She started to tell this to Ben, after he greeted her in the book-lined room on the safehouse's second floor, but he didn't seem impressed.

"I hate to tell you this, Ruthie, but much of the history you learned in school is now invalid. Certainly everything after 1941 is. And the rest of it might be thrown out the window when the next reality wave happens. We think of history as something fluid, not fixed. Your background in history will give you an understanding of one timeline, but you have a lot to learn about all of the other possible timelines."

"You mean the Variations?"

Ben smiled. "I see you've picked up a little of what you need to learn. Did Miles tell you about the Variations? How much did he tell you?"

"Only that they were discovered by two men called Carlos and Caesar. Carlos is your team's mentor, helping you establish the seventh Variation, which is supposed to be the only one that doesn't include mankind's extinction. Caesar leads a team that is trying to stop you, for reasons that I can't even imagine."

"That's it exactly. Everything we do is based on the work of Carlos and Caesar. As young men, they traveled up and down the timeline, causing large and small changes to history to happen and recording the results. They mapped and numbered all the known variations and identified all the known linchpins connecting them."

"Linchpins?"

"Linchpins are the historical events where Variations branched off from each other," Ben explained. "Change the circumstances at one of these linchpins, and all history from that point on changes in a sudden reality wave, a tsunami that erases everything that previously existed in that timeline and replaces it with a new sequence of historical events."

"Is the old timeline really gone?" Ruthie asked. "Or do both the old and new timelines still exist, in alternate realities?"

"I wish I could say that's a possibility," Ben said. "I know science fiction writers for years have been writing about a multiverse of alternate realities — an infinity of possible histories all coexisting side-by-side. Unfortunately, it doesn't seem to be the case. There is only one timeline, one history, one past, present, and future. It can be changed, rewritten by Travelers using their timebands. When that happens, the old sequence of events ceases to exist. People who had lived and died in the old timeline can be wiped out of existence, never to have been born."

A chill went down Ruthie's spine. "If I hadn't put on Jack's timeband," Ruthie said, "I might have been erased by the reality wave — and I would never have known it."

"Probably. I suppose there's a slim chance that your parents might still have lived to meet and give birth to you, but there's a far greater chance that their lives would have been so affected that you never would have come into existence at all. Putting on the timeband saved your life."

Ruthie was silent for a moment, thinking back. "Miles was trying to remove the timeband from my arm when it started pulsing red. That was the warning that a reality wave was coming, right? Even after it started flashing red, he kept trying to get the timeband off of me, but there wasn't time."

"Don't think harshly of Miles. In that moment, he had to consider what was a kinder fate for you — to be wiped clean out of existence by the rushing wave of new reality, or to be uprooted from the world you knew and to lose all connections with your past life — no family, no friends, everything you knew would be gone. If you were in his place, would you have done any different? There was no time to ask you which you would have preferred. He tried to make the choice for you, the only reasonable one under the circumstances."

Ruthie considered this. Ben was right, she had to concede. Miles didn't really know her at that moment. To him, she was just one of the millions of people — past, present, and future — who had existed in the old timeline but wouldn't in the new. The reality wave wouldn't have killed her; it would have caused her never to have been born, which was not the same thing at all. Miles must have known how difficult a new life as a Traveler was going to be for her. He had gone through it himself, a survivor of an entire nation that now never existed. Yes, there had been quite a few times today when she had found herself wishing that she hadn't been wearing the timeband when the reality wave passed through, and had instead faded into sweet oblivion with everything else she had ever known.

"All right," Ruthie said. "I don't want to dwell on that. What have you got for me, Professor?"

"Let's start with a linchpin in the year 1755. The Battle of the Monongahela, during the conflict you probably know as the French and Indian War. General Edward Braddock, the British commander, is mortally wounded in the unsuccessful attack that he leads. There is a volunteer officer with him, a Virginian with the honorary rank of colonel. He rides back and forth across the battlefield rallying Braddock's troops, and in the process his coat is holed several times by musket balls. The officer is unwounded, and goes on to do a few famous things in his remaining years."

"George Washington."

"Correct. Now let's take a look at what happens if it had been Washington, and not Braddock, who is mortally wounded in 1755..."

For the next few hours, Ben took Ruthie through multiple histories that never were, empires that she never heard of that rose and fell. What would have happened if the British won at Saratoga, or if Napoleon had prevailed at Waterloo. How history would have changed in the Czar had not been overthrown in Russia, or if the Japanese had sank the American fleet at Midway. Ben showed Ruthie where the possible linchpins of history were, events that made the difference between one Variation being followed or another. At the Beer Hall Putsch in Munich, police shot and killed several leaders standing in the front rank of the would-be rebels, but the man who was standing between two of the fatalities lived and was arrested instead. How many millions of lives would have been altered if Adolf Hitler lay dead in the streets of Munich, instead of living to write *Mein Kampf* in his prison cell?

Most fascinating of all were the alternate histories of what still seemed like the future to Ruthie, the years following 2007. These were not based on mere speculation — Ben and his teammates had traveled to these eras, as far as their timebands would take them, to map out the decline and fall of Western civilization, and the extinction of the human race. In Ruthie's timeline, which they called Variation Six, there is a regional conflict in Africa in 2101 that spirals out of control and becomes a global war involving all the major powers on Earth. China, the mightiest economic power on the planet at the time, takes on the Western alliance of Europe and North America, and the resulting conflict unleashes misery and human suffering on a scale far beyond anything the world had ever seen. The war quickly escalates into full-scale exchanges of nuclear and biological weapons. Billions die as the great cities of the world are destroyed in a matter of days. Even after the fighting ends, when the warring nations are too decimated to continue, the dying continues from plague and famine. In the nuclear winter that follows, the last vestiges of civilization disappear, and within fifty years the human species is extinct.

"That's the oblivion your world was heading toward," Ben explained. "We don't think it was inevitable. There were several linchpins that we thought might turn Variation Six into Variation Seven, both before and after 2007. Jack, Miles, and I were getting ready to pitch a proposed mission to Sarah to try to create a new timeline when this most recent reality wave hit. Now the whole thing is moot; we're in Variation Three, not Six, and we have to come up with a new plan."

"I'm not sure I understand how to Variations work," Ruthie admitted. "There must be an infinite number of possible timelines — anything a Traveler does in the past must constantly create new Variations. I don't see how you can possibly categorize them and number them."

"Actually, it's much harder to change history than you think," Ben explained. "The timeline is naturally resistant to change, and it tends to fix things on its own without having an entirely new reality come into existence. Small changes don't matter much in the great scheme of history. Even big changes have a natural tendency to cancel themselves out over time. If you were to succeed in preventing Richard Nixon from becoming president in 1968, for example, someone with very similar politics would have been elected instead. The new president would have enacted almost the same policies that Nixon did, made the same mistakes, and probably would have suffered the same fate. In the long run, it wouldn't have mattered much; the world would have continued on the same course with or without him.

"Think of the Variations as wagon ruts in the road. The wagon wheel of history ends up falling into one rut or the other; it's inevitable. With the proper push at the proper moment, the wheel can jump from one rut to another. But there aren't that many Variations that a timeline can follow; Carlos and Caesar proved that long ago."

"So where is this Variation going to lead us?" Ruthie wanted to know.

"Not sure. We have sketchy descriptions of it from some of Carlos's early researches. We know it ends badly for the world; none of the Variations except Variation Seven make it past 2200 A.D. With Nazi Germany as one of the major superpowers in the twenty-first century, I'm not surprised there's little hope for human survival as a species. But as soon as we're ready, Sarah will start sending some of us out on field trips to gather data about this Variation. We'll need a full picture of the future course of history before we start planning how to nudge it back closer to Variation Seven."

"What would Variation Seven be like?"

"A true Golden Age on Earth," Ben says. "Sometime in the late twenty-first century, the industrialized nations find the will to use their technological achievements to end human misery. War, disease, poverty, oppression — all are solved in a matter of decades. Then mankind goes on to colonize the stars, and we are at last a multi-planet species. Supposedly Carlos achieved Variation Seven, long ago, and from his descriptions we have a general idea how this future utopia is achieved. But Travelers allied with Caesar wrecked the timeline, throwing it back into one of the other doomed Variations. We've been working to restore Variation Seven ever since."

Ruthie shook her head. "I don't understand. Who are these other Travelers, and what is their motivation?"

Ben shrugged. "We don't know. They're nihilists, bent on the destruction of everything. They use their timebands to subvert everything we're trying to achieve. It's the battle between Good and Evil, Order and Chaos, played out with a small number of participants on the grandest battlefield imaginable — all of modern history, all over the world. If there's an explanation for what they do, I'd like to hear it. Until then, we have no choice but to continue to try to beat them."

Ruthie went to bed that night with her head filled with the details of events that had never happened, histories of great civilizations that might have been, if only some minor detail of history had gone differently in some small way. She was impressed by Ben's encyclopedic knowledge, but she knew she could never hope to keep that much information straight in her head, especially when most of it pertained to things that never even happened. It had been a struggle in college to master a rough outline of the historical past — how could she ever learn multiple histories that included not only the past but the future?

Yet she was not ready to give up yet. Early the next morning, when Jason pounded on her door again long before sunrise, he found that Ruthie was not only awake, but fully dressed and ready for their run.

After their run, Jason instructed Ruthie to get showered and dressed, and then meet him for the next part of the training session in the safehouse's "back yard".

"Not downstairs in your, um, dojo?"

"No. You'll understand when you get there."

When Ruthie arrived, a half hour later, she found Jason setting up paper targets on an improvised shooting range. "Ever fired a gun before?"

"No," she said. "I don't like guns."

"Doesn't matter. One of the requirements for being on this team is proficiency with firearms. The bad guys may be shooting at you, and you need to be able to shoot back. In later lessons we'll go over some of the other weapons you might have occasion to use as a Traveler, but we'll start with handguns." He led her back to a table where several weapons had been placed, along with some safety glasses and ear protection. He picked up a handgun and showed it to her.

"This is a Glock 17, manufactured in Austria from about 1980 on." He slid the magazine out to show her it was unloaded, replaced it, and handed it to her. Ruthie took it reluctantly. Even though she lived in Chicago, a city known for its high rate of gun violence, Ruthie had never wanted to own a gun, not even for self-protection. But now she realized that she would have to learn to use a gun and carry one, and possibly even fire one to save herself or her comrades. Again she wondered if this was really what she wanted to do, and if it had been better if she had never put on the timeband in the first place.

"So how did your training with Jason go this morning?" Denise asked as their afternoon session began. Once again they were meeting in the empty storeroom, sitting on yoga mats.

"All right, I guess," Ruthie said. "Today was shooting practice. I learned how to load a gun, shoot it, take it apart, and clean it. I found out I'm actually not a bad shot when it comes to shooting paper targets."

"That's good."

"Yeah. Now if Caesar only has paper targets on his team, I've got nothing to worry about."

Denise laughed, and Ruthie laughed with her, although she didn't think she had been joking. Could she ever fire a loaded gun at a living person? Only a few days ago Ruthie would have been sure that she could not. But that was a different Ruthie, living a life that she would never be able to go back to. What would the new Ruthie be capable of?

"We're going to start off with more deep meditation again," Denise said. "Get better acquainted with the information the timeband is feeding you. There's a lot of new stuff in your head that you need to sort out, and before we do any more traveling, you need a better feel for how this all fits. So close your eyes, breathe slowly and deeply, and focus on what your timeband is telling you."

After an hour of deep meditation, Denise took Ruthie out into the "back yard" again to attempt some short trips into the past. This time, Ruthie found she could control the timeband with much better accuracy. She still was missing her intended targets, but now she was missing by only days instead of centuries. On each trip, Denise's timeband was still slaved to Ruthie's, so no matter how poorly Ruthie did, Denise could always bring her back to where they had started. It was still frustrating to her that she couldn't control her timeband with absolute precision, like Denise and the others could, but Denise praised her for the improvement she was showing.

As her training continued, Ruthie got to know her new teammates better, and she learned more about how they ended up on the team. She found out, for example, that Denise and Ben were lovers, and that some time ago, Denise and Jason had been lovers. The relationship between Denise and Jason had ended by mutual agreement long before Denise started spending time with Ben, but it was still obvious that Jason harbored some resentment toward Ben. It was unusual to ever see the two men working together, and Jason hardly ever spoke to Ben unless he had to.

It was Jason who had recruited Denise to be on the team. Denise was a first-generation Chinese-American, living in Milwaukee in 2011 when she met Jason. She was a grad student in theoretical physics, and she had already been dating Jason for three months before he revealed to her that he was a time traveler. By this time there was a vacancy on the team; an earlier team member, in failing health, had decided to retire from Traveling and give up his timeband; Jason proposed that it should go to his girlfriend. The other team members interviewed Denise and decided that her knowledge and skills would work well on the team, and she was accepted.

Jason himself was originally a frontiersman in the early 1800's, exploring the western territories of the young United States. He was already in prime physical condition when Carlos first encountered him, a skilled fighter and proficient with all the weapons of his day. In the years since joining the team he made studying the martial arts his passion, training with the greatest masters of several eras. He eventually became the operations chief for the team, planning and executing all of their most daring missions into various time-periods.

Prior to Ruthie, Ben was the most recent addition to the team. He had been recruited to replace another history specialist who unfortunately had been shot and killed while on a mission to France in 1917. While on an expedition to collect data in 1964, the team learned of a black history student at a newly-integrated university who would die at the hands of a lynch mob. Sarah went back in time to meet Ben, told him of his impending fate, and suggested that he might instead wish to study history by actually traveling to different eras. Had Ben declined, he might still have avoided the hangman's noose with the foreknowledge that Sarah gave him, but he decided to accept her offer anyway.

Of Sarah herself, Ruthie found out little. She had apparently been on the team much longer than anyone else, and dated back to an earlier team, all recruited by Carlos himself. Ruthie got the impression that it was Sarah, and Sarah alone, who knew where and when Carlos was, and how to get in contact with him. She knew that Sarah was much older than the rest of the team, who all seemed to view her as some kind of a stern mother figure. Everyone tried their best to please Sarah, who was rarely free with compliments.

Ruthie gathered that Jack had been Sarah's second-in-command on the team, and now that Jack was dead, that responsibility seemed to fall to Miles. It was with Miles that Sarah wanted to talk strategy, bouncing ideas off of him in private conferences. Miles took over many of Jack's other responsibilities at the compound, trying to keep the place in good working order. Miles was also the team's best scrounger, making supply runs to various eras to bring back anything team members required. As a result Ruthie got to see very little of Miles. During the first week of Ruthie's training, she had seen Miles only briefly on two occasions. The rest of the time, she was told that Miles was away, either gathering data or collecting supplies in some future year.

"How did I do?" Ruthie asked Denise. It was the eighth day of training with the timeband, and Ruthie finally felt like she was getting the hang of time travel.

"Not bad. I gave you three destinations to Travel to. The first one, you were only off by twelve minutes; the second, by eighty-five seconds, and the last one you missed by nine point two seconds. You're doing great."

"Great? That's fantastic! I can do it! I can travel through time!" Ruthie was grinning from ear to ear. What had first seemed so difficult was now easy for her. She could reset those glowing red numbers in her mind and push the timeband into sending her there with near-perfect precision. "So? Can I solo now?"

Denise shook her head. So far, Denise had been with her on each and every attempt, her timeband slaved to Ruthie's. It had been days since Denise had to take over and bring Ruthie home from an errant trip into the past or future, but Denise had still stubbornly insisted on keeping her timeband linked to Ruthie's for these training sessions. "Not yet. Maybe in a couple of days, if you continue to progress."

"'Continue to progress?' Denise, I missed my last target by nine point two seconds! That's nothing! I'm ready to solo now!"

"I don't think so. It doesn't matter if you miss by nine seconds or nine centuries. The fact is, you still missed your target, and it's not safe to let you Travel without an instructor until you hit your target exactly. Also, your trips today came after an hour of deep meditation, when your mind was utterly calm and focused. It's much harder to Travel accurately when you're agitated or distracted."

"Denise, please! I need to prove my worth to this team! How long will Sarah wait for results? I'm sure that Jason's been telling her how lousy I am at martial arts and firearms, and I doubt if Ben's been giving her glowing reports on how well I've mastered a dozen alternate histories. If she doesn't hear that I can use my timeband without an instructor watching over my shoulder, I'm sure she's going to ask for it back. I'm surprised she hasn't already."

"Sarah doesn't expect overnight success. Neither should you. Come on, we're done for today. Let's get something to eat."

Denise turned to walk back to the house, but Ruthie wasn't finished yet. "No. I've got something to do first. I'll be back." She checked to make sure that Denise's timeband was no longer linked to hers.

"Ruthie! Don't!"

Ruthie saw the panicked look on her friend's face, but she ignored it and picked a date to Travel to: October 1, 1580. It was exactly four hundred years before the day she was born. Then she pushed fiercely in her mind and willed herself to Travel to that date. Except for the short trip of a few minutes that she had made in the Chicago police station basement, it was the first time she had attempted to Travel without another timeband linked to hers.

But at the moment that she willed herself to Travel, she realized that she had lost control of the destination target. Denise had been right — she was too agitated to Travel properly, and she was heading for a random destination in time. What's worse, there was no way for Denise or anyone else on the team to know where she was ending up, and they could not come to get her to bring her back.

Ruthie found herself standing up to her knees in snow, with thick flakes coming down all around her. The date was January 30, 1712, and she started shivering uncontrollably. All she was wearing was a light nylon windbreaker, T-shirt, blue jeans, and sneakers. The temperature on this date must be well below freezing, and Ruthie had lived through enough Chicago winters to know not to be outside in one unprotected. Angry at herself for Traveling blindly into a winter snowstorm, she attempted once again to find October 1, 1580.

But once again, she found she couldn't keep her attention fixed on the target and will herself to Travel at the same time. When she gave the mental push to Travel, she lost control of the target date again. She knew she had to keep calm to achieve both parts of the task, but she was not anywhere close to calm. She was scared and angry and overwhelmed by the power of the timeband, and she was feeling very, very alone.

Ruthie found herself in darkness. She knew at once she was no longer in the snowstorm, for the bitter cold had been instantly replaced by the muggy heat of summer, but it took a few seconds for her eyes to adjust to the sudden reduction of light. It was no good trying to get her bearings from the clock and calendar in her head; in her fright, all the data from the timeband was swirling around in a chaotic mess, and she couldn't even concentrate enough to find the date or time in the bombard of new data being fed into her brain.

But soon a few things became clear. It was night, and the sky was overcast, an orange tint coloring the low-hanging clouds. She could see buildings around her and feel pavement under her feet, so this must be the future rather than the past. She must be in some version of the city of Chicago. As her vision improved, she could see that many of the nearby buildings were no more than ruins — partial brick walls still standing where the rest of the structure had collapsed, or been bulldozed flat. The orange tint to the clouds was from fires burning in the distance. Parts of the city, it seemed, was burning. And there were sounds in the distance that seemed to be muffled thunder, or maybe explosions, one after another.

Near her feet she found a twisted pole that was once a street sign. At one end were crossed placards that identified this intersection as Clark and Belmont. But the area looked nothing like the busy intersection, not far from the Cubs' ballpark, that Ruthie once knew. This area was blasted almost flat, as if a tornado had come through, or a war.

Ruthie forced herself to be calm so she could make sense of the timeband data. She needed to know where in time she had ended up, a first step to eventually returning to the safehouse. She tried to take control of her breathing, slow her heart rate, just as she had been able to do while meditating with Denise. Slowly the numbers in her head stopped spinning long enough for her to see what it was that the timeband was trying to tell her. What was the year? The year, the timeband data said, was 2031. The month, it said, was August, and the date…

Voices suddenly came out of the darkness, many voices, all talking excitedly. Ruthie saw a half-dozen flashlights coming at her, all pointed at her, and the bright circles of light blinded her again.

Again she lost control of the timeband data, just when she was so close to pinpointing her location in time, and she began to panic.

Her instinct said to run, but there was nowhere to run to. The voices were all around her, and Ruthie realized that while some of them were in English, most of the words she could pick out sounded like Spanish. The flashlight beams started to spread out around her, and though she still could not see who was holding the flashlights, she understood she was surrounded.

"Who do we have here?" a voice said, louder than the rest. The speaker sounded male, young, with a distinct Hispanic accent. "What's an Anglo girl doing here on *Tigre* turf?"

All the flashlights were shining on Ruthie's face, and she blinked rapidly in the glare of their lights. "Please," she said. "I took a wrong turn. I need to get home — I don't want any trouble."

"You're a long way from home, *chica*. I think you're a government spy. Is that what you're doing here? Spying for the government?"

Ruthie realized she was in an increasingly desperate situation, but there seemed to be no way out of it. As her heart started beating faster, it became harder and harder to make sense of the timeband data. All she had to do was give the timeband a command to move her back into the past, or freeze this moment of time, or do any number of things that could get her out of danger. But it was danger that was keeping her from doing any of that. There was no way she could control the timeband until she calmed herself, but instead she found herself becoming more and more frightened and agitated by the threats being made by the leader of the mob surrounding her.

"I don't know anything about any government — please let me go." Her voice was a ragged sob.

"Oh, we can't let you go. Not until *El Tigre Rojo* gets here. He'll decide what we do with government spies. Maybe he will let you go. Right, men?"

All around her, Ruthie could hear the sound of mocking laughter behind the flashlights. Apparently the idea that *El Tigre Rojo*, whoever he was, might let her go was amusing to the mob.

"Tie her up, men," the leader says. "We'll give her to *Rojo*, and he'll decide how long she gets to live."

Several sets of hands reached out of the darkness, grabbing Ruthie's arms and legs and forcing her to the pavement. Her arms were forced behind her back, and thick plastic bands were fastened around her wrists. Another set secured her ankles together. Then one pair of powerful hands lifted Ruthie up by the waist, and she was thrown over the shoulder of a big man. Helpless, she was carried to the back of a nearby van and dumped inside. The back gate of the van was left open, but it did Ruthie no good; she could do nothing more than wriggle on the van floor.

Over and over again she tried to access the timeband, but it was no use. Each time she was almost calm enough to visualize the timeband data, something would distract her — a scream in the distance, the faraway sound of gunfire, the rumble of a bomb explosion. Then she would fall victim to panic again, and the numbers in her head would blur and spin away. What was the use of having a device like the timeband on her arm if she was powerless to use it?

Ruthie wished she had not been so stupid as to try to Travel solo. There was a reason Denise had refused to permit her to try it, and now she understood. If something went wrong — and it had — there was no way for her teammates to come and rescue her. She could be in any year in history, and by the time her teammates found her, if they even bothered to look for her, she would probably be dead. Of course they would be looking for her. Not that Ruthie mattered much to them, but the timeband on her arm was beyond price, and they would want it back.

The night crept by. Now that she was no longer the focus of a half dozen flashlights, Ruthie's vision improved to the point where she could now clearly see her captors. They looked like a ragged motorcycle gang, all dark leathers and shiny chains, and every one of them carried weapons, mostly assault rifles, pistols, and knives. This part of Chicago, she surmised, was a battleground, and whatever government still claimed to be running the city, or even the country, it was clear they did not control this piece of turf. This neighborhood belonged to the *Tigres,* and their lord was someone named *El Tigre Rojo*: the Red Tiger. And eventually, the Red Tiger arrived.

El Tigre Rojo was a large man with a short stubble of hair surrounding his round head and chin. His black leather jacket had stripes of red on each sleeve, and he appeared at the back of the van with a nasty-looking machete in his hands. "Who are you?" he rasped in a thick Spanish accent.

Ruthie could barely speak, her throat was so thick with fear, but she managed to squeak, "Ruthie McDonald," to the gang leader.

"How about we let the men have some fun with her?" one of the chief's lieutenants asked. "Then we kill her?"

"No," *El Tigre Rojo* said. "It's almost dawn, and there will be drones out in the morning. I don't want any government agents seeing that we have her in our camp. Get a rope. When the drones appear, let them see her hanging from a lamppost."

"No," Ruthie began to moan, and she began to tremble uncontrollably. "No no no no no." Again, she tried to make her timeband work, but it was futile. In her state of panic, there was no way to achieve the mental control that was required to operate the timeband.

Moments later, a rope was found, and someone hastily tied one end into a noose. Then someone else reached in to pull Ruthie out of the van. She tried to wriggle away from him, but it was no use. She was hauled out of the van and roughly carried to where the noose was being readied.

"Get your hands off of her!"

Ruthie looked and saw the most amazing, beautiful sight she had ever seen. There was Jason, standing at the base of the lamppost that was meant to be her gallows, and his two fists were raised in defiance against the assembled gang.

All around were shouts of confusion, and then Ruthie heard *El Tigre Rojo* bellowing, "Get him!" The *Tigres* drew the weapons and began to fire at Jason.

The man who had been carrying Ruthie dropped her to join in the attack on Jason, but somehow, Ruthie didn't fall to the ground. Instead, she was floating, suspended in air, watching the battle unfold. All around her, there was a muffled roar, and everything seemed frozen in place, all except Jason. He was a whirlwind of motion, dodging bullets, kicking *Tigres* in the face, wrenching rifles from their hands and tossing them away. He was a one-man demolition crew, speedily disarming and disabling the entire gang of thugs before any one of them could act against him.

It was the most amazing display of martial arts prowess Ruthie had ever seen, more than she ever could have imagined, and she was watching it all while suspended a couple of feet off the ground. As Jason continued to pummel the heavily-armed gang, Ruthie understood what she was seeing. Jason had adjusted the rate of time flow so they seemed to be moving in extreme slow motion, although to them, Jason would be no more than a blur. And he must have linked her timeband to his, so she could see what was happening from his perspective, rather than the *Tigres'*. What seemed like more than a minute of combat to her must be happening in less than a second, for she had hardly fallen at all from the moment the man carrying her had released her.

Suddenly it was all over. Jason had disarmed and beaten every one of the *Tigres*. Every single one of them was unconscious but still standing; they had not had time to fall yet. The last thing Jason did was to rush over and catch Ruthie, set her up in a sitting position on the end of the van, and cut her bonds with a knife from his belt. His lips were moving, but Ruthie could not hear the sound of his voice.

As soon as she was free, Ruthie rushed forward and wrapped her arms around Jason, sobbing. When she opened her eyes again, she saw that they had returned to the safehouse, just outside its wooden walls.

"Thank you," she whispered, but Jason took her wrists and pulled her away from him. Without a word, he turned and headed back toward the safehouse.

"Jason? Thank you for what you did!" Ruthie said. She was still in a state of shock from everything that had just happened, but she wanted Jason to know that she appreciated the rescue.

Jason turned and glared at Ruthie. "I think the first words out of your mouth ought to be, 'I'm sorry.'"

"I am sorry. I shouldn't have tried to solo when Denise told me not to…"

"Damn right. She knew you'd panic and wouldn't be able to come back on your own. We all knew it. If it were up to me, I'd have left you there, and you'd probably be swinging from a lamppost. Come on, get inside the walls. With the way your day is going, a bear would probably come along and eat you."

Ruthie didn't know if Jason was kidding or not. She hurried through the gate into the back yard of the safehouse.

"How did you find me?"

"Standard search protocol. The four of us divided up possible destinations. Denise took the next two centuries into the future, Ben took the previous two centuries of the past, Sarah covered the time earlier than two centuries ago, and I wound up scanning all the centuries after —"

"Hold it. Sarah went searching for me, too?"

"She did. Miles wasn't back from his current mission yet, and it takes four people to do a search like this properly."

Ruthie was truly surprised that Sarah was part of the search effort. Sarah had never struck Ruthie as being "hands-on" about anything — she was always giving orders to the team and delegating responsibilities to others. This must have been an exceptional event to get Sarah to leave the desk in her office and venture out into the field.

"But I could have been anywhere in those centuries — how did you know where to look?"

"I didn't. So I slowed the rate of time flow down to about three million times slower than normal. At that rate, I sped through two hundred years in less than half an hour. Everything around me was little more than a blur, but the timeband would ping me when it detected another timeband in proximity to it. To anyone who happened to be looking in my direction, I'd be nothing more than a flicker of light and shadow. When the timeband told me I was close to you, I returned time flow to normal and worked on getting back in synch with you. Luckily you hadn't moved far from your original location, or I'd have never found you. Come on in the house and get a cup of tea. The others will be returning from completing their searches, and you're going to have to apologize to each one of them, personally and individually."

"I will." She followed Jason back into the house, heading toward the kitchen. "Jason? When you found me and linked my timeband to yours, you could have taken me home immediately. True?"

"Yeah. So?"

"You didn't have fight that entire street gang. Why did you?

Jason shrugged. "I needed the workout. Besides, it was fun."

"Weren't you taking an unnecessary risk?"

"No. At the time differential I had set, they had no chance to touch me. I could have taken on a hundred more of them before any one of them had time to reach me. You saw how slowly they were moving. I was moving faster than bullets."

"Yes. I did see. You linked my timeband to yours first so I could see. If you hadn't, I would have seen you the same way they probably did — a blur that appeared and disappeared in less than a second. You wanted me to see you in action. You wanted me to see you disable a dozen armed thugs with your bare hands."

"Maybe I did want you to see. Call it part of your training. Did you learn anything?"

Ruthie didn't answer. But she was thinking that she learned not to question the orders of her instructors when it came to using the timeband. She still had a lot to learn.

Over the next few minutes, the other three searchers returned to the safehouse, one by one, and Ruthie apologized sincerely for making them search for her. Denise arrived first, and she was too furious with Ruthie to listen to any apology; she stormed out of the kitchen and slammed her bedroom door in Ruthie's face when Ruthie came to try to smooth things over.

Sarah was next, and she stood and listened sternly as Ruthie swore that she would never, ever attempt again to solo with the timeband until Denise thought she was ready. Ruthie could not tell how mad Sarah was with her, for Sarah's face was like a stone mask, but she was sure that Sarah was not pleased.

Finally Ben arrived. He brushed off Ruthie's apology with a laugh. "We've all done it when we're first starting out. I panicked and got lost when I was still in training. Hell, I'll bet even Sarah did, when she first got her timeband. Don't worry about it. It happens."

"Thanks. Everyone else has been treating me like I committed some kind of capital crime by trying to solo."

"Well, you see now how dangerous it can be. But we needed a little excitement to liven up the day — it's way too boring around here lately. But tell me about where you ended up. We've got very little data about that era in this Variation, and anything you remember could be valuable knowledge."

Ruthie's mood brightened a little; maybe some good could come out of her accidental trip into the future. "It was August 2031, I think — I never did get a good look at the exact date. It was night, and some kind of a war was going on. I could see fires and hear explosions in the distance. Most of the buildings were ruins. The neighborhood was run by a gang called the *Tigres*, and they were Hispanic, I think. I heard a lot of Spanish. Their leader was *El Tigre Rojo*, and they thought I was a spy for the government."

"Good," Ben said, sounding like the history professor again. "So we know that in 2007, Chicago is under control of a Nazi-aligned dictatorship, but by 2031, civil war has broken out, and true control is in the hands of local militias, organized along the lines of street gangs. This is filling in our outline of the twenty-first century timeline nicely. We'll have to take a few more trips into this and surrounding eras to get a clearer picture of the breakdown of civilization in this region, but this is a promising start."

"You want to go back there?"

Ben nodded. "It's what we do. Sarah will make the call, of course, but if were up to me, I'd authorize a few well-armed forays into a few selected years and make discreet observations. Slip in carefully, get as much data as possible, and then slip back to the safehouse without drawing attention. It's what you're in training to do, but not before you're ready."

"Oh." Ruthie didn't relish going back to the *Tigres'* turf, not even in a suit of armor with a bazooka.

"I understand you've just been through a traumatic experience," Ben went on. Ruthie doubted if he really did; he wasn't the one who was nearly murdered. Then she remembered that Ben had once almost faced a lynch mob himself. But that wasn't quite the same thing; Sarah and her crew had saved Ben before he ever saw the mob and the noose; that was an eventuality that Ben never had to actually experience. "But Ruthie, this is what our job is all about. We're the ones who keep history on the right track, and the way we do that is by gathering information about what the future is going to be like. We try to do it as safely as possible, but sometimes we put ourselves in dangerous situations. If you want to keep the timeband and stick with our team, this is what you'll be expected to do."

Ruthie didn't know what to say. She did want to keep the timeband, but she knew it would be a long time, if ever, before she felt ready to return to the nightmare future that she had just been rescued from.

The next day, Ruthie was up early again, expecting to find Jason waiting for her for their morning run, but he didn't show up. He caught up with her several hours later, while Ruthie was working out on the stationary bike in the basement. "I thought I'd let you sleep in today," he said when he saw her. "After yesterday, I thought you might appreciate the break."

Ruthie thanked him and continued her workout. She hadn't wanted a break. She wanted to complete her training. She wanted to feel ready to be a productive member of the team, and she didn't want everyone treating her like a fragile princess who needed protecting.

After lunch, she reported for her regular session with Denise. Denise hadn't spoken to her since Ruthie's attempt at an apology the day before, and while the silent treatment was now behind them, it was clear that Denise still was not happy with what Ruthie had done.

"Are we clear?" Denise said to Ruthie at the beginning of the session. "Absolutely no solo trips with the timeband until I authorize it. Do I have your solemn promise?"

"Yes, Denise." Denise was seven inches shorter than Ruthie and at least thirty pounds lighter, but somehow she made herself seem larger and more threatening in Ruthie's eyes. "I promise."

"Good. I'll bet when you were a teenager and learning to drive a car, the first thing you did when you got your learner's permit was to cruise around town in your dad's car all by yourself, even though it wasn't legal for you to do so yet. Am I right?"

"I guess so." Actually it had been her mom's car; Ruthie's father had been long absent by that point, but it wasn't really the occasion to explain her family history now.

"Well, listen carefully, Ruthie. The timeband is not a Buick! That thing wrapped around your wrist is the most dangerous object ever created! It's a weapon of mass destruction! With one careless thought, you could get yourself killed, and that's far from the worst thing that might happen. If you use it recklessly, you could destroy whole civilizations — undo all the good that this team has ever achieved! Do you want that on your conscience?"

Ruthie shook her head. Denise was right; she had acted stupidly. But how long was Denise going to make her suffer for her mistake?

"Look, I know you want to be part of this team," Denise continued. "You've told us your reasons, and they're all the right reasons. Personally I think you've got all the makings of a great Traveler, and someday soon you'll be pulling your weight and more. But right now you've still got a lot to learn, and I don't think you realize yet how much you have to learn. We can't afford any more mistakes like yesterday. Jason told me how very close he came yesterday to recovering just your dead body, rather than one live trainee."

"That's something I wanted to ask you about. Suppose Jason had been too late to save me, and showed up after they had already — you know. Couldn't he just go back in time to when I was still alive, and rescue me then?"

"No. You've got to understand synchronicity. If he had found you hanging from a lamppost, dead, he could have gone back to when you were still alive, but he wouldn't be able to rescue you. You'd be out of synch. You would be in his past, and he'd be coming from a future that you wouldn't live to see. Think of it this way — you exist at many different moments in time, going all the way back to the day you were born, but only one of those is your 'now', the moment where your consciousness resides. It also happens to be the same moment that is 'now' for me, so we're able to interact. But if one of us were to use our timeband, we'd be out of synch with each other, and we couldn't interact again until we synched up again. That's why when Jason located you, the first thing he had to do was get back in synch with you again, and hope it was in time to save your life. If you die while wearing the timeband, you're permanently dead — there's no way any of us can save you."

"Okay." Ruthie remembered finding Miles in the holding cell in the Chicago police station. Miles couldn't see her because they were out of synch. She hadn't considered the possibly fatal consequences that might come from being out of synch.

"All right. Let's talk about what happened yesterday."

Ruthie didn't want to rehash what she had done wrong during the previous day's lesson, but it was clear from Denise's tone that there was no avoiding it. "Go ahead."

"When you were practicing with me, you were controlling your timeband like a pro, with nearly insignificant errors, but when you lost your temper with me, all of a sudden you were traveling through time randomly, with no control over your destination. How come?"

"I couldn't concentrate. Couldn't focus. All of the timeband readouts blurred together, and I couldn't fix them in my mind to modify them. I guess when I get angry or scared, I can't use my timeband. Is that what I'm supposed to learn?"

"Wrong. Emotions shouldn't stop you from Traveling successfully. Experienced Travelers are able to Travel accurately even when they're in a state of near-panic. The difference is experience. You've only had a timeband on your arm for a few days. The rest of us have had our timebands for years. You just need to keep practicing with me, keep doing the mental exercises and the meditation, and before long you'll learn how to be in control of your timeband even when you're boiling mad, or scared out of your skin. I promise you, you'll get there."

"If you say so."

"I do. Let's try a few short trips, and then we'll gradually work our way up to some harder stuff. Link my timeband to yours, and let's go back exactly five years. Ready?"

Denise pronounced that day's session as productive when they finished, but Ruthie wasn't so sure. She still felt unsure using the timeband, and with each jump through time she feared she might arrive not at her intended destination, but far in the future, where she might be attacked by Nazi cops or post-apocalyptic street gangs. During the evening session with Ben, she was distracted by recurring thoughts of danger and doom, and in the end she had to apologize to Ben for comprehending little of what he was trying to teach her.

Feeling miserable, she wandered out into the garden. It was late, just a little before midnight, and she was sure that Jason would be expecting her for their daily run before sunrise in the morning. But she didn't feel sleepy. She had too much on her mind. Perhaps it was time to tell Sarah that this had all been a mistake, and she should return the timeband and let the team set her up in some safe period of history.

All of a sudden the front gate opened. Ruthie was so startled that she almost used the timeband by reflex, fleeing into a random moment in the past or future, but it was only Miles, returning from an assignment. He was wearing a fedora and pinstripe suit and carrying a cardboard box. "Grocery shopping in 1923," he explained when he saw her. He put his box down and joined her on a bench in the garden. "How's it going?"

"Fine," she said, and there was something in her voice that let him know that she was not fine. He turned to get a better look at her face, and he could see the moonlight reflected in a track that a tear had left as it ran down her cheek.

"No, it's not fine. Tell me about it."

"It's just so — so overwhelming. Denise keeps saying how I'm doing a great job learning how to use the timeband, and I keep overshooting by ten years. I tried to solo yesterday, and I almost got killed. The whole team had to search for me. Jason is a sadist when it comes to his training sessions. Ben expects me to keep dozens of alternate histories straight in my head. Sarah hates me. And I find myself wishing that I... that I..."

"That you had been wiped out in the reality wave, too," Miles said, and Ruthie nodded. "I know. I felt the same way at first, after the reality wave that rewrote the end of the War for Southern Independence hit, and wiped clean everything that I had ever known. And I had joined the team by choice, and already had an understanding of what to expect from a reality wave. I still felt like I had been orphaned by some huge natural disaster."

Ruthie looked at him, not sure whether to believe that this calm, self-assured man ever felt as badly as she did now.

"But I got over those feelings," he continued. "I came to realize that I had a family, a new family, this team. They're good people, Ruthie. And they do like you. Even Sarah. She's told me several times already how wrong she was to doubt that you would fit in on the team."

"She's never told me."

"And she probably won't, not for a long while. That's the way she is. She won't butter you up with complements, but you wouldn't still be here unless she thought that you're going to make a valuable addition to the team. This team is everything to her, and she feels as strongly about it as a mother lion does about her cubs. In her eyes, you're already one of us, and she'll fight fiercely to keep you safe and secure."

"What's her story?" Ruthie asked. "I know pretty much what there is to know about everyone else, but no one will tell me anything about Sarah."

"Sarah was Carlos's wife. Still is, I guess. No one knows all the details, but we think Carlos and Sarah explored time together long before the first team was assembled, in the years after Carlos had his disagreement with Caesar. It was Sarah who recruited the first team members, and under Carlos's leadership, they started to work to undo the terrible alterations to the timeline that Caesar and his followers perpetrated. But then Carlos and Sarah separated. No one knows why; no one has ever heard Sarah talk about it. Sarah remained in charge of the team, and Carlos went into hiding. This happened long before I was recruited. We still get messages from time to time from Carlos. He keeps track of our progress, and gives suggestions on how to proceed. But most of us have never even seen him."

"I still feel like I'm never going to measure up in her eyes," Ruthie said., "Miles, what am I going to do? I'm not cut out to be a time traveler."

Miles noticed that Ruthie was shivering. The night was chilly, and Ruthie had been sitting here without a proper coat or jacket. Miles took off his jacket and wrapped it around her. "We're going to have to get you some decent winter clothes soon," he said. "You're going to have to have more than just Denise's hand-me-downs." He left his arm around her, and Ruthie nestled against him for warmth.

"What I mean to tell you," Miles continued, "is that you still have a family. We want to be your family. It's a little dysfunctional at times, but whose family isn't? You know you can quit any time if you wish, give up the timeband and live out your life in whatever time-period you choose, but we would miss you if you did. I'd miss you."

Ruthie looked up at him, eyes moist with tears.

Miles didn't say anything else, just tightened his arms around her and kissed her.

This continued for some time, and it seemed like the most natural thing in the world to Ruthie. She realized she had wanted to do this for some time, even before the morning of the bomb explosion and the reality wave, when all she knew about Miles was that he was a polite customer who tipped well. For the moment all her doubts and self-pity were forgotten, and she felt safe and secure in Miles's arms.

Some time later, when they broke apart, Ruthie said, "We'd better go inside."

"Yeah." They got up from the bench and, hand in hand, they headed toward the house. "Besides, your training with the timeband isn't done for today."

"Oh?"

"That's right," Miles said. "You wouldn't believe what two people with timebands can do in bed."

Ruthie found out. Slaving her timeband to his, she found that at the end of lovemaking, they could jump back to the beginning, refreshed and ready to do it all over again, with variations. Ruthie lost count of how many times she and Miles replayed their night together — she was sure it was well past variation seven — before they finally called it quits and slept instead.

Of course using the timebands in this way left them badly out of synch with the rest of the team, and when they awoke in the morning they had to jump to late afternoon to catch up to them. From the others' point-of-view it seemed that Miles and Ruthie had gone missing for most of a day, but they surmised what had probably happened. When they reappeared, there was no keeping secret what had transpired, and Miles and Ruthie were the object of much good-natured joking from the others for the rest of the evening. Even Sarah didn't reprimand Ruthie for missing an entire day's training.

Ruthie felt happier than she had at any time since she had first arrived.

From that point on, training seemed to go much better. Over the next three weeks, she finally got the hang of how to control her timeband with precision and dexterity, and the day came when Denise announced that Ruthie was finally ready to solo.

She handed Ruthie a slip of paper. "There are five locations in time listed here. At each of these moments I've left a digital watch. You need to bring them all back to me. If you make your jumps exactly right, the watches will prove it. Are you ready?"

"I'm ready." She felt more than ready. She was eager to show what she could do.

"And Ruthie — stay away from murderous street gangs, okay?"

At the end of the exercise, the watches showed that each of Ruthie's jumps had been right on the mark.

The next day, Ruthie got her final exam. Sarah herself slaved her timeband to Ruthie's and went along for the ride, telling her what destination in time to jump to and silently evaluating her skill. Ruthie felt more nervous than she had when she got her first driver's license, with the examiner giving her the road test. When it was finished, Sarah said nothing to her except, "Meet me in the common room in thirty minutes." Neither her face nor her tone of face gave any clue as to how well or poorly Ruthie had done on the exam.

Ruthie passed the next half hour anxiously pacing the floor in her bedroom. She had thought she might try to get in a short nap, but she was far too nervous to rest or relax. What if she had failed the exam? Things had been going so well in the training sessions with Denise — surely she couldn't wash out of the program now? And if she did, would she ever see Miles again? The two of them had remained close ever since their first night together, and not only was Ruthie more determined than ever to keep the timeband, she was sure she didn't want to give up Miles either.

Exactly thirty minutes later, Ruthie came down the stairs to the common room. The furniture was arranged differently; the large cherrywood table was pulled to one end of the room, and two chairs were set up behind it. The larger one was for Sarah, and another one, to Sarah's right, was occupied by Miles. He had a notepad in front of him and a pencil ready in his hand. To one side of the room were three more chairs, where Jason, Ben, and Denise were sitting. The rest of the furniture in the room had been taken away. Ruthie understood that she was expected to stand, and she did, at the far end of the room, facing Sarah and Miles. "I'm here, Sarah," she said.

"Thank you, Ruthie. I see we are all assembled. We don't hold many formal meetings of the team, but this is the occasion for one. We are here to do a final review of the training program of Ruthie McDonald."

Miles began taking notes. Ruthie hadn't expected anything so formal, and she was sure this was all in preparation for her removal from the team. She hadn't been this apprehensive about a formal hearing since she was called into the dean's office in college for taking part in an unauthorized beer party on her dorm floor.

"Ben, shall we start with you?"

Ben stood up, a small wire-bound notebook in his hand. He glanced at a page in it and said, "As far as I'm concerned, Ruthie's progress has been satisfactory. She's got a good foundation in U.S. and European history. She's smart and has a good memory. She's not quite up to speed yet on all the known Variations, but few of us are. From a tactical and operational perspective, I think she'll make a good addition to the team. She has my recommendation." He smiled at Ruthie, and Ruthie smiled back nervously.

"Thank you, Ben," Sarah said. "Denise?"

Denise rose to her feet and said, "Well, after that minor setback three weeks ago, Ruthie has made steady progress. She's demonstrated complete control over all timeband functions, and she's been able to operate her timeband solo, without being linked to an instructor. I think she's good to go. I recommend her without hesitation."

Sarah nodded. "She passed my examination as well, without error." Ruthie felt greatly relieved — this was the first indication she had gotten from Sarah that she had passed the exam. Maybe she was going to get to stay on the team, after all. But there was still one instructor left to give his report. "What do you say, Jason?"

The tall man stood up and looked in Ruthie's direction. Ruthie didn't like the way he was looking her over, as if he was getting ready to deliver the death blow. He turned back to Sarah and said, "To be honest, if she's ever in a fight, she's probably going to die. Her unarmed combat skills are almost non-existent. She completed my basic firearms course, and her marksmanship scores are barely passing. But to her credit, she's physically fit, and she's shown a willingness to learn. I like her determination and her perseverance. There's a mental toughness there, deep down, that she might not even be aware of. She went through a pretty bad scare a while ago and didn't fall apart. If she's willing to continue the training regimen and keep working on her combat skills, she's got my vote."

"Ruthie," Sarah said, "if you're allowed to continue on this team, would you do as Jason recommends?"

Ruthie nodded, too overwhelmed to speak.

Sarah turned to Miles. "I wish to know your view also, Miles, even though you weren't one of her instructors. But since you've been acting as my deputy, ever since we lost Jack, it's important that you give your opinion as well. Do you recommend in favor of Ruthie, as well?"

"You know what I think, Sarah. Ruthie's worked hard for this timeband. Harder than any of the rest of us had to work for it, I might add. I think she's more than earned a spot on this team."

"Very well." Sarah stood up. "We've heard from all the team members, and I have nothing to add to dispute their reports. Ruthie McDonald, upon the recommendations of your instructors, you are hereby graduated from training, and you are officially a full member of this team, with all rights, privileges, duties, and responsibilities of the same. Congratulations!"

Immediately everyone flocked around Ruthie, giving her their warmest congratulations. Miles hugged and kissed Ruthie, and then Ben and Denise each hugged her. Even Jason embraced her and kissed her on the cheek. Finally Sarah came over to her and said quietly, "I knew you'd make it."

Ruthie threw her arms around Sarah and embraced her fiercely, and Sarah held her arms around Ruthie for a long moment before letting her go. Tears filled Ruthie's eyes.

When Ruthie stepped back from Sarah and dried her eyes, she found the common room had been completely transformed. Multicolored crepe paper streamers had been hung from the ceiling, and everywhere were helium-filled balloons of every color of the rainbow. Ruthie was startled. "What happened? Is it someone's birthday?"

Denise laughed. "No, silly. It's your graduation party!"

Jason popped his head in from the kitchen. "It's a team tradition. Every time someone graduates from training, we throw a party. This is it."

"Nobody told me!" Ruthie complained.

"Of course not!" Denise said. "Then it wouldn't be a surprise. Surprise!"

"But I don't understand. How did all these decorations get set up? I only closed my eyes a moment. How — oh. I get it."

"I should hope so, after all of your training with the timeband. Ben and Miles did all the decorating in an instant, while the rest of us were still congratulating you. It only takes a nanosecond to decorate when you're wearing a timeband."

"But where are they?"

"You'll see them soon enough. Getting all that work done in frozen time leaves you really out of synch. I'd say we'll see them in about a half an hour or so."

Ben did appear, out of thin air, about thirty minutes later, about the same time Jason's appetizers were coming out of the oven. "Nice job on the decorating," he said. "Where's Miles?"

"Miles said he had another errand to run. He didn't say where he was going."

That mystery was solved about a quarter of an hour later, when Miles came in the front door carrying a stack of flat cardboard boxes. The smell of cheese and tomato immediately filled the air in the room.

"Oh, my gosh," Ruthie said. "That smells exactly like..."

"Chicago-style pizza, circa 1985. The Nazis might be running America, but they didn't outlaw pizza. Luckily I didn't need to show a passbook to order carryout on Belmont Avenue. In honor of our newest teammate, I bring you what I assume is a favorite hometown delicacy. Dig in, everyone."

"Do I smell pizza?" Sarah came out of her private office, a big smile on her face. "Nothing but the best for our Ruthie on her big day."

By this time Ruthie was weeping openly. She had never felt so much at home anywhere as she did at this moment. Miles was right; she did have a family, and she loved them all.

Chapter 8

The next day, Sarah called Ben, Miles, and Ruthie into her private office.

"The three of you are going on a field trip," she explained. "This will be Ruthie's first mission as a member of the team, but it shouldn't pose any great risks. We need to learn exactly when and how the most recent reality wave got started. The earliest discrepancy that we know about is the attack on Pearl Harbor, in December 1941. We need to learn if the wave started any earlier than this, or if the linchpin actually was Pearl Harbor itself.

"So this mission is to June 7, 1941, six months before Pearl Harbor. Your job is to spend several weeks in the time-period, making observations and looking for discrepancies to history as we know it. Miles and Ruthie, we have forged documents that will identify you as James and Alice Vickers, a married couple visiting Chicago from Cincinnati. Ben, you'll be posing as —"

"Don't tell me. I'm going to be their Negro houseboy, right?"

Sarah looked at him patiently. "I was going to say manservant, but you have the general idea. Face facts, Ben. In 1941 there weren't very many black history professors. You would attract attention if you were doing anything other than menial labor in that time and place. This way, you'll have a reason to be with Ruthie and Miles, and no one from that time will think it odd or unusual."

"You don't need to explain it to me," Ben said. "I understand, but I don't have to like it."

Ruthie was sure she didn't like it. Ben had become her friend, as well as her teacher, over the last few weeks. Even though she knew it was just play-acting, she would have a hard time treating Ben as a servant, and an even harder time adopting the class prejudices of that time to treat him as an inferior.

Also, she knew that Miles would have just as hard a time displaying racial prejudice, for by now she knew him well enough to know that he was anything but a racist. At first Ruthie had been afraid that Miles might be just that, since he was a Southerner from a timeline where the South hadn't lost the Civil War. But she soon learned that in his timeline, the South had never gone through the harsh Reconstruction period, had never had anything like the Ku Klux Klan or a system of Jim Crow laws, and slavery had gradually been eliminated with the full support of the Southern people. Decades of racial hatred and violence had been avoided in Miles's timeline, and Miles was free of prejudice against African Americans or any other race.

"We need you on this mission, Ben," Sarah told him. "You're the team historian; you'll be able to spot anything amiss with the timeline quicker than anyone. Miles is on the mission because he's the only one who's actually lived through a similar time-period; it was the late 1930's when he first became a Traveler. And Ruthie is familiar with Chicago, she's studied history as well, and most importantly, we need to know how well she does on her first field trip."

"I won't let you down," Ruthie said.

"I know you won't," Sarah said benevolently. "And I'm counting on you to keep these two out of trouble." Miles and Ben adopted expressions of mock outrage and protest.

Sarah's voice became all business again as she continued, "Now I'm going to go over the ground rules for this mission. Ben and Miles know them already, but I'm repeating them for everyone's benefit. This is a data-collecting mission. Observe as much as you can, take notes when you can do so unobserved, and gather historical documents to bring back here. Do not call attention to yourselves. Do not reveal that you have knowledge of anything beyond what a typical inhabitant of that time would know. Avoid doing anything that would have significant consequences in history, or change the timeline in any large or small way. Avoid any use of the timeband that would confuse or puzzle eyewitnesses. If anything goes wrong, jump back to this year and rendezvous at Wrigley Field. Understood?"

All gave their agreement. The list of rules and cautions made Ruthie nervous all over again. She had felt excited about time-traveling to a different era and taking on a new false identity — especially since she would be doing this with Miles — but Sarah's regulations reminded her how high the stakes were, and how dangerous this could be if she failed.

The basement was the safehouse's costume and prop room, and here the three of them found their traveling clothes for the mission, as well as period trunks and other accessories for travel. Once they arrived in 1941 Chicago they would purchase more complete wardrobes for themselves, but they found enough in the basement to get them started. Money for the team was never a problem; they had huge amounts of currency from various eras stored at Wrigley Field, as well as gold coins and bullion. Acquiring large sums of money was easy when you knew ahead of time which stocks were going to go up, or which horses would finish first.

Once they were properly outfitted for the trip, Miles led them to a point outside the compound wall which he had previously marked with an X in the dirt. "Sarah asked me to do a little advance scouting to make sure we could arrive unobserved. This exact spot in 1941 will be a blind alley off of Clark Street. There's little chance anyone will spot us if we pop into existence there."

Miles slaved the other two timebands to his, and in an instant the three of them, each carrying a traveling trunk, were transported to a narrow alley, between two blank brick walls and rows of garbage cans. Lying on the pavement, clutching a bottle in a paper bag, was a wino in ragged clothes, his back up against a garbage can. He looked up at the trio that had suddenly appeared before him, trying to focus his bleary, intoxicated eyes.

"Almost unobserved," Ben corrected Miles. "Go back to sleep, oldtimer. No one here but us hallucinations."

The unfortunate did as he was told, muttering softly and incoherently to himself. Miles led Ben and Ruthie out of the alley and into the sunlight on Clark Street. Ruthie checked her mental dashboard. The glowing red numbers read June 7, 1941, followed by 2:13 P.M.

Wrigley Field — the real one — stood across the street from them. It didn't look much different than the ball park Ruthie knew so well from her own era, where she had spent a number of summer afternoons in the bleachers. "The Cubs are on the road today," Ben reported. "I checked. Otherwise there would be a lot more people on the street right now. If you're interested, they'll beat the Braves in Boston today, five to one."

Ruthie didn't care about baseball scores; she knew the Cubs were doomed to lose in almost any era. Instead, she was looking around her at a city that was more than sixty years removed from the one she knew. It looked like something out of an old black-and-white movie, but it was vividly real, and in living color. The streets were jammed with huge black automobiles, and newsboys were actually shouting, "Extra, extra!" on the street corners. Men in suits and fedoras and women in long dresses walked past them on the sidewalks, taking no notice of them.

"Not so much gawking," Miles said, and Ruthie realized she was doing exactly that. "People will wonder what we're looking at."

At the street corner, Miles hailed a cab. As the driver helped Ben load the baggage into the cab's trunk, without any audible grumbling from Ben, Miles told the driver, "The Drake Hotel, please." This was the plan that they had formulated; they would take a suite at the famous hotel as part of their disguise, a well-to-do couple from out-of-town traveling with their servant.

Almost out of force of habit, Miles also bought a paper from the newsboy, which he read in the back seat of the cab on their way downtown.

"Anything in the paper?" Ruthie asked him.

"Just what you'd expect. Plenty of war news from Europe. Convoys being attacked in the North Atlantic. FDR's going to make a radio address tonight."

Ben looked like he wanted to say more, but he shot a glance at the cab driver, who was close enough to overhear every part of their conversation. "If you ask me," the cabbie broke in, "we ought to go over there and show *der Führer* what he can do with his master race. I was over there in 1918 when we kicked the Kaiser's butt, and we can do it all over again if you ask me. Begging your pardon, ma'am." He looked back apologetically at Ruthie.

"Quite all right," she answered, getting into her role.

Soon the cab had pulled up to the curb outside the Drake, and once in the lobby, Miles had no difficulty getting a luxury suite with an adjoining bedroom for their servant. He signed the hotel register as "Mr. and Mrs. James Vickers, Cincinnati, Ohio."

"Coming, Mrs. Vickers?" Miles had caught Ruthie gawking again, this time at the opulent splendor of the hotel lobby, and well-dressed ladies and gentlemen making their way through it.

"Right away, Mr. Vickers," she said with a laugh as she latched onto Miles's arm and fell into step behind the bellman with their bags. Ben just shook his head.

The next few days were like a glamorous vacation for Ruthie. She and Miles played their roles as wealthy visitors to the city to the hilt, dining in fine restaurants, shopping for expensive clothes, and going to the theater. Somehow Miles had managed some introductions to some of the elite of Chicago society, and they soon found themselves with invitations to fancy, elegant parties. Ruthie felt like she was on stage again, not just playing a part but improvising the script as she went. And she had to admit she was rather good at it.

"Yes, I know the Harrisons," Ruthie said to the woman she had just met, a platinum blonde with diamonds on her necklace. "Mrs. Harrison is a good friend of mine, and her husband belongs to the same club as my husband." Ruthie had no idea who either Harrison was, but she guessed that anyone with any social standing in Cincinnati probably knew the Harrisons, and she hoped the blonde woman didn't know them that well.

"Really?" her new friend said, and she sounded impressed. "When you are home again, mention my name to Anne Harrison, will you, Mrs. Vickers? My husband's work takes us east every now and then, and the next time we are in Cincinnati, I should like an introduction."

"Of course." Ruthie smiled, but she had already forgotten the blonde woman's name and thought it rather unlikely that she would ever be speaking to Mrs. Harrison, whoever she might be.

Miles came over, a drink in either hand. He looked elegant in his tuxedo, Ruthie thought. Handing Ruthie a glass of champagne, he said to the blonde woman, "Would you excuse us?"

"Of course."

They drifted off to an unoccupied corner of the huge hall. "You look like you're having fun," he said.

"I am. At first I was scared to death that I'd be discovered as an impostor, but then I realized everyone here is a phony as well, pretending to be more important than they really are. As long as I keep pretending that I belong here, no one seems to be the wiser."

"That's all there is to it. Believe me, in this crowd, people will believe you are who you say you are. The last thing they'll suspect is that you're a time traveler from the future. But keep your eyes and ears open. If anything doesn't seem right to you, if it doesn't fit with what you know of the history of this time, remember it and let Ben know. The slightest detail that seems off may be a clue to a changed timeline."

"I'm not sure I'd know if what's supposed to be part of this timeline and what isn't."

"I know," Miles said. "It's like finding a needle in a haystack, except that there may not be a needle and it will probably look like hay if you do see it. Just be observant and do the best you can."

"Okay."

"You look great, by the way."

"Thanks." She knew she did look great in a floor-length peach-colored designer gown with plenty of expensive jewels. She wore elbow-length gloves that matched her gown and also served to keep the timeband well hidden. "So is there anyone here at the party you think I should be talking to?"

"Let me see." Miles scanned the crowd. "You see that man in the slicked-back hair and the expensive suit over there?"

"The one that all those men over there seem to be paying attention to? Who is he?"

"He's only the top gangster in Chicago. His name is Frank Nitti."

"That's Frank Nitti? Al Capone's buddy?"

"The same. Capone is currently in Florida, dying of syphilis, but Nitti is the man who heads up what's left of Capone's empire. You want to meet him?"

Ruthie hesitated. "I don't know — the idea is exciting, but couldn't it be dangerous as well?" Ruthie was quite familiar with the stories associated with Chicago's infamous mob history, and she imagined ending up as part of another St. Valentine's Day Massacre.

"Ruthie. You're wearing a timeband. If anyone starts going for their tommy guns, we could be gone before they even open up their violin cases."

"Oh, yeah. Sure. Let's go meet a mobster."

As Miles and Ruthie approached the knot of men in dark suits clustered around the long polished bar that dominated one end of the banquet hall, Ruthie noted with relief that there were no violin cases in evidence. However, she was quite sure that Nitti and his lieutenants, if that's who they were, probably all had weapons under their dinner jackets. So did Miles, she remembered. Miles had suggested that she might want to conceal a small pistol in her purse, but Ruthie had declined. While she had continued to make progress in firearms training with Jason, she still did not conceive of any situation where a gun in her possession would do her any good at all, and she was just as comfortable without one.

Miles took Ruthie by the hand and squeezed between two beefy guys standing near Nitti. "Mr. Nitti?" he said, extending his free hand. "James Vickers. I'm visiting from Cincinnati, and I wish to pay my regards. This is my wife, Alice."

"Pleased to meet you, Vickers," the gangster said gruffly. He extended his hand to Ruthie. "Mrs. Vickers." Ruthie took his hand. Nitti's grip was firm, and she thought he held her hand several seconds longer than she would have liked before releasing it.

"I'm a businessman, Mr. Nitti," Miles said, "and sometimes I need to do business with associates of yours. A good word from you might go a long way."

"I'm sure it might, Mr. Vickers, but this is a social occasion, and I don't do business when I socialize. Drop by my office Monday morning, and we can talk over how we can help out each other."

Miles smiled politely. "I do apologize for disturbing you, sir," he said, his Southern drawl quite noticeable. Ruthie had never been to Cincinnati, and she wondered if anyone there sounded as Southern as Miles did. "I only wanted to make an introduction, in hopes that we might have a chance to chat at whatever time is convenient for you."

"Of course," Nitti said, waving Miles away with a gesture of his hand. Then he looked directly at Ruthie. "Enjoy your stay in Chicago, Mrs. Vickers."

"Thank you," Ruthie said, but Miles was already tugging gently on her elbow. After they retreated to the safety of a deserted alcove, Ruthie started laughing uncontrollably.

"Ruthie?" Miles said. "Are you all right?"

"Better than all right," she said as she regained control of herself. "This is wonderful fun. Who else can we meet?"

But while Ruthie and Miles partied, the most important part of the mission was hard at work back at the hotel suite. If this operation was to be a success, it would be up to Ben to discover the origins of the latest reality wave. To do this, he had the table in the suite's sitting room filled with stacks of newspapers, magazines, and library books, and he was scouring the current news reports for anything that didn't match the history as it should have been happening. Ruthie and Miles kept him supplied with the information sources he needed, but mostly they left Ben alone to conduct his researches.

When Miles and Ruthie returned to the hotel suite that night, well after midnight, they found Ben still poring over stacks of newspapers. "Still up?" Miles asked.

"Just finishing up for the night. How was the party?"

"Incredible," Ruthie said, and she meant it. Perhaps it was just the effects of all the champagne she was feeling — she knew she had had one or two glasses more than she should have — but she really felt this had been one of the best nights she had had in a long, long time.

"Ruthie got to hang out with Frank Nitti," Miles explained. Ruthie knew that Miles had had at least as much to drink as Ruthie had, but he didn't seem the least bit drunk. She wondered how Miles did it.

"The gangster? Tell me all about it in the morning, if you still remember."

"How's the research going?" Miles asked Ben.

Ben shook his head. "I don't know. Superficially, everything seems exactly as it ought to be. If something's changed from the way history records this time-period, it's beyond my ability to detect from here. Maybe there isn't a difference, and the source of the reality wave doesn't happen until later. I just don't know."

"You'll figure it ought. I have faith in you."

"Thanks. I wish I shared your confidence."

For the next week, things continued much the same way for them. Miles and Ruthie partied with Chicago's famous and infamous, and Ruthie was pleased at how adept she had become at blending in with the elite of 1941 society. Meanwhile, Ben continued his researches at the sitting room table, but he did not have any substantial progress to report for his efforts.

Late one night, while in bed, Miles said to Ruthie, "I need to apologize to you."

"What for?"

She could hear the guilt in his voice as he went on. "That first day, when you first put on the timeband, and the reality wave flipped us into Nazi America — we got separated in the police station, and those men..."

"I remember," she said, wondering where this was leading.

"You had to deal with it on your own, and after you stopped time to escape, you came to get me out of my cell. But you know, I could have gotten out of the cell on my own, and come to rescue you."

She had known it. She realized it sometime during her training with Denise, when she started to realize all of the time-tricks that you could accomplish with the timeband. As soon as the timeband came out of sleep mode, he could have jumped back a few centuries, to a time before the city had even been built, walked a few feet, then jumped forward to the same moment and reappeared on the outside of the cell. There were probably many other things someone experienced with the timeband could have done. She didn't know why he had hadn't, but she expected Miles would tell her when he was ready.

"I should have come to help you at once," he went on. "But at the moment, I just couldn't. Jack had just been killed. He had been my partner and my friend for years. We were as close as brothers — closer. Right then, I wasn't thinking about anything but myself and my grief. I knew I should be doing something to help you, but I suppose I thought that since you were in a police station, you would be safe. If I had had any idea what they would try to do to you — "

"Shh." Ruthie laid a finger across his lips. There was no need for Miles to apologize; Ruthie had already gone all over this in her mind and come to the conclusion that, under the circumstances, Miles had done nothing wrong. "Don't say another word about it. It's over, and there's nothing to apologize for. Just because you're wearing a timeband doesn't mean you have to be a super-hero and rescue every damsel in distress. You can rescue me next time, okay?" She pulled him closer to her and kissed him.

Eight days into their mission to June 1941, Ben looked up from a stack of the Congressional Record on the sitting room table. "Miles?" he asked. "Can I get your opinion on something?"

"Sure. What do you need?"

"I've been reading some speeches that some Congressmen gave on the floor of the House earlier this year that deal with U.S. trade policy with Japan. I think I've caught some statements that don't ring true to me. Read through these and see if you notice anything fishy about them."

Miles took the documents and made himself comfortable in an armchair. Ruthie had been watching them, and she looked with dismay at the volume of reading matter that Ben had given Miles. This would occupy the two of them for hours, she knew.

After reading a couple of paragraphs, Miles looked up and saw Ruthie's unhappy expression. "Ruthie? Is something wrong?"

"Well, you and Ben are probably going to be discussing Japanese foreign policy until late in the evening. I'd like to go out and do something."

"Okay. Go shopping. Take a couple thousand in cash and have a good time. When you come back, I'll take you to a nice restaurant."

That wasn't what Ruthie had in mind. She had gone shopping already, several times, and the hotel closet was now filled with gowns and furs and jewels, more than she had ever imagined owning in her wildest dreams. "No. I mean I want to really do something. We've got timebands. We ought to be doing good with them, not just research."

"What did you have in mind?"

"Did you ever hear of the *Eastland* disaster?" Ben and Miles both looked at her blankly; neither had grown up in Chicago. "In 1915, a ship full of passengers capsized right here in the Chicago River. Over eight hundred people died. We could go back to 1915 and prevent it from happening — tell people not to board the ship, or warn them that it could tip over. We could save hundreds of lives."

"We have our orders," Miles said. "Sarah told us this was to be a fact-finding mission only. No interference with the events of this time-period. She was quite specific about that."

"Besides, changing history can have unintended consequences," Ben said. "You might be saving the life of someone who goes on to become a serial killer, or a politician that starts a war that otherwise would never have happened. These things have to be researched carefully before you take any actions that might change the timeline."

"But eight hundred lives! Most of them were Western Electric workers on their way to a picnic, with their families! If we've got the power to do something, it would be criminal not to!"

"Relax, Ruthie," Miles said. "It's a good idea, and it's something we should do. But not now. One advantage to being able to travel in time is that you never have to act in haste. I promise you, once this job is done, we'll look into doing something about the *Eastland* and save those people. From their point of view, it makes no difference if we do it today or a year of subjective time from now — they get saved just the same. But we'll do it right, with no mistakes. Now take my advice. Go shopping, or go sight-seeing, and let us get our work done."

Armed with a purse full of currency from their seemingly limitless stash of money, Ruthie headed for the expensive shops on Michigan Avenue. She was still unhappy when she left the hotel, but soon her mood passed, for she felt like a movie star on a Hollywood set as she walked down the crowded sidewalk, dressed in a beautiful outfit from this era. She knew she looked good, too, dressed as she was. She never failed to get appreciative glances from the men as she walked past them, though she pretended not to notice.

All of a sudden she realized, with alarm, that no one was looking at her. At first she assumed it was her imagination that allowed her to feel that she had suddenly become invisible. But then first one pedestrian, then another, bumped into her without comment or apology. She was horrified to realize that no one on the street could see her at all. Not only that, they could bump up against her and still not take any notice.

She walked up to a traffic cop, stopping cars to allow pedestrians to cross the street, and waved his fingers in front of his eyes. No reaction. She yelled, "Can you see me?" in his ear. The policeman didn't even blink, but he stepped aside to allow traffic to proceed through the intersection again. Ruthie had to hurry to the curb as she realized that the drivers in oncoming cars couldn't see her either.

Safe again on the sidewalk, Ruthie tried to figure out what was happening. Remembering her training, she realized there was one set of conditions that would explain this phenomenon. Somewhere, close by, had to be another Traveler, out of synch with her. Someone with a timeband in her subjective past had to have visited this time and place. All of the 1941 Chicagoans within range of their timebands would only be able to perceive one of the two Travelers, and the Traveler who had been here first, from his or her subjective point-of-view, would have precedence. Ruthie, coming from that Traveler's future, would not be able to affect this moment or even be seen by anyone with range.

Unnerved by this sudden invisibility, Ruthie tried to figure out which of the dozens of people on this crowded street was a Traveler like herself. She half-expected to see Denise or Jason, or even Sarah herself, among the strangers walking past her on the sidewalk. But she saw no familiar face, saw no sign of a sparkling meshlike timeband on someone's forearm.

Who else could it be? She knew that there had been earlier team members who had the timebands before the current members had joined the team. She didn't know their faces — except for Jack. She half-hoped she would see him in the crowd, walking the streets of Chicago on a mission he had taken years before his violent death. But she didn't see his gruff face anywhere. But even though she didn't recognize anyone, she wondered if the other Traveler might be one of her predecessors on the team.

But the more she considered this, the unlikelier it seemed. One of the protocols that the team followed strictly was keeping a log of all uses of the timeband. Sarah had insisted on it, and every one of Ruthie's training jumps was recorded in a master logbook that was kept at the compound. Ruthie felt sure that Sarah would not have sent them on a mission to a time and place that had been already visited by anyone on the team, just to make sure an incident like this couldn't happen.

So, by the process of elimination, Ruthie realized that she must be in the presence of one of the Others — the Travelers who opposed her team, and followed Caesar. Somewhere, close by, was one of the group that set off the reality wave that erased her home and family from history, not to mention exploding the bomb that killed Jack. Ruthie felt close to panic before she remembered that there was no possible way that the other Traveler could see her. The Other was in her past; she was in the Other's future. Whichever one of these people on the street was the Other, it was only an afterimage of a person who had been here and gone. They were not in synch; they could not interact.

Ruthie tried to memorize all the faces she saw around her, in hopes that if she encountered the interloper again, she could recognize the person. But there were too many, moving too quickly past her. And then, suddenly, everything seemed normal again. A man bumped into her on the sidewalk and politely excused himself. Another, seeing her standing there with a worried expression on her face, asked if she was all right.

Ruthie nodded quickly, then hurried back to the hotel to tell Miles and Ben.

Chapter 9

When Ruthie returned to the hotel suite, she found Miles and Ben where she had left them, sitting around the table studying stacks of documents. For a moment she was reminded of those mornings in the diner, when Miles and Jack would be doing the same thing with their piles of newspapers. Miles looked up and saw Ruthie's troubled expression. "What's wrong?"

"The oddest thing just happened," Ruthie began, and then she told her two friends about the strange incident from beginning to end.

"This could be bad," Ben said. "It could be nothing, but it could also be very bad."

"How?" Ruthie asked. "Whoever the other Traveler was, he or she was in my past, right? I could see him — if I knew which one he was, that is — but he couldn't have seen me. From his point of view, I wasn't there yet."

"That's true, but why should another Traveler be here at all? Remember, there are only twelve timebands, and an entire world with many centuries within range. What are the odds you're going to cross the path of another Traveler simply by chance? The odds are too astronomical for it to be a coincidence."

"Besides," Miles added, "we have no way of knowing how out of synch you and the other Traveler were. You could be years apart, or only a few seconds. Let's hope that all you encountered was the leftover afterimage of some visit by a Traveler that happened long ago, subjective to us. But the worst-case scenario is that there's someone out there looking for us, looking for the exact moment in time to be synchronous with us."

"Is that possible?" Ruthie asked. "How would someone know when to find us?"

"They shouldn't be able to," Miles agreed, "but let's say somehow they learned we would be going on a mission to 1941 Chicago. They don't know exactly when we would arrive, so they show up a little earlier than us, maybe by just a few hours. They search the city, don't find us. They they jump ahead an hour and look some more. Then another jump of an hour. Eventually they're

111

going to be futureward of us, instead of the other way around, and they'll see the traces of when we've been. They could enter this hotel room, come back to this moment, and watch the three of us talking now."

A chill went down Ruthie's back as she realized that the Others could be eavesdropping on this very conversation.

"Relax," Ben said. "If they find us, they're in our future. We'll be nothing but past images to them."

"Wait a minute," Ruthie said. "If I was within range of another Traveler, shouldn't my timeband have detected it and reported it to me, along with a measurement of synchronicity deviation? I didn't get any kind of an indication like that." She remembered the readings she had noticed that time in Miles's cell in the police station, when she was out of synch with him.

"No," Miles said. "All the timebands on our team are set to identify each other when they're within range, but timebands belonging to the Others wouldn't have that feature. They wouldn't automatically signal ours when they got within range. Yet another proof that it wasn't a friendly Traveler that you encountered."

Ben started gathering up the books and papers. "This mission is over. We need to get back to the safehouse immediately. Someone's out there looking for us, and it's only a matter of time before they get in synch with us and locate us. We've got to go now."

"I'm sorry," Ruthie said. "If I hadn't decided to go out for a breath of fresh air —"

"It's not your fault," Miles told her, taking her hands in his. "You may have just saved us. If you hadn't encountered the Other, we might have had no warning at all that they were searching for us. And we may not be in any danger anyway. But we can't take the risk."

Within minutes their trunks were packed with as much as the timebands could handle. A timeband could transport not only its wearer but also whatever the Traveler was physically carrying, up to a weight limit of about fifty pounds. Ruthie hated to leave behind some of the expensive clothes she had bought here, but the books and papers they had gathered were more important to them right now than her dresses. Quickly they made their way down to the hotel lobby. The suite had been on the tenth floor, and they didn't want to jump back in time while they were still more than a hundred feet in the air, as they would be if they reappeared in a time that was before the building had been constructed.

Ordinarily they would take a cab to Clark and Addison, where the current Wrigley Field stood, and jump back to their safehouse. But Ben felt it was important not to stay in this era a moment longer than necessary, so instead of leaving the hotel, they instead found an unoccupied cloakroom on the ground floor and made the jump back to 1504.

They appeared once again in a grove of trees, not far from the Lake Michigan shoreline. Miles suggested they leave most of their baggage here; they could come back for it later. From here it would be a walk of several miles to their safehouse, but Miles and Ben knew these woods well, and they told Ruthie it would take them only a couple hours to reach Wrigley Field. Ruthie was still feeling jittery from her possible close encounter with an enemy, and she nearly jumped out of her skin when two men stepped out from the trees and directly into their path.

"Don't react," Miles warned her at once. "Show them your hands, and make no sudden moves." Both Miles and Ben put down their bundles and presented their empty hands to the strangers, who Ruthie could now see were not time travelers, but American Indians. Both men were nearly naked, wearing only loincloths and some feathers in their long black hair, and each carried a spear with a sharpened tip. Ruthie immediately followed the lead of her two friends and presented her open hands to the Indians.

"They're Potawatomi," Ben explained. "We've encountered members of their tribe before. They're probably out hunting small game, and they have no interest in our activities unless we present a threat."

One of the hunters spoke a few syllables to them. "Do you know what he's saying?" Ruthie asked Ben.

"Not a clue. Hopefully he's saying, 'Don't hurt us, and we won't hurt you.'"

"I hope you're right."

The two Potawatomi continued to look suspiciously at the three Travelers for more than a minute, and then they slowly moved off into the trees again. "It's all right," Miles said after the hunters had completely disappeared. "You can breathe again." Ruthie realized she had been involuntarily holding her breath.

"Wonder what they make of us?" Ruthie said. "It will be years before the first explorers from Europe make it this far west. They've never seen white or black faces before."

"So far, the original inhabitants of this area have always been friendly to us," Miles said. "On the other hand, we did put up that big wall around Wrigley Field just to be on the safe side."

Upon their return to the safehouse, Sarah convened an emergency meeting of the whole team to hear the debriefing and discuss the situation.

Ben gave the rundown on how the first few days of the mission went, and what they thought they had accomplished. There really wasn't much for him to report; he had a few questions about some curious pieces of data that he had uncovered, but no satisfying answers. Then he invited Ruthie to tell what had happened to her on Michigan Avenue, which she did as completely as she could remember. Sarah, Denise, and Jason listened closely, their faces showing how seriously they, too, were taking the situation.

"Okay, here's what we know to be true," Sarah said. "We know that some time in our past, another Traveler visited downtown Chicago on June 15, 1941. This is an unrecorded time jump. If it had been made by someone in this room, Ruthie would have recognized the Traveler. If it had been made by someone previously on this team, we would have a record in the log of the jump. We have to conclude that this was one of the Others. We don't know by how much the synchronicity of this Traveler deviated from Ruthie's. Unless we have reason to believe otherwise, I'm going to assume the worst possible case is true: some Traveler, or Travelers, were hunting for our group. They had an idea when and where our people were, and they were looking for them."

"I say we turn the tables on them," Jason said. "Ruthie doesn't know the Others by sight, but some of us do. They're probably still in 1941 looking for us — why don't we send a team there to look for them?"

Once again Ruthie struggled in her mind with the concept of synchronicity. To time travelers, you could be together in the same time and place and still not be existing in each other's "now". When Jason was wondering what the Others were doing "now", he didn't mean in the same century, but what they were doing in their current moment of awareness, wherever that might be along the timeline.

"Too risky," Sarah said. "We'd be hunting for them over the same time and place when they were hunting for us — it would be a throw of the dice who found who first, and who would come out alive. Besides, we have a far greater problem to consider."

She paused, then said slowly, "Either it's an amazing coincidence that we happened to cross the path of some unknown Traveler who passed this particular time and place long ago in our past — and I am not about to trust my life to a belief in coincidences — or there's one or more hostile Travelers out there with advance knowledge of our movements. And when I try to contemplate how that could happen, the only conclusion I can reach is that they are getting the information from one of us."

The room became deathly quiet. Each person involuntarily looked around at each other, silently evaluating if there could be any possible truth in that statement. Ruthie felt that all eyes were on her. She was the newcomer in the group; no one except Miles really knew where she came from, or where her true loyalties might lie.

Jason spoke first. "That's a load of crap, Sarah. I refuse to believe that one of us is a traitor. There's got to be a better explanation."

Ruthie didn't want to believe it either. But she couldn't help thinking that if one of them was willing to sell out the team, it could be Jason. He seemed to have the most anger bottled up inside of him, especially since his former girlfriend was in love with Ben. And yet — they had to trust Jason. He was the most experienced fighter in the group. If he wanted them all dead, he could have killed them all anytime he wanted to.

"Jason is right, Sarah," Denise said, visibly shaken by Sarah's theory. "If one of us was leaking information to the Others, then we would all be dead by now. Even the location of this safehouse would no longer be secret, and the Others would be able to attack us in force and kill us all."

"All but one," Ben added with emphasis. "I think I have to agree with Sarah. Certainly there are other explanations, but the security of this team and its mission demands that we consider the worst-case scenario to be the true one, until we can prove otherwise. Too much is riding on our success. Not just our lives, but the entire future of humanity."

"What do you say, Miles?" Sarah asked.

Miles drew in a breath before answering. "I think you and Ben are right," he said at last. "We may indeed have a security leak — especially if the purpose of the bomb that killed Jack wasn't to assassinate Ron Klaussen, as we assumed, but instead to disrupt our operations in that era. But I think Jason and Denise are right, too. We can't function as a team if we refuse to trust one another. We can't keep looking over our shoulder wondering who's going to slip a knife in our back. For better or worse, you are all my teammates, and I need to trust you all unconditionally. If I can't, then it's time for me to unlock this timeband and turn it over to some other poor schmuck to try his luck at saving the world."

Ruthie felt she had to say something, so she said, "I feel the same way. You've all made me feel so welcome on this team; I can't believe anyone is secretly planning to do the rest harm."

Sarah thought about this for a moment, then she said, "Very well. Until we have reason to believe otherwise, we're not going to go around suspecting each other of betrayal. But I am going to insist on tighter security. Motion detectors in and around the compound are going to be fully active at all times, and we're going to drill what we do in case of intruders popping in unannounced. Jason, you're in charge of that. Also, no solo jumps out of this era. We go in groups of at least two, and each person will be armed. If some Others out there are hunting my team members, I want them able to defend themselves. Understood?"

There was no dissent, although privately Ruthie wondered if this was all a bit of an overreaction, all just because for a couple of minutes she was invisible on a street corner. But she kept that opinion to herself.

Chapter 10

Later that day, Sarah began Ruthie's indoctrination into the nature of their enemies. "We probably should have done this earlier," Sarah said, "during your training, or at least before you went on your first mission. But there was so much for you to learn then, and, well, better late than never, I guess. Anyway, here's some pictures of some faces I'd like you to learn."

She showed Ruthie a file of several photographs, plus a number of hand-drawn sketches. "These are the Adversaries, as near as we can tell. We can never be sure of who makes up their current membership, nor are we entirely sure that these individuals we've identified actually are Travelers. But in the past we've spent some time trying to track them down, and this is what we've surmised."

There were several photographs of a gray-haired man with thick glasses and a short beard. "This is Caesar," she continued. "His real name is Angelo Rosetti, but no one calls him anything but Caesar. He is the original proponent of the ideology of the Others — that the human race is a corrupting influence on the Earth, and that civilization has become too degenerate to be allowed to survive. The planet should be wiped clean so some other species can take our place."

Ruthie looked at the photograph in amazement. "There are actually people who follow this nutcase?"

"He's not a nutcase," Sarah reminded her. "He's highly intelligent and very persuasive. Probably one of the brightest men I've ever met. So bright that he developed this strange, destructive philosophy that only he can comprehend. He and Carlos argued for years over whose view of humanity was correct. Eventually they decided that they could no longer work together when it was obvious that they were at cross-purposes. Caesar took several members of their original team of Travelers with him, and they left to try to undo everything Carlos was trying to create."

"Who was he originally, before he became a Traveler?"

Sarah smiled. "That's a little hard to explain. His original timeline was quite a bit different than yours. This was a timeline where the United States never came into existence, where the world was governed by a number of theocratic empires unlike anything in your history. It dated back to the defeat of Britain by the warships of the Spanish Armada, and from there history took a number of twists and turns unlike anything in the history you're familiar with. In this reality, Caesar was the equivalent of an intermediate government official, a sort of provincial governor, with jurisdiction over various academic and research functions. This is how he came into possession of a timeband. In experimenting with its functions he set off the reality wave that erased his entire world, and while trying to restore it — always a nearly hopeless task — he encountered Carlos. This is how their partnership began."

Ruthie studied the man's face. He didn't look like a dangerous man. He looked like someone's grandfather, like a kindly greeter at your neighborhood Wal-Mart. He certainly didn't look like someone who would want to end human civilization. She tried to remember if this face was in the crowd on Michigan Avenue, wearing the timeband that had rendered her invisible to everyone else. She couldn't remember seeing him, but that didn't mean he wasn't there.

"There are no more than four other Travelers allied with Caesar," Sarah went on. "You know there's a physical limit to how many timebands can exist: twelve. We've got six of them — Carlos makes seven — so there must be no more than five Others. Just like our side, their membership may be subject to change, but we try to keep track of who's wearing the other timebands."

"How do we even know who they are?" Ruthie asked. "I imagine it must be hard to even locate them, considering they can be anyplace and any time."

"True, but don't forget that if we find where they've been, and stay futureward of them, we can see them and they can't see us. This is how we were able to take these pictures of them. It's a strange experience to be in a room with your enemies, listening to what they're saying and taking digital photographs of them, but they can't see us at all."

"But that's what they probably were able to do with Miles and Ben and me," Ruthie said, alarm in her voice. "Once they figured out we were in 1941 Chicago, they probably were able to find our hotel room after we left, and they've heard our discussion and seen what we're working on."

"It seems likely," Sarah agreed. "We can assume that our opposition now knows you're on our team. They can't learn much about you, since their reality wave probably wiped out almost all of your past, but they do know that we have a new recruit, and they can recognize you by sight. That's why I want to make sure that you can recognize them."

She showed Ruthie another photograph. This appeared to be a man in his late thirties or early forties, possibly Arab or Mediterranean ancestry, with thick curly black hair and dark eyes. "This is Stan Atwas," Sarah said. "He's been with Caesar for some time, and we can only assume that he is still on their team. He's their top assassin. We know for a fact that he engineered several reality waves by killing pivotal figures in history. He's an excellent marksman, as well as a skilled master of other forms of killing at closer range. He's also a master linguist and skilled with advanced electronics. He is committed to the destruction of everything we've been trying to put together. He is the primary reason why we are now nowhere near achieving Variation Seven."

Ruthie studied the face carefully, trying to commit it to memory. If she saw that face again, she resolved to try to get as far away as possible.

"Be very careful if you see Stan," Sarah added. "Of all the operatives working for Caesar, I would bet money that he is the one who set the bomb that killed Jack."

The next two photographs were each of a woman, though it took Ruthie a moment to realize that they were of the same woman. In one she had short red hair; in the other she had long blonde hair and looked years older. "Ellie Gagnon is the actress of their group. It's her job to infiltrate organizations and make changes from within. She is skilled with every known means of persuasion — and that includes being an accomplished seductress. She's also cold-blooded and ruthless, so treat with utmost caution if you encounter her. Ellie is also responsible to undoing much of our work, with several reality waves of her own to her credit."

The next photograph was taken from a distance, in bad light. The figure in it was no more than a dark silhouette, seen in profile. But someone with artistic ability had drawn some sketches based on the photograph, providing more detail and a full-face view of the man. He was pudgy-faced and balding, with bushy eyebrows. "This is Harvey," Sarah said. "Last name is either Bloom or Broom, we're not sure which. If he's still with the group at all, he is the most reclusive of them. We don't have any good photographs of him; he doesn't seem to do much Traveling outside the Others' stronghold, wherever and whenever it is. He's the group's historical strategist. The others bring him information, and he makes their decisions on how to best screw us over. He's brilliant and unpredictable. It's doubtful that you will ever encounter him in the field, but you never know."

The last photograph was of a young black woman in her twenties. "We think she's wearing the last timeband," Sarah explained. "She was seen in the company of Ellie and Stan in two different time-periods, so we have to assume she's a Traveler. But don't have a name for her yet, nor do we know what her function on the team is yet. We don't even know if she's still on the team, or if this is just old data. Our best guess is that she's a trainee."

"Like me," Ruthie said.

"Like hell. You finished your training with flying colors; don't you remember your graduation party? This is just a postgraduate course. Anyway, that's the five of them. Think you saw any of them in 1941?"

Ruthie looked over all of the pictures carefully. None of them seemed to match the faces she saw on the street corner in Chicago. "I'm afraid not," she confessed. "But there were dozens of people going by me on the sidewalk. Any of these Others might have been there and I wouldn't remember seeing them."

"I know. Also, there's a radius on the effect that would have gone right into the nearby buildings. Someone could have been on the other side of a wall, in one of the stores, and you would have come under that timeband's temporal shadow without even seeing the Traveler. But I want you now to know these faces, and watch for them. If you ever seen one of these again, I want you to run home right away and tell your Aunt Sarah."

Ruthie smiled. "I will."

The alarm went off in the middle of the night, a loud piercing firebell that woke Ruthie up out of a sound sleep and pleasant dreams. Miles was awake even quicker, pulling her out of the bed they shared and getting her to her feet. Ruthie grabbed the pistol out of the nightstand drawer. She hated the thing, but it was now standard operating procedure for team members to arm themselves as soon as the alarm went off.

"Ready?" Miles asked. He had his own handgun held ready as he crouched beside their bedroom door.

Ruthie flipped the safety off. "Ready."

Miles threw the door open, and both Miles and Ruthie leaped outside, guns pointing in opposite directions. As they had practiced each made their way down the corridors to their assigned posts. Emergency lights had come on automatically with the alarm, casting a strange purplish light on everything.

Heart pounding, Ruthie arrived at her assigned location, where the bedroom corridor intersected the one leading to the kitchen. Keeping her revolver trained on where the suspected intruder might suddenly appear, she pressed the call button on the intercom unit on the wall. "Post six," she reported. "All secure."

"Stand by, post six," she heard Jason's voice respond.

Several tense minutes passed. There was not a sound to be heard anywhere in the big house. Ruthie held the weapon in her hands, trembling in her short pajamas. For a moment she could not believe the absurdity of it all, how only a few weeks ago she was a waitress and struggling actress, and now she was holding a gun in a darkened hallway ready to shoot someone in her pajamas.

Then the regular ceiling lights switched on, filling the hallways with bright white light instead of the dim purplish variety. "All right, everyone!" she heard Jason call down the hall in a loud voice. "Drill's over. Common room, everyone."

Ruthie put the safety back on her gun and headed to the house's large common room. The others filed in as well, similarly accoutered in sleepwear and handguns. Only Jason was fully dressed, with a pistol in a shoulder holster.

"What time is it?" Denise asked, yawning.

"Oh-four-hundred, sunshine," Jason said. "If I were planning on assaulting the safehouse and murdering everyone in it, that's the time I'd plan to hit. Would you prefer they make an appointment for four in the afternoon? We could serve them tea."

"Can the comedy, Jason," Sarah said. She appeared to have been awakened out of a sound sleep like everyone else, but she wasn't complaining. "How did they do?"

"Good enough. Everyone was at their posts in under a minute. If this had been a real assault, some of you might actually have lived through it. I doubt that there's any way to fully protect ourselves from a real invasion, especially when our attackers can stop time and move between the seconds, but it's the best we can do."

"Then what's the point?" Ruthie asked. "If they learn where we are and want to kill us, then we're all dead, aren't we?"

"Maybe," Jason said, "Still, it pays to be prepared. If they come to get us, I want to be able to go down fighting. Anyone have a problem with that?"

No one did, and Sarah said, "Keep on drilling us, Jason. I don't mind losing a little sleep if it makes us even the least bit safer, and our work is too important to have it end just because we were careless. Now, let's get back to bed."

Ruthie did go back to bed, but it was some time before she could fall asleep again.

Drills in the middle of the night were not the only change in the routine at the safehouse. Sarah no longer invited the whole team to the big common room to discuss ideas and strategy. She spoke individually with them instead, calling each into her private study once or twice a day. Often it would be to get opinions on what another team member had proposed. Sometimes Ruthie had the feeling that some of what Sarah was relating was deliberate misinformation, trying to make sure that no team member had the true and complete picture of what the team was planning to do, except herself. It seemed that Sarah had decided that the only team member she could unconditionally trust was herself.

And it was obvious that plans were shaping up, filtered as they had to be through Sarah's suspicions. One day, three weeks after the mission to 1941 had suddenly ended, Sarah called Ruthie into her study alone.

"I have a mission for you," Sarah said. "You'll be going with Denise. Your timeband will be slaved to hers. She has the destination coordinates; you don't need to know them."

"Right," Ruthie agreed, understanding the reasons for the secrecy. "I'll need to know how to dress."

"The clothes you wore on your last mission will do fine." So she would be returning to 1941, or close enough. "Listen, Ruthie, I don't want you to tell anyone else that you'll be leaving. Not even Miles. I'll explain it to him after you've gone. This shouldn't take long, perhaps little more than a week. Most of the time you'll spend traveling by train to and from Washington, D.C."

"What do we do when we get there — or is that something else you're only telling Denise?"

"No. This is the part that you know and she doesn't. As you've probably figured out, we're not going to try to restore the Pearl Harbor attack to history. Whatever the Others did to prevent the Japanese from succeeding that day we'll let stand. Ben thinks our best bet is to focus on starting a new reality wave shortly after Pearl Harbor. We'll change a few pivotal minds about the U.S. going to war against Germany, and thus change the outcome of the war."

"Okay," Ruthie said, wondering if this was really what Ben told her, or if Sarah was deliberately giving her misinformation. No way to tell.

Sarah gave Ruthie a thick manila envelope, sealed with tape. "Guard this with your life," she told her. "This contains documented proof of the existence of Nazi death camps in eastern Europe. Photographs, eyewitness testimony, all incontrovertible evidence. Information no American in early 1942 possessed. Your part of the mission is to deliver this envelope to three key members of the U.S. Senate and convince them of the truth of the Holocaust. We believe that armed with this information, they will lead a movement in Congress to demand a declaration of war against Germany. The resulting reality wave will take the timeline out of Variation Three and closer to Variation Seven."

"You want me to start the reality wave?" Ruthie asked incredulously. "Are you sure? This is something for someone with more experience — Miles or Jason or..."

"No. This is your mission, Ruthie. Miles and Jason have already done their part. It was Jason who infiltrated the Nazi concentration camp called Auschwitz and brought back the contents of this envelope. Miles was his back-up." Ruthie had wondered where the two of them had been when they were absent for several days last week; now she knew.

"I'm counting on your skill as an actress to pull this off," Sarah continued. "The men you are to contact are going to be naturally disbelieving. The person who delivers this to them has to win their trust. A woman will have a far better chance of this than a man. Denise will be at a huge disadvantage in this era. She's Asian, and many Americans will assume she must be a Japanese spy — never mind that she's Chinese, not Japanese. We don't think there's as much anti-Japanese hysteria now as there had been when the Japanese attack on Pearl Harbor succeeded, but it's still going to be a factor. So that leaves you or me — but I'm going to stay here and coordinate our efforts. Besides, I think you'll be better in the field than I would be. You're younger and prettier. That's why it has to be you. Agreed?"

Ruthie nodded, still not feeling like she was the right person for the responsibility. The thought of having the power to change the outcome of World War Two was staggering.

"I wouldn't ask you to do this unless I had complete confidence in your ability to pull this off," Sarah said. "And if it makes you feel any better, yours is not the only mission I'm sending out. If you fail, someone else may succeed. But I don't think you'll fail."

She gave Ruthie a piece of paper with three names on it. "Memorize these names, then destroy the paper. They are the three Senators who you need to convince. Then go on down to the costume room and pick yourself out some traveling clothes."

As Ruthie got up to go, Sarah opened up a desk drawer to take something out. "Oh, and take this with you, too." It was a Colt revolver.

Chapter 11

The date, Ruthie determined once they had arrived, was March 20, 1942. Denise did not tell Ruthie of the destination date beforehand, only that she should dress for early spring. And a good thing she did — it was cold on this morning as the two women carried their suitcases from the cab into Chicago's Union Station to board a train to Washington.

It was cold in other respects, too. Much had changed in the city since she had viewed it in June 1941. The U.S. was at war — with Japan, but not Germany — and posters with war themes could be seen everywhere. Americans were being reminded to conserve for the war effort, to enlist in the armed forces, and to be on guard against enemy sabotage and espionage. Ruthie thought the mood of the people seemed chillier, too, now that the nation was at war. As they waited in the crowd to board the train, Ruthie thought that some of the strangers were eyeing Denise with suspicion. Even though Chicago had a large Asian population, mostly from China, Ruthie couldn't help but imagine that some of those stealing glances at them were figuring that Denise was here to spy on behalf of the Emperor of Japan.

Once on board the train, the envelope with the incriminating evidence tucked safely in a hidden compartment of her traveling bag, Ruthie reviewed in her mind the names that Sarah had given her. Lister Hill, Democrat from Alabama, the majority whip of the Senate. Charles McNary, Republican from Oregon, the Senate minority leader. Tom Connally, Democrat from Texas, chairman of the Senate Foreign Relations Committee. Three influential members of the Senate, coming from three different ideological backgrounds. She would need to show the evidence of the Holocaust to each of them and try to convince them that war with Germany was the only ethical choice. If she could convince all three of them, they would certainly convince the Senate to introduce a resolution of war against Germany — wouldn't they? Ruthie's knowledge of the workings of government at this level was sketchy at best, but she was willing to give it her best try. Sarah wouldn't have devised the plan if it didn't have a chance of succeeding, she told herself.

She still hadn't told Denise what they would be doing once they arrived in the nation's capital, and Denise hadn't asked. Probably, Ruthie decided, Denise had been given her own mission in D.C. to accomplish, which she wasn't supposed to tell Ruthie about. It was even likely that Denise's assignment was the primary mission, and Ruthie's was only the back-up in case Denise failed. Ruthie didn't know, and chose not to ask Denise about it. Sarah had decided for the good of the team, each should be ignorant of what the other's assignment was. Ruthie hated for it to have come to this, but she had to admit that Sarah was probably right.

More than anything else, Ruthie wished that Miles were here. Ruthie had been nervous about her first mission to 1941 Chicago, but the fact that she only had to follow the lead of Miles and Ben, both experienced time-travelers, gave her confidence. In the short time she had known Miles, she had come to depend upon the quiet strength and calm that Miles displayed, and she had to admit that she missed his presence. Ruthie liked Denise, and having her here made her feel safer, but it wasn't quite the same.

For this mission, Ruthie had chosen to resurrect her Mrs. Alice Vickers identity, since she still had identifying papers to support it. But now, she decided, Mrs. Vickers was a wealthy young widow, traveling on her own with her lady's maid. Denise didn't like playing the servant any more than Ben did, but it did give the two women a justification to be traveling together.

Ruthie had never taken a long-distance journey by train before, even though in her previous life she had taken an el train to work nearly every morning. She found she enjoyed the old-fashioned romance of the railroad of this bygone age, watching the landscape rush by as she ate her meals in the dining car. She wished that she could take the time to see more of the country this way, but she was not here to be a tourist. She had an important assignment, and thousands or millions of lives might depend on her success or failure.

Soon after they arrived in Washington and had gotten checked in at the hotel, Ruthie decided to see what she could do about changing her appearance. She remembered the two photographs Sarah had shown her of Ellie, agent of the Others. The woman had short red hair in one picture and long blonde hair in another. If Ellie could wear disguises for the benefit of the Others, then Ruthie thought she should do the same for her side. She found a shop near the hotel that sold wigs, and she selected a pageboy blonde wig that she could tuck her long dark hair under. The Others had probably already had pictures of her from the visit to 1941 Chicago. If they came looking for her, she was going to make it harder for them to recognize her in 1942 Washington.

"Thank you for seeing me on such short notice, Senator."

"My pleasure, Mrs. Vickers." Tom Connally stood behind his big desk as Ruthie entered the office. Spread out on the desktop were the photographs, maps, and diagrams of the Nazi death camps of Europe, along with paper-clipped stacks of pages of sworn testimony from survivors and witnesses. Everything was dated no later than 1941 — even though many of them had been acquired from sources in the future, nothing in the material suggested that time travel was necessary for them to have been collected. "Please, have a seat. Do you mind telling me where you obtained these pieces?"

"I represent an international relief organization, headquartered in Switzerland," Ruthie said glibly, repeating the lie she had carefully practiced. "Individuals obtained this evidence at great risk to their own lives and smuggled it into neutral European countries. We need evidence of Nazi atrocities to be seen by the officials at the highest levels of our government, before it is too late for thousands more victims of this evil regime."

"Well, rumors of these — atrocities, as you call them — surface every now and then," the senator drawled. "They are hardly news. This is the first time I've seen pictures, though. They are truly horrific. But, as I don't need to tell you, America is already at war. How do you expect America to go to war with Herr Hitler, when we're already fighting the Japanese warlords in the Pacific?"

Ruthie felt frustrated. She had already had this same conversation with Senator Hill and Senator McNary. How could she convince this intelligent man of something that she already knew was more than possible — that the United States of America could summon the will and resources to fight two major foes on opposite sides of the globe simultaneously, and defeat them both. But in this timeline, America had embarked on a different course, willing to fight one enemy but not both. She had to find a way to convince this influential man of Congress to give the history she knew a chance.

"Senator, I believe that America could fight both the Japanese and the German at the same time, if we thought it was necessary. I'm certain of it. And it is necessary. Eventually both Britain and Russia will fall to the Nazis, and then there will be no one left in Europe to oppose Hitler's program of mass genocide."

"Genocide," Connally repeated. "That's a word I haven't heard before."

"It means the extermination of an entire race or nation of people," Ruthie told him, the anger rising in her voice. "Hitler will be judged by history as guilty of that most awful of crimes, and the United States will be an accessory to that crime if it does nothing to stop it, now that the proof of it has become available."

"We've hardly done nothing, ma'am. The Lend-Lease Act, for example —"

"Will ultimately fail. Do you really think Hitler's ambitions end on his side of the Atlantic? How would you like to see the Nazi flag flying over America?"

"Now you go too far, Mrs. Vickers," Senator Connally said, chuckling softly. "That day will never come."

Yes, it will, Ruthie thought. She recalled the corrupted Swastika and Stripes she saw flying in Chicago, the nightmarish police station she had escaped from. It took all of her self-control to keep from making a scene in the senator's office.

"Please think carefully on what you are deciding, Senator," Ruthie said carefully. "The fate of the world may hang in the balance. Thousands, millions of lives..."

"I will consider what you've shown me," he said, rising to his feet. Ruthie did the same. "I'll see if this information can be corroborated independently. If there's any indication that anything like this is actually happening in Europe, I'll schedule hearings in my committee for this summer. We'll see what happens from there."

"Is there anything that can be done before that, Senator?" Ruthie asked. "The situation in occupied Europe is desperate. Hundreds of innocent people are dying every day."

She thought that something she said, maybe something in her tone of voice, had gotten through to the Texas senator. He blinked and looked away for a moment, then he said softly, "It takes time to get things done, Mrs. Vickers. But I'll see what I can do." He looked again at the scattered documents on his desk, then back at Ruthie. "If my committee does hold hearings on this matter, I trust that you will be available to appear as a witness?"

"No," Ruthie said quickly, and Connally looked surprised at her abrupt answer. "I mean, I'm not the person who ought to be testifying. I'm only a messenger; I don't have firsthand knowledge of the situation. In these documents are the names and titles of individuals who should appear before your committee. Some of them are refugees who have witnessed the brutality of the Nazis with their own eyes. I'm sure your committee could locate them, and their testimony would be far more effective than mine."

"I understand. Still, you've already been an eloquent spokeswoman for their cause. I hope we meet again."

Ruthie nodded, knowing that would almost certainly never happen. "Thank you for your time, Senator." Ruthie left the material on the senator's desk, left the office, and headed for the street. While Tom Connally had been polite toward her, she still felt that she had made little impact on him, and that nothing would come of this meeting. She felt utterly defeated, and she wondered what to do now. Should she try to see other senators, or try again with Hill and McNary? Should she try to see the President? Or should she resign herself to having done her best, and return to the safehouse to report to Sarah?

She had arranged to meet Denise for lunch at a restaurant within walking distance of the Capitol. Denise had mentioned spending the morning at the Library of Congress. Apparently she did have her own set of private instructions to follow, given to her by Sarah. Ruthie hoped Denise was having better luck than she was.

Ruthie had only walked a few blocks when she suddenly felt the air thicken around her, as if she'd somehow become trapped in a giant bowl of invisible Jell-O. She knew the sensation well, having experienced it first in the Nazi police station, and then many times afterward while training with Denise. Not only had the air thickened around her, but also all sound on the busy street ceased, replaced by a soft dull roaring noise. And all motion stopped — cars, trucks, people all stopped moving exactly where they were.

Ruthie understood what had happened, but she had no idea why it happened. What had happened was that her timeband had stopped the rate of time flow, so that she remained stuck in a single moment of time. But she hadn't given her timeband the command to do that! Had she done it by accident? Mentally she ordered the timeband to restore normal time flow. Nothing happened; everything around her continued to remain frozen. In her mind's eye she saw the various read-outs that her timeband was sending to her, and she immediately noticed that she was receiving an indication that her timeband was in linked mode. Another timeband in range was controlling her own. But that was supposed to be impossible. No timeband could force hers into linked mode against her will — that was what she had been told in training. Yet that was what was obviously happening. She tried releasing her timeband from linked mode, but it stubbornly refused to respond.

Ruthie looked around, and immediately she saw the source of the trouble. Among all the people in the area on this busy Washington street, only one person was moving. It was a woman, walking directly at her. From a distance of about twenty yards away, Ruthie could spot the faint lights blinking on the timeband on her arm. She looked at the face. The hair was different, once again, but Ruthie was sure that the chestnut-haired woman was Ellie, the Other in the photographs that Sarah had shown her.

Ellie's lips were moving, but the sound was not reaching Ruthie's ears. Sound waves couldn't reach her in this frozen moment of time, though Ruthie now knew why light waves could. It had been explained to her in training that the timeband never actually stops time completely, but the rate of time flow is reduced to an incredibly tiny fraction of normal. The speed of light is reduced to about the speed of a quick jog, so that light still can travel with a perceptible delay.

Ellie continued to close the distance to Ruthie, motioning to her unintelligibly with her hands. Ruthie pulled the Colt revolver that Sarah had given her out of her purse. Though she had practiced with it and other weapons over the past few weeks, she had never fired it at another living person. Gripped by fear, she fired it now.

The report of the pistol seemed almost deafening against the odd quiet roar that surrounded her. She felt the recoil from the gun, saw the flash of light from the muzzle. Then she saw with astonishment that the bullet was suspended in midair, about an inch or so from the end of the revolver barrel. Apparently whatever effect the timeband had to allow time to flow normally for the

Traveler and whatever she was holding did not extend very far beyond her. The gun could fire normally, but the motion of the bullet ceased to be visible once it had exited the gun.

This didn't seem to come as a surprise to Ellie, who didn't even flinch when Ruthie fired at her. Ellie continue to advance on Ruthie, who did the next thing that occurred to her; she ran.

Ruthie ran as fast as she could away from Ellie, which was difficult in the thick atmosphere. Air did not seem to get out the way of her fast enough, and fighting against its resistance was tiring. As she ran, she struggled to regain control of the timeband. She knew there was a limited range for one timeband to control another, and Ruthie tried to run far enough away to be out of range. She took a glance behind her to see where Ellie was, but Ellie wasn't bothering to run. The Other continued to walk steadily toward Ruthie, not bothering to wear herself out against the air resistance in this timeless state.

As she turned her head back to see where she was going, Ruthie caught a glimpse of motion out of the corner of her eye. Another person was moving against the backdrop of frozen people, coming toward her from a new direction. This was a man dressed in black, with curly dark hair. Ruthie only saw him clearly for a brief second, but she was sure this must be Stan from Sarah's photographs. She feared him more than anyone, and so with a new burst of speed she turned, angling her flight to take her away from both pursuers.

Once again she attempted to command her own timeband, and this time it responded to her thought. Sound and motion returned around her, and she was running at full speed down a Washington city street as curious onlookers watched her. Well, Ruthie thought, if they were surprised to see a woman suddenly appear from nowhere, this will give them something else to wonder about. She commanded the timeband to shift her a full century into the past.

Chapter 12

Still running at full speed, Ruthie found that the surface beneath her feet changed suddenly from hard concrete to wet, slippery mud. Her feet flew out from beneath her, and she fell, face first, into a rain puddle. She lay there for a long moment in the muck, afraid to get up in case she was still being chased. But she didn't hear anything like running footsteps anywhere near her, and she rose to her elbows, wiping the mud out of her eyes.

A chicken was walking nearby, bobbing its head up and down as it regarded Ruthie through one disgruntled eye.

Despite her recent scare, Ruthie could not help but laugh at the comical sight. She took a reading on the current time and date, and found that it was April 17, 1843, at 8:12 P.M. local time. Slowly she got to her feet and wiped the worst of the mud off her dress and face. Her brand new wig, which had not helped in the least to hide her from her enemies, was a total ruin, and Ruthie pulled it off of her head and threw it away. Brushing out her own long hair with her fingers, she took a look around.

She was on the outskirts of the city of Washington, not nearly as large a metropolis as it would be in the twentieth century. In the distance she could see the white marble buildings of government — no dome yet on the U.S. Capitol; that had not yet been added. Beyond that, she could discern the more familiar outline of the White House. But here, perhaps a mile away, there were small houses surrounded by vegetable patches and fruit orchards. Chickens roamed freely, as well as the occasional cow or sheep.

She wasn't hurt from the fall, though these clothes were a mess. She tucked the revolver safely back in her purse and considered her options. She thought returning to 1942 would probably be a mistake. Ellie and Stan would probably find her if she returned, and that would be bad. Denise would figure out that something had gone wrong when she failed to show up for lunch, and she would head back to the safehouse without her. That was what Ruthie should do, but unfortunately, she was half a continent away. If she shifted all the way back to 1504, when Miles and the others were waiting for her, it could take her months to make it to Wrigley Field on foot, if she made it at all.

Going into the future, when air travel between cities would be commonplace, was also not an option. That would mean going into the era of Nazi control of America, and she did not plan on doing that again if she could help it. No, her best bet was to stay in this era or a similar one and try to make it back to Chicago using the transportation available to her. In 1843 that would be another train ride, probably far less comfortable than the ride in 1942 that took her to Washington. She didn't even know how far west she could take a train in 1843, or how difficult it would be for a woman traveling alone to make the journey. And she realized glumly, all the money she was carrying probably wouldn't pass in this era. She didn't even think the United States used greenbacks in the 1840's — she seemed to recall that didn't start until the Civil War — and she doubted that anyone would believe that the bills she was carrying were real United States legal tender.

While she was standing there in the mud, weighing her unhappy options, a woman came out of the nearest house and called to her. "Goodness gracious, child, are you all right?" She was a stout woman with gray hair and a white apron, and she stared at Ruthie, the mud covering her, and her unusual clothing. Her skirt length, fashionable in 1942, had seemed conservative to Ruthie by 2007 standards, but here in 1843 it must seem quite scandalous. Ruthie opened her mouth to try to explain to the woman what she was doing there, but she found that nothing came out; she had no conceivable explanation to give.

"Come in, come in the house," the woman urged her, not waiting for any explanation. "You can't stand there, soaked to the skin. You'll catch a chill and die of fever."

"Thank you," Ruthie said. "I must look frightful. I was hurrying, you see, and I guess I slipped in your mud puddle, and..."

"Yes, yes, I can see that. Come inside. Wouldn't want the neighbors to see you out here, dressed like that. What sort of a costume is that?"

"That's — sort of hard to explain." The woman led Ruthie into the house, which had a small parlor near the front door with a large fire already in the fireplace. She didn't seem particularly interested in Ruthie's attempt at explanations, though, which suited Ruthie well, since she didn't have one handy.

"Edward, heat some water for me," the woman called to her husband. "We've got a poor girl here covered with mud. I'm Harriet Cole, by the way."

"Pleased to meet you, ma'am," Ruthie said, trying to sound polite. She needed to give her name now, but there didn't seem any need to disguise her identity in this distant era. "I'm Ruthie — Ruthie McDonald."

Edward Cole, a white-haired man in his sixties, came into the room. "Harriet, what's the — oh, my. Aren't you a mess?"

"Don't just stand there, Edward. Heat up some water so Miss McDonald can get cleaned up properly. Come with me, dear. Let me find something you can change into while Edward gets you some hot water."

Mrs. Cole took Ruthie upstairs to a spare bedroom, and she found an old nightgown for her and some blankets to wrap herself in. "You really don't have to do this for me," Ruthie protested.

"Nonsense. It's no trouble, and you can't go wandering the streets of Washington City covered in mud. Get yourself cleaned up, then come downstairs and have a cup of hot tea."

In a few minutes Mr. Cole had a basin of warm water for Ruthie to clean her face and hair, and soon she was back downstairs to join the Coles in the parlor by the fire. She had to admit that the hot tea tasted good, especially after the sudden plunge into muddy water, and she started feeling drowsy in the warmth of the firelight.

"Where do you live, dear?" Mrs. Cole asked.

"Me? Oh, sort of far away. I'm kind of passing through." Ruthie thought it sounded like a very clumsy lie, but she had nothing better prepared.

"Is there anyone in the city we can send word to, who can come to get you? It's dark outside now, and I wouldn't want you to travel anywhere unescorted."

"No, no one," Ruthie admitted. "I'll be all right on my own. Don't worry about me."

"Hush, dear," Mrs. Cole insisted. "No good Christian would turn a poor girl out of their house on a night like this. But I am confused about what you were doing here, and where you might be going in those clothes."

Ruthie saw Mr. Cole lean over and whisper something in his wife's ear, and Mrs. Cole just shook her head sadly in response. They probably think I'm some sort of streetwalker, Ruthie thought. Or worse, a madwoman. They'd really think that if I tried to tell them the whole truth. *Well, you see, Mr. and Mrs. Cole, I'm a time traveler from a hundred and fifty years in your future. If I could just be on my way, I'll pop back to my own century.*

But of course she couldn't say that, so she just smiled instead and thanked them again for their hospitality. It seemed that the Coles realized that no useful answers were forthcoming from Ruthie, so they decided to stop prying and leave her be. She noticed them from time to time looking at her timeband with curiosity, but they asked no questions about it.

Feeling comfortable and safe in the warm blankets by the fire, sipping on the hot tea, Ruthie's eyes began to shut, and she caught herself nodding. Mrs. Cole noticed this as well, and she suggested that Ruthie go up to the spare bedroom and get some sleep. "You are more than welcome to spend the night," Mrs. Cole insisted. "Tomorrow we can figure out where you belong, and we'll try to get you there."

Not likely, Ruthie thought as she sleepily climbed the stairs. But the offer of a warm bed sounded very good to her right then and there. By her internal clock it was still only late afternoon, time jumps notwithstanding, but being chased by Ellie and Stan had exhausted her, not to mention the stress of the mission and this unexpected detour, so she accepted the Coles' offer gratefully. She climbed into the soft bed and fell asleep almost at once, promising herself as she did so that she would not worry about her travel plans until tomorrow.

She was awakened some time later by Mrs. Cole's voice. "Ruth? Wake up, dear. Your uncle is here for you."

"Uncle?" Ruthie was confused. "I don't have an —"

A dark silhouette of a man entered the room, followed by Harriet Cole, holding a candle close to her face. Ruthie heard the man say, "You're safe now, Ruthie. I've come for you."

As Mrs. Cole moved closer, the candlelight illuminated the man's face. Ruthie felt the prick of a needle in her shoulder just as she recognized the stranger as the renegade leader of the Others, Caesar.

Then blackness took her, and the world went away for a while.

When she awoke again, Ruthie was alone in a small room. She was still dressed in the nightdress borrowed from Mrs. Cole and covered in her blankets, but nothing else in the room suggested the nineteenth century. She was lying on a cot that seemed to be nothing more than bright orange nylon fabric stretched over a metal frame. There were no windows in the room, nothing but dull beige-painted walls and a tile floor of the same color. No other furniture could be seen, but attached to the wall opposite the cot there was a flat-screen television. Above it was the slightest indication of a camera lens set into the wall. Other than that, the room was entirely bare.

Instead of a normal door, there was an indentation in one wall that suggested a sliding door that would open up and slide into a pocket in the adjacent wall. There was no knob or any control on this side, and Ruthie didn't think it would conveniently open as she approached it, like on *Star Trek*. No, everything about her surroundings suggested that she was a prisoner locked in a cell.

Almost by reflex, she checked the readouts in her head to find out what year this was, sure it was no longer 1843. The readouts were gone. Her worst fears were realized when she looked at her arm. They had taken the timeband.

Ruthie felt sick with panic. Without the timeband, she was stranded in an unknown era, probably separated by centuries from Miles. She desperately wished he was here, or any of her new family. This was worse than what had happened that day of the reality wave, when she lost her home and family, the world she knew. Because on that day she got a new home and a new family, as well as a remarkable new power, but today she was all alone in the hands of her enemies, and all her power was gone.

The television switched on. The face on the screen was Caesar's, looking like someone's pleasant grandfather sitting behind a large oaken desk. "Good afternoon, Miss McDonald," he said. "I see you're awake. Did you sleep well?"

Ruthie didn't say anything.

"No nasty aftereffect from the sedative? There shouldn't be, but not everyone reacts the same way to the drug. I'm sorry it was necessary to sedate you like that, but I doubted that the farmhouse was the best place for long explanations involving the mechanics of time travel, and we didn't think you would have gone willingly with us otherwise."

"I want my timeband back."

"And we have every intention of giving it back to you. We're not going to keep you a prisoner, Ruthie. But it is important that you hear what we have to say, and that's why we've gone to these lengths to make sure you hear it. After we're done, the timeband is yours again and you're free to do as you wish with it."

Caesar's voice was mellow and soothing. He didn't sound like a raving madman, the way Ruthie had half-expected from Sarah's description. He sounded quite rational, but Ruthie was not about to fall for his tricks. She stayed silent, waiting for Caesar to continue.

"If you're fully recovered from the effect of the drug, Ruthie, come out and join us. There's a change of clothing for you in the next room, and if you follow the hallway you'll find where we're assembled waiting for you. Come join us." The door slid open.

Ruthie got up from the cot, the tile floor cold against her bare feet. The next room looked much like the first one, except this one had no television or camera. Instead of a cot, this room had a single table, made of what looked like a hard plastic. Folded neatly on the table was a blouse, skirt, underwear, socks, and shoes, all in a style would have been common in 2007. Deciding that if she was going to meet her captors, she would prefer to be fully dressed when she did so, she took off the nightdress and tried on the clothes. Of course they fit perfectly; she would have been surprised if they hadn't.

Once she was dressed, she approached the door in the wall opposite to where she had entered. This door did slide open automatically, sensing her approach. Beyond it was a short hallway which led into a well-lit larger room.

The room looked well-furnished, with plenty of comfortable furniture in soft, muted colors. There was a soft carpet on the floor, and the walls were wood-paneled. At one end of the room was the large oaken desk Ruthie had seen on the television; by another wall was a well-stocked bar. Caesar stood from behind the desk when Ruthie entered the room. Seated around the room on couches, watching her arrive but not getting to their feet, were the four other people from Sarah's briefing: Ellie, Stan, Harvey, and the unnamed young black woman. All wore timebands.

"Greetings, Ruthie McDonald," Caesar said warmly. He approached her and extended his hand. Ruthie looked at it but decided not to shake it. Caesar barely noticed the slight and continued to gesture with the extended hand, indicating the entire room. "Welcome to 2088. This is my team: Ellie and Stan, whom you met earlier, in a manner of speaking. And this gentleman is Harvey, and this is Tonya. You may call me Caesar."

Three of them nodded in greeting to her from where they sat, but Ellie stood up and walked over to Ruthie. "A pleasure to meet you in synch at last, Ruthie. I've viewed your past image, recently, but it's nice to be able to meet in a way that you can actually see me and talk to me." Ruthie thought she detected a slight French accent in Ellie's speech.

Ruthie was sure she didn't like the idea of these people traveling to a time she had visited and spying on the afterimages of her time there. But she did understand that this was one of the basic properties of time travel, and there was nothing she could do about it. "You saw me in Chicago in 1941, I presume," she said, her voice cold.

"And Washington some months later," Ellie replied, a smile on her lips. Ellie's hair was no longer chestnut, as it had been when she had chased Ruthie; now it was blonde and cut short. "You did well there. We were impressed."

Ruthie couldn't tell if the woman was being sarcastic or not. She stood there glaring at Ellie, refusing to respond.

"Please, my dear Ruthie, have a seat," Caesar implored. "Make yourself comfortable. Would you like something to drink? Some juice, or coffee, or something stronger if you like?"

Ruthie didn't want anything from them, but the sedative had left her with an uncomfortably dry throat. "Water, please. Just water."

Tonya, sitting closest to the bar, got up to pour a glass of water from a pitcher. Ruthie sat down on an unoccupied couch as Tonya brought her the water. "You didn't kill me when you had the chance," Ruthie said, "so I suppose the water's not poisoned."

"Kill you?" Caesar said with mild surprise. "No, we wouldn't do that. No matter what Sarah and her assistants might have told you. You're our guest, Ruthie. Listen to what we have to say, and then you get the timeband back. What happens after that is up to you."

"Where am I?" Ruthie asked. The water felt good on her dry throat.

"You're on an island in the South Pacific, which I named Lemuria. Otherwise uncharted. The year, as I said, is 2088. Our location is sufficiently remote that we've been able to withstand practically any reality wave without adverse effect. Even the most recent one. Harvey, give Miss McDonald her trophy, if you would."

Harvey had been sitting on a far couch, with what looked like a futuristic laptop propped up in front of him. He had been so entirely absorbed in what he had been doing that he barely looked up when Ruthie first entered. Now he pressed a key, and a thin sheet of paper slowly ejected out of one side of the device. He got up and passed the page over to Ruthie.

It was a facsimile of the front page of *The New York Times* from May 7, 1942. The headline read, "FDR SIGNS WAR RESOLUTION; US DECLARES WAR ON NAZI GERMANY." Ruthie had to squint to read the article itself, since the page had been reduced from its actual size, but it appeared that her meetings with the senators, which she thought had failed, had instead bore fruit. Hearings in the Senate had turned popular sentiment in favor of joining the war in Europe, and a hastily-written declaration of war was passed by Congress and signed by President Roosevelt. "This started a reality wave?" Ruthie asked.

"Oh, yes," Harvey reported. "I'm still gathering archival records from the past hundred and forty-six years, but the course of future history has definitely changed. There are a few slight discrepancies, but it appears the timeline has been kicked back into Variation Six. Germany loses World War Two, the Allies are triumphant, and so on and so forth. Not bad for your first try, Ruthie."

Caesar clapped his hands in applause, and the other four joined in moments later. Ruthie was startled by this sudden and strange acknowledgment from her captors.

"I don't get it," she said. "You people set off the reality wave that caused the Nazis to conquer America, and now you're cheering me because I set it right?"

Caesar sat beside Ruthie. "You're suffering under terrible misapprehensions. We didn't cause the previous reality wave. You've been lied to, again and again, by Sarah and her operatives. They want you to believe we're the bad guys. We're not."

"Really." Her voice was cold; she didn't believe a word of it.

"It's true, Ruthie," Ellie said. "They want you to believe that we're a bunch of lunatics bent on destroying the world. But it's the other way around. We're the ones who are trying to save it."

"From whom?"

"Carlos," Caesar said firmly. "It's Carlos who has these insane dreams of a planet wiped clean of what he calls the human vermin."

"Funny. Sarah said almost the same thing about you."

Caesar chuckled. "I'm sure she did. One of us is obviously lying to you. I need to convince you that it's her. Will you listen to my tale?"

"I don't see that I have any choice."

"Again, you're our guest, not our prisoner. If you insist, I'll give you back your timeband this minute and send you back to America to rejoin your so-called friends, but you may never have this opportunity again to hear the entire and complete truth from us. Ten minutes is all I ask, Ruthie. After that, you are free to make up your own mind whom to trust."

The plaintive tone in Caesar's voice took Ruthie by surprise. It sounded as if he were begging for her to grant him a favor, when it still seemed to her that she was in their power, not the other way around. It made her feel a little braver and more in control. "All right, ten minutes. Caesar. The meter's running."

"First, you've probably been told that Carlos and I were once partners in time exploration," Caesar said, rising to his feet and absently pacing a bit. "That much was true. We were friends for many years, and together we traveled up and down the timelines, testing our theories of the evolution of human societies by making small changes at pivotal moments, and charting the results. In the course of our explorations, we discovered the whereabouts — and whenabouts — of the other ten timebands, and we recruited assistants to use them to help us in our researches.

"As we grew older, I observed signs of psychological instability in my friend Carlos. The psychosis progressed slowly, and for some time I thought I would be able to stop him from hurting himself or others by my presence and intervention. But I hadn't reckoned on Sarah.

"Sarah was our brightest pupil and leading assistant. She also became Carlos's lover and ultimately his wife. Sarah, I realized too late, was as ill as Carlos was, only in a different way. Sarah worshipped Carlos and fed his insanity, telling him that his twisted view of the world was in fact correct. Together they tried to impose Carlos's insane theories of the undesirability of the human race onto the timeline, and then she lied to myself and the others on our team about what they were doing. When I tried to stop them, she turned Carlos against me. She ordered the assassination of myself and others whom I trusted. Some of my associates were killed and their timebands taken, and only Stan and I escaped alive. Sarah and Carlos gathered a new team around them, operatives who were taken in by Sarah's lies.

"As I understand it, Carlos's mind continued to deteriorate. Eventually he became completely incoherent, a raving lunatic. Sarah had to hide him from the rest of the team; otherwise no one would be left to follow them. Sarah is still trying to follow the mad plans laid by her insane mentor, and those of us whom you see here are still trying to stop her, as best we can."

Caesar stopped talking, and the room fell silent. Finally he said, "I still have some time left on my ten minutes, Ruthie. What else do you need to know?"

Her mind was rejecting what Caesar had told her. It had to be a lie! "What's Variation Seven?" she asked, not knowing where else to start.

"There are eighteen known Variations that the timeline can follow between the years 1471 and 2290," Caesar stated with certainty. "I've visited them all. Only one ends in the extinction of humanity — the rest continue into the twenty-fourth century and beyond. That Variation, which Carlos and Sarah are determined to achieve, is Variation Seven."

"If that's true," Ruthie said hesitantly, "do the others know? Ben and Denise and Jason — and Miles?"

"We don't know," Caesar said. "Maybe they do, maybe they don't. It's possible that each has been fooled by the same lies that you have so far believed. Possibly one or more of them knows the true nature of things, and sides with Carlos anyway. We have no way of knowing for sure. But since you are the newest addition to their group, we thought that you might be the easiest to help see the light. You've been exposed to Sarah's lies for the least amount of time."

"You expect me to believe that everything I've come to believe in recent weeks is a lie?" Ruthie said. "And you don't even have anything to prove your story? I'm just supposed to take you at your word?"

"Of course not, Ruthie. Show her, Ellie."

Ellie opened a drawer in a nearby table and took something out. "Put your arm out," she commanded. Ruthie did so without thinking, and Ellie snapped a timeband on her arm.

It was her timeband — Ruthie knew that without asking, for at once the device started making the familiar cybernetic connections with her nervous system, much more quickly than the first time she had put it on. Within a few moments the timeband was fully operational, putting data directly into her brain. Ruthie found the readout that gave her the date and time: September 8, 2088, at 2:15 P.M. local time.

"Shall I slave her timeband to mine and take her there?" Ellie asked Caesar.

"No. Let her go on her own. She'll be back. Ruthie, your destination is seven weeks ago. July 20 of this year, at 9:45 A.M. Jump back there and see what happened on that day. You'll be out of synch with other Travelers, so you won't be able to affect events, but you'll be able to see and hear what took place in this room."

"What will I see?" Ruthie asked.

"I think it will be self-explanatory. But if you're not interested in learning more of the truth, take the timeband and jump anywhen you want. No one here will stop you. My ten minutes are up."

Ruthie thought about this for a moment, then commanded the timeband to take her to the exact date and time that Caesar had given her. The room now looked exactly as it had a moment earlier, though now sunlight was entering the room through a different window at a different angle. She was now alone in the room, but everything else about her surroundings seemed the same.

One of the doors to the room slid open, and two men entered. The first was Caesar, wearing a different suit of clothes but looking no different than he had in what was just moments ago to

Ruthie. And the second man — Ruthie's heart skipped a beat when she saw who it was.

It was Jack.

Neither man could see Ruthie. This was to be expected, since Ruthie was out of synch with them, coming from seven weeks into their subjective future. A future that Jack would not live to see, since from his point-of-view, this was taking place only days before his death. The two men were talking, continuing a conversation that had started in the hallway.

"Then you're convinced?" Caesar was saying.

"I am now," Jack replied in his tough Brooklyn cop voice. Ruthie couldn't help remembering the last time she had seen him, dying in her arms after the bomb blast. "You've convinced me. Sarah's a danger that has to be stopped."

"I'm glad to hear that, my friend." Caesar offered his hand to Jack, and Jack shook it. "Do you know how you'll proceed?"

"Carefully. If Sarah suspects in the slightest that I'm on to her, she'll have me killed. I don't doubt that at all. When the time is right, I'll approach my partner, Miles, and explain it all to him. Miles is a good man. I'm sure he's not mixed up in this. The others — well, I'm not sure about them."

Ruthie wanted to leap for joy when she heard Jack say he didn't think Miles was part of the conspiracy to destroy the human race. How could he be? But if Jack thought Sarah needed to be stopped, then it must be true. Caesar must have been telling the truth.

"You're a good man, too, Mr. Bruno," Caesar was saying. "Talk to your friend Miles. Convince him to join us. Eventually we'll help all those that Sarah and Carlos have duped to reject them, and we can keep Variation Seven from ever happening."

Ruthie had heard enough. She gave the timeband a command, and instantly she had returned to be in synch with Caesar and the others, minutes after she had left them. She didn't even realize she was crying until Caesar offered her a tissue.

"Was that proof enough for you?" Caesar asked her gently.

"I don't understand," Ruthie said. "The bomb that killed Jack — the reality wave minutes later —"

"As I tried to tell you before, those were not of our doing." Caesar put his hands on Ruthie's shoulders and looked into her reddened eyes as he spoke. "We didn't set off any bomb in Chicago in 2007. The person who did wasn't trying to kill Ron Klausson, or any other inhabitant of that era. The target was Jack Bruno. Jack was silenced because he had agreed to help us. The attack was coordinated with a change in a key linchpin, decades earlier, to create a reality wave that would wipe clean any trace of the crime. This was done by one or more of the members of your own team. Believe it, Ruthie. It's the truth."

She did believe it now, and, sobbing, she buried her head on Caesar's shoulder. The old man held her as if he were her own grandfather. It was a long time before she could regain control of herself, but Caesar let her cry as long as she needed to.

Ruthie and Caesar talked for hours, late into the night. Already Ruthie had begun to think that this old man was the most remarkable person she had ever met in her life. Sarah had told her that the man called Caesar was dangerously insane, a threat to the entire future of the human race, but now that she had met the actual person, Ruthie understood how far from the truth that had to be. Of course this could all be an act, and Caesar might be an evil genius who was pretending to be pure of heart, but Ruthie didn't think so. Caesar seemed to be the genuine article — a kind, caring man who was worthy of the respect and love that his team obviously felt for him. He let Ruthie ask questions, which he answered fully and without evasion. And he wanted to know about Ruthie, but he would not invade her privacy. He deliberately refused to ask her questions about the other members of Sarah's team, or their plans.

"I know you don't wish to betray your friends," Caesar said as they ate sandwiches and drank iced tea. "I will not ask you to. But there is much I'd like to know about you, Ruthie. About your life before you put on the timeband. I know very little about your past, and I'd like to get to know you. Tell me as much or as little as you wish; I understand if there are many things that you are reluctant to share."

There were many things that Ruthie usually didn't share with so new an acquaintance, but over the course of the evening, Ruthie found herself opening up and telling Caesar things that few individuals knew about her. About growing up with an alcoholic mother and an absent father. About her lack of success as an actress and her series of low-paying jobs to make ends meet between auditions. And finally, she told him about meeting Jack and Miles, the terrible day when Jack died and she became a Traveler, her difficult training sessions before being accepted on Sarah's team, and falling in love with Miles.

Caesar listened patiently, nodding with sympathy at the details of Ruthie's life. The more she talked, the more she found herself trusting Caesar fully. But at the same time, a small voice inside was warning her not to trust him, that no one was to be trusted. Ruthie didn't want to listen to this voice. She had to trust someone, and at this particular moment, there seemed to be no one more worthy of her trust than this white-bearded gentleman who had drugged and kidnapped her just hours before.

The next morning, Ruthie awoke in the comfortable bedroom they had given her. She dressed quickly and walked through the large, sprawling house looking for Caesar or his team. But the house was nearly empty, and it took her several minutes before she found the only resident still on the premises. Harvey was in the same wood-paneled room that they had been in yesterday, still working on his computer. "I think everyone's on the beach," he said, looking up briefly from the screen. Ruthie guessed that whatever Harvey was doing, he found it more interesting than working on a tan. She thanked Harvey and headed for the front door.

Once outside, Ruthie found that she was indeed in a tropical paradise. There was a brilliant sun in a cloudless sky, a sky just as blue as the vast ocean that stretched out beyond the green line of trees that surrounded a small lagoon. Caesar was in the water, swimming the width of the lagoon from side to side, and Ellie was in a beach chair, sipping on a cool drink. When she saw Ruthie, Ellie waved to her to come join her on the vacant chair next to her, and she poured Ruthie a drink from the pitcher on a small table.

There was a warm breeze blowing in from the ocean, and Ruthie slipped off her shoes and let her toes feel the hot beach sand between them.

"Where's Stan and Tonya?" she asked.

"On a mission. They left last night, but they should be back soon. Please join me, Ruthie. A beautiful day, no?"

Ruthie nodded and seated herself next to Ellie. The glass that Ellie offered her was mango juice, sticky sweet but delicious.

As Ruthie sipped the juice, Ellie said, "I hear that you and Caesar had a chance to talk last night."

"Yes. He seems like a very nice man. Not at all what I expected."

"You expected some kind of a monster, with blood dripping from his fangs? No. That is not our Caesar. In my career, I have met some very bad men, and some very good men. I think I'm somewhat of an expert on the subject. Caesar is the very best — the most sincere, the most noble, the most courageous man I have ever known. I would walk through fire for him."

"Oh." For an instant, Ruthie thought she understood exactly what Ellie meant. There was something about Caesar's quiet, gentle manner that could inspire such devotion in his followers, and Ruthie found herself longing to be allowed to become one of them. But if she did, that would mean turning her back on Sarah and her team, and that included Miles. Could she do that? Ruthie wanted to trust Miles, but how well did she really know him? And Ben and Denise and Jason — she had become fond of them all, but if Caesar was right, at least one of them killed Jack, and they might all be willingly helping Sarah's mad plans to end the human race.

"There's still so much I don't understand," Ruthie said. "When you found me in Washington, you took control of my timeband. How? I was taught that was impossible — that no one can link your timeband to theirs without your consent."

Ellie smiled slyly. "We know a few tricks that Sarah's team doesn't know. We've found a way to mask the signal from our timebands so that your timeband thinks it's in the presence of a friendly Traveler, and it will allow another timeband to take command even if you haven't given permission. It's a trick that usually works once and once only. If I tried it again, your timeband's artificial brain will have already figured out the ruse, and it's doubtful it would work again. Luckily no one on Sarah's team has figured out how to do this — or have they?"

"I don't think so. If they have, they haven't shown it to me."

"Well, it's possible they're keeping it a secret from you. But I think it's more likely that they haven't figured out how to do it yet. What else are you wondering about?"

"I jumped a hundred years into the past," Ruthie said, "and your team found me easily. When I got lost once during training, it took Sarah's whole team to scour the centuries to find me. How did you find me so fast?"

"Well, it wasn't that easy to find you, but it still was a simpler matter for us than it would have been for Sarah's operatives. Some of us can track through time. If you know just how to look, you can see the disturbances in space-time that's left after a Traveler travels. A few of us are skilled enough to track someone all the way to their destination in time. Think of it as seeing the wake of a boat in the water and knowing where the boat has gone from it. Your jump back to 1843 left ripples in time that some of us could still sense. Stan is very good as it, though, and he followed you immediately. He was only out of synch with you by a few seconds when you slipped in the mud."

Ruthie thought about this, but one question still nagged her. "Why are you telling me all this? If these are things you've managed to keep secret from Sarah, aren't you afraid that I'm going to reveal everything I've learned when I go back to her team? Because I have to go back, you know." Even as she said it, she realized that she might be making a terrible mistake. What if these Travelers, so recently her enemy, had no intention of allowing her to return to Sarah's team — to Miles? What if they intended to keep her prisoner here or, worse, kill her? What if the only reason why Ellie was revealing so much was because she knew that Ruthie would never have the opportunity to bring what she's learned to Sarah?

Ruthie's mind rejected these thoughts as unlikely possibilities. Caesar, Ellie, and the rest had only shown kindness to her. She was being treated as a guest, not a prisoner.

Ellie guessed what Ruthie was thinking. "Don't worry. Caesar told us not to keep any secrets from you. When you go back to Sarah's hideout, wherever it is, you can tell her whatever you want. But I'm guessing that you won't be so eager to to blab to her everything you've learned. By the time you leave her, I think you'll understand who really is your friend, and who isn't."

Ruthie knew that Ellie was right. While she wasn't ready yet to change sides, she had already come to believe that nothing was as black and white as it had seemed when Sarah had spelled out the situation to her. These people were no danger to her, and she found herself more and more unwilling to do anything to harm her new friends.

"Tell me something else," Ruthie said. "A few weeks ago, when I was in Chicago in 1941, there was another Traveler there. I turned invisible on a street corner on Michigan Avenue because some other Traveler had been there first. That was one of your team, wasn't it?"

"I think that was probably me. We had hoped to contact you in Chicago, but we never were able to get exactly in synch with you before you left abruptly."

"How did you know we would be there? And in Washington, the following March? Who was the leak in our organization?"

Ellie smiled. "That's the one thing I'm not allowed to tell you. You'll know who it is eventually, of course, but for that person's safety, we have to keep his or her identity a secret for now. Suffice it to say that one other member of your team has already switched loyalties, and leave it at that."

Ruthie was taken aback. "You don't trust me?"

"I feel sure I can trust you, Ruthie," Caesar said, stepping onto the beach. As he approached the two women, he took a towel from a pile on the beach sand and began drying himself off. "Yes, I heard the last part of your conversation, and forgive me for eavesdropping. I do trust you, Ruthie. But I'm not certain that's good enough to gamble another person's life on. For now, all you need to remember is that someone else on your team has already decided to help us. And at least one other person is willingly helping Sarah, and killed Jack. The rest — hopefully they can still be convinced to join us. But who's who — that's for you to discover."

Suddenly there was a roaring noise from the far end of the island, a sound that startled Ruthie but did not seem to surprise Ellie or Caesar at all. Ruthie turned to see a large winged craft, unlike any that she had ever seen before, slowly lowering itself to the ground upon the fiery jets from four downturned rocket engines. The massive flying machine disappeared behind the house before making its landing.

"What's that?" Ruthie asked.

"That," Caesar said, "is Stan and Tonya returning from the mission I sent them on. Come on in the house. Let's hear their report."

Chapter 13

Back once again in the wood-paneled room that seemed to serve as the central meeting place of Caesar's team, Ruthie seated herself on a couch next to Ellie as Tonya and Stan entered. Both of them were wearing some kind of futuristic flight suit, olive green in color and tailored to fit very close to the body, and each carried a full helmet with a tinted plexiglass visor. Ruthie noted that no one seemed to object to her being present at this debriefing; it was like everyone had already accepted Ruthie as part of their team — a status that took weeks to achieve on Sarah's team.

"Was Stan piloting that — whatever it was that we saw land?" Ruthie asked Ellie.

Ellie shook her head. "Tonya's the pilot on our team. Stan was the passenger."

Stan took a seat closest to where Caesar was sitting, and Tonya found a seat further in the back. "What did you learn?" Caesar asked Stan without preamble.

"As we expected, Sarah's agents showed up in 1942 Washington at the time and place of Ruthie's disappearance. This was less than six hours, subjective, from when we encountered her and she jumped back to 1843. We were only fourteen hours futureward of them."

"A very fast response on their part. Which agents responded?"

"Foote and Terwilliger met Han on the scene. The three of them began a systematic search of the years pastward from Ruthie's disappearance. We checked the time of Ruthie's arrival in 1843, but our opponents missed finding her there. So far, they have not witnessed her 'abduction' by you, nor do they realize that Ruthie is now our guest. I watched them up to the point where they abandoned the search and left the scene, presumably to return to their own headquarters. Tonya and I left then, to report back to you."

Ruthie was filled with joy that Miles was one of the team members who had searched for her. She wanted to ask Stan if Miles had broken off the search first, or if he had insisted in vain that they continue looking for her. In her imagination, Ruthie saw Miles pleading with Jason and Denise to keeping looking, but the others were the ones who convinced him it was hopeless.

Caesar nodded and smiled. "Good work, Stan, Tonya. Go get some sleep. I won't need you for the rest of the day." Ruthie realized that while she was sleeping, Stan and Tonya had been working, flying from the Pacific to Washington and back, and watching the afterimages of the search party that Sarah had sent to look for her.

The elderly team leader turned to Ruthie. "So, Ruthie, we're fairly certain that your teammates have no idea where you've disappeared to, and the secret of this location is still safe. The choice is now yours. You are welcome to stay with us. We can always use an extra hand, and the fact that you already have been trained to use a timeband is an extra plus. Join us, and help us counter the mad plans of Carlos and Sarah. But if you feel you must, you are free to return to your friends who work for Sarah. No one will try to convince you not to go, and Tonya will fly you to wherever you need to go."

Ruthie thought about Caesar's offer. It was very tempting — now that she had met them, she found that she liked the gentleman called Caesar and the people who worked for him, and to live and work on this tropical island would be as close to paradise as she could imagine. But there was no doubt in her mind what her answer had to be. "Caesar, believe me, nothing would make me happier than to stay here and work with you. You've all been wonderful to me, and I can't believe that any of you might be lying to me about what Sarah's trying to achieve with Variation Seven. But I do have to go back. As you said, I do have friends on that team, people who I care about and who care for me. I have to sort out whom I should trust. I have to see Miles again — even if Sarah has lied to me, I can't believe that Miles is a party to it. Besides, if I stay here, Sarah will continue to send out her agents looking for me, and eventually they might find me — and you. I can't risk them discovering the secret location of this island. I do need to go back — but in time, I may return."

"Exactly as I expected you to say," Caesar said. "Please enjoy our hospitality for another day, and I'll have Tonya fly you back to America tomorrow."

Their transportation to and from this remote island was a craft unlike any Ruthie had ever seen before. It bore some resemblance to a jet airplane, but the wings were designed to fold up into the long fuselage that ended in a elongated tapering nose. Huge engines under the wings were able to pivot to different angles, like a jump jet, and one more massive engine was located in the tail of the craft. This, Ruthie learned, was what a single-stage-to-orbit space plane looked like in 2088.

Tonya would be the pilot for the trip from the South Pacific to Chicago, which would take less than an hour. Ellie was coming along for the ride. Ruthie had gotten to know the two women well in the last two days, and she found it hard to believe she had ever thought of either of them as the enemy.

Tonya had spent only the last year of her life as a Traveler. She and Ruthie found, to their mutual delight, that they were not only from the same timeline, but born in the same year, 1980. Tonya was born in Detroit and had been recruited by Caesar while she had been serving in the U.S. Army as a helicopter pilot. Caesar needed to fill a vacancy on his team, and Tonya thought that traveling through time was a much better proposition than serving in Iraq, especially after Caesar explained to her that her future, if left unaltered, included being blown up when an insurgent's rocket would strike her helicopter in the next few days.

Ellie had come from a far different timeline, having been part of Caesar's team for over fifteen subjective years. In the history of the world as Ellie had known it, North America had never been successfully colonized by Great Britain; Jamestown had been one of several failed attempts during the sixteenth and seventeenth centuries. Instead, America became a hodgepodge of colonies of various European countries, each achieving independence singly. There was no United States of America, but in its place were many different nation-states. Ellie had been born in 1829 in the Republic of New France, in an area that Ruthie would have called Indiana. She had been a skilled intelligence agent for the Prince's Guard in the First Texas War when she unexpectedly came into possession of a timeband. Not long afterward, Caesar encountered her and offered her a job on his team.

Ruthie had asked Tonya and Ellie to take her back to the downtown Chicago of 2088, and then she would make her own way alone back to the safehouse. Though Ruthie had come to believe that Ellie and Tonya were not the enemy, she still thought it best not to disclose the exact location of Wrigley Field to them. It was a very dangerous game she would be playing now, trying to decide whom to trust and whom to beware. If she betrayed the team's secret location to the opposition now, she might be endangering the lives of those who might actually be her friends.

"Everyone strapped in tight?" Tonya called from the pilot's chair. The small cabin could seat as many as ten if needed, but the two passengers on this flight sat up at the front, directly behind Tonya. Both Ruthie and Ellie wore the same olive-green jump suit as Tonya, which Ruthie was told functioned as an emergency pressure suit in the event that the cabin pressure was lost. Ruthie wondered if Tonya was going to start a countdown, but she only said, "Here we go!" The powerful engines beneath them came to life, pushing the space plane up into the air about twenty feet, where it hovered in midair for several seconds. Then the engines tilted back, sending the craft barreling forward at high speed. Tonya brought the nose of the craft up, ignited the huge main engine in the tail, and launched them up toward Earth orbit. Ruthie felt squashed under the weight of an invisible giant as she sank back into the foam of the passenger couch.

Just when she felt she was about to scream from the incredible acceleration, the pressure stopped. Tonya had cut the engines off, and Ruthie felt the sensation of weightlessness. Through the cabin window, she could see the blue Pacific stretched out below her, the curve of the Earth's surface plainly visible. "Quite a ride, isn't it?" Tonya beamed, her voice giddy over the headphones. "I'll be firing the retrorockets in about ten minutes for our descent to Chicago, so until then, enjoy the zero-G."

Ellie had already unbuckled her own restraints and had floated up from her couch. Ruthie did the same, and she joined Ellie at the cabin window. "Beautiful," Ruthie said. It was the only word she could think to say; no other words seemed sufficient to describe what she saw. Ellie nodded in agreement. Though she had seen this particular view of the Earth on many earlier occasions, it was obvious that she marveled at it as well, and would every time she came up here.

"Stomach okay?" Ellie asked.

"So far." For the earliest astronauts, zero gravity was something that few could endure without vomiting, but by 2088 medication had been discovered that cured that problem, for the most part. Ruthie had taken her pill before boarding.

"Remember, I expect to see you at the rendezvous point, seven days from now. You know when and where to meet?"

"October first, 1930, at noon," Ruthie said. She wouldn't easily forget that date; it was her birthday, minus fifty years. "At the Water Tower in Chicago." The Water Tower was the only structure to survive Chicago's Great Fire. Even if another reality wave struck in the next seven days, the Water Tower would probably still be standing.

"Be there. And bring your boyfriend. He's cute."

"Miles?" Ruthie hadn't told them any details about her relationship with Miles. But she realized that Ellie had spied on them, out of synch and invisible to them, during their visit to 1941. Ruthie wondered how much she'd seen.

Ellie must have guessed what Ruthie was thinking. "Relax, I'm no peeping Tom. But I saw enough to know there's something going on between you two. So bring him along. We'll swing him over to our side. Jack had planned to do just that, but someone got to him first."

"I know," Ruthie said, remembering hearing what Jack had told Caesar. "I hope this all works out — so many things can go wrong."

"Back to your acceleration couches, ladies," Tonya called from up front. "Time to begin our descent to Chicago."

It was still called O'Hare International Airport, but now it was a true spaceport, sprawling across what had once been several suburbs west of Chicago. The space plane made a fiery descent high over the upper Midwest, spiraled down from extreme altitude to kill its velocity, then settled gently to the surface in the exact center of its landing grid, a picture-perfect landing.

As they exited the spacecraft and entered the terminal, Ruthie was exposed for the first time to what life was like in what she considered to be the future. Everything looked new and strange to her. All around her in the airport corridors were animated advertisements that seemed to be little more that a cacophony of light, sound, and color, and what she supposed to be music in this era sounded to her to be little more than weird rhythmic noise.

Fashions were strange — they seemed ugly to her eyes, and in some cases even immodest.

Ruthie noticed, with a little bit of relief, that even Ellie and Tonya were on unfamiliar ground here. The last reality wave had come through while they were all on the island, so no one had really experienced this particular version of history and its consequences yet. But Harvey had researched it as carefully as he could over the computer networks during the last forty-eight hours, and they had all been briefed on what to expect. Ruthie listened to Ellie and Tonya compare notes on what differences they noticed from other versions of 2088 that had experienced earlier. She gathered that, as far as the two women could tell, the world had reverted back to something close to, but not exactly the same as, what it had been before the reality wave that had caused the Nazis to win World War Two. This was the future that Ruthie's world was heading toward, had history not been abruptly changed.

They took a ground shuttle to what was still called the Chicago Loop, and after a six-minute ride at bullet-train speeds, they began to say their good-byes on the subway platform. Ruthie had become quite fond of Ellie and Tonya during the past two days. Perhaps it was because, in this strange new life, she had very few friends, and of those she really didn't know whom she could still trust. She needed friends, and she needed the friendship of Ellie and Tonya. She was so happy that they had accepted her as a friend, and they wanted her to join their group.

But now she was going back to her other friends, some of whom she knew she could no longer trust. She was scared, and she wouldn't be doing it at all except for the fact that Miles was there. She had to get back to Miles, tell her everything she had learned, and hope he would tell her that she had done the right thing.

Several hours later (or almost six centuries earlier), a weary and footsore Ruthie arrived at the front gate of Wrigley Field. It was now almost three days, subjective time, since she had gone missing from 1942 Washington. Ruthie knew that her team had known almost at once that she had gone missing; no doubt as soon as Denise realized that she was gone, she had jumped ahead in time and managed to get fast transportation from Washington to Chicago, then jumped back to report Ruthie's disappearance.

Ruthie had made the hike from the future site of downtown Chicago to the safehouse alone for the first time. The last time she had made this trip with Miles and Ben, and they had shown her the various trail markings they had made in the trees, rocks, and other features to help them find their way back. Ruthie had little difficulty following the trail now, and as she hiked, she made up in her mind exactly how much she should tell Sarah and the others about where she had been during this time.

She decided it was best to stay as close to the truth as possible. She would tell them about encountering Ellie and Stan on the street in Washington (leaving out the fact that Ellie took control of her timeband; if they didn't know that was possible yet, it was best they didn't learn now). Ruthie would tell how she escaped by jumping back to 1843. She'd even include how she fell in the mud puddle — the incident was embarrassing, but that was what would help make it believable. She was taken in by Mr. and Mrs. Cole, and she spent the night in their house. Then the next day, after investigating the futility of trying to arrange transportation to Chicago in that time-period, she jumped ahead to the late twenty-first century and eventually took a sub-orbital commercial flight to Chicago. She would leave out entirely being drugged by Caesar and the two days she spent in the South Pacific.

When she told this story to Sarah and the others, no one expressed any doubts at all about its truth. All of them, especially Miles, were simply glad to see her back. "We had begun to give up hope of seeing you again," he said, nearly crushing her in his embrace. All of them greeted Ruthie just as warmly, and it hurt Ruthie to think that some of them were actually deceitful killers, and she didn't know who was sincere and who wasn't.

She was surprised that Sarah didn't seem incredulous about the tale that she told, but apparently Sarah accepted the events as reported by Ruthie at face value. "Your mission to 1942 seems to have succeeded," Sarah explained. "You started a chain of events that led to the U.S. entering the war in Europe, and the postwar conquest of America by Germany was avoided."

"I was on a field trip to 2025 when the reality wave came through," Ben reported. "You couldn't believe the changes that brought about. I'll be analyzing the data for weeks!"

An impromptu celebration broke out in the safehouse, and Ben and Denise uncorked some champagne bottles to toast the return of the prodigal. After an hour or so of happy partying, Ruthie whispered into Miles's ear, "I need to see you alone."

"Now?" He expected that she would want to be alone with him, but the party was still going on.

"Right now. Let's sneak out."

Ruthie led Miles out of the common room. Some of the other team members noticed they were leaving but made no comment, no doubt figuring that the couple wanted to spend some time together in private. She took Miles out the front door, and Miles looked puzzled but didn't object when she led him through the front gate in the outer wall and out into the woods. But he looked even more puzzled when she asked to take control of his timeband, and then jumped with him thirty years into the past.

"Brrr! It's cold!" Miles said, reacting to the several inches of snow on the ground.

"Sorry." She jumped them ahead to a more temperate season. "Is that better?"

"Much. What's going on?"

"I know we've got cameras and microphones and motion detectors in the woods. I'm hoping we're far enough back so they're not in place yet."

"They shouldn't be. Tell me why we're here."

She told him. Everything. She told him about her stay on Caesar's island. About jumping back to hear what Jack had said to Caesar. She left nothing out, and then she waited for his reaction.

Miles stared at her in silence, then paced away from her, running his fingers through his hair in agitation. He turned back toward her, glaring at her in silence.

"Miles?" Ruthie said nervously. "Say something. Please. Your silence is worse than anything you might say to me."

"How do you expect me to believe this?" he said at last. "For the past eight years of my life I've been waging war on Caesar and his followers. Everything I've done during that time has been undone by them. And I've tried to undo everything that they've done, every chance I could get. Now you're telling me we should be on the same side?"

"I know it's hard…"

"Hard? Ruthie, it's impossible!"

Ruthie was taken aback by the vehemence of Miles's position. She hadn't known how long it might take to convince

Miles to change sides, but she had hoped that eventually he would join her in helping Caesar, once he had heard that Sarah had been lying to them. She hadn't expected Miles to be so firmly opposed to what she was trying to tell him.

But she had to convince him. If she couldn't, she would truly be lost, trapped amongst her enemies. "Miles, listen to me. Jack understood Sarah is wrong. I heard him say it. He said he would try to convince you. He didn't live to get a chance to do that. He would have tried. That morning at Jack's memorial service, I said I wanted to continue to wear his timeband so I could carry on his work, and save the world if I could. Now I know that Sarah was who he was trying to save the world from. That's what I need to do, and I'm going to need your help."

"Ruthie, think of what you are asking," Miles said. "You want me to betray our friends…"

"One of your 'friends' killed Jack."

"You don't know that! How can you be so sure that they weren't lying to you? They would tell you anything to get you to switch sides."

"They didn't need to get me to switch sides," Ruthie said, her voice level. "I was their prisoner; they could have killed me easily enough and taken my timeband. The fact that they didn't proves something."

"Not much. They wanted you more than just for your timeband. You have information they want — the location of our safehouse, for one thing."

"Relax," Ruthie said. "I didn't tell them that. They may already know it; someone else on our team is already giving them information. But even if they were simply lying to me to get me to switch my allegiance, how do you explain what I heard Jack say?"

"I don't know. Maybe it wasn't Jack. Maybe it was one of them made up to look like Jack. Maybe they drugged you or hypnotized you so that you thought you saw Jack. They're very clever. They're masters of deceit."

Ruthie walked up closer to Miles and took his hands in hers. "Miles, you have to trust me. I wasn't deceived. It was Jack. I heard him say that he was turning against Sarah and he wanted you to turn against her, too. I know it's a lot to ask you all of a sudden. All I need from you now is to keep an open mind. Someone is lying to us

— it might be Sarah, it might be Caesar and his crowd. We'll find the proof that we need, and then we'll know what to do. All right?"

She kissed him, and after a moment's hesitation he put his arms around her and returned the kiss. She wanted to believe that everything was all right now, but she knew it probably wasn't. In fact, everything was even more confused than ever. How would she ever know whom to trust, and whom to beware?

Life within the safehouse compound returned to normal — if living in a twenty-first-century mansion tucked behind walls in an unexplored sixteenth-century prairie wilderness could be called normal. But Ruthie had decided, to her surprise, that she did consider this life normal now for her, comfortable and familiar, and yet she also knew that it was also a lie.

Ruthie resumed her martial arts workouts with Jason, studied alternate timeline history with Ben, and practiced using the timeband with Denise. Even though she was no longer considered a trainee, Ruthie had asked to continue the lessons to increase her value to the team. But she had an ulterior motive: the training gave her the opportunity to continue to watch her teammates close up, and try to figure out where each one's true loyalties lay.

Jason seemed to be her early candidate for the person who executed the bomb attack that killed Jack. He had both the skill and the temperament for the job; she knew that he had assassinated historical figures in the past in order to force the timeline into a new Variation. Would he have dared to do the same to his own teammate? Ruthie had not been very fond of Jason; he had always seemed like a bitter, self-absorbed man who carried a lot of anger bottled up inside him. And yet — her antipathy toward Jason hardly constituted proof of his guilt. She would need for more proof before she could be sure that he had placed the bomb to kill Jack.

She suspected either Ben or Denise of being the person leaking information to Caesar's team. Perhaps they were working together; that didn't seem unlikely. Ruthie had become fond of both of them as a result of traveling to the twentieth century with each of them, and she especially couldn't believe that either could have anything to do with the bomb attack. She hoped that one or both would turn out to be her secret ally, but she had as little proof of that as she had of Jason's guilt.

And Miles — Miles had unfortunately grown cold toward her since her confession in the woods. Ruthie could only imagine that Miles was sizing up their teammates in his own mind, and possibly reaching the same conclusions. But he refused to speak to her about it, or about hardly anything else, for that matter. As before, he spent a great deal of time talking in private to Sarah — and Ruthie couldn't even begin to imagine what those talks were about, or what Miles was thinking while he was conferring with her.

The nighttime drills continued, every other night or so. These made Ruthie especially nervous — everyone running around in the dim light with loaded weapons, the perfect situation for a tragic "accident" to happen. Ruthie always felt a sigh of relief when the normal lighting came back up and everyone put the weapons down. So far each drill had run as planned, with no one getting accidentally shot in the dark, but Ruthie couldn't help thinking that if the wrong person learned that she had been speaking to Caesar, she might not live through the next drill.

Five days after Ruthie's return, Sarah summoned the entire team into the commons room. "I have a new mission for the team," she announced. "Since it involves the entire team, I'll present it to you all at once, instead of speaking to you individually. Ben, will you give us the background?"

The young man opened his notebook and flipped pages until he found what he was looking for. "I believe I've identified the primary linchpin between Variation Six and Variation Seven. It comes sometime around 2024, when two major competing ideologies clash with each other in the United States and other industrialized nations. If we can intervene at precisely the right moment, we can tip the scales toward Variation Seven."

"I've consulted with Carlos as well," Sarah said, which took everyone by surprise. "He agrees. Basically, the major conflict of the twenty-first century will be the struggle for supremacy between the pro-technology and pro-environmental movements. Carlos mapped this course of history out decades ago, and his researches show that in order for Variation Seven to be achieved, the forces promoting the rise of a global technological society have to come out on top."

Ruthie looked at Ben, to see if he agreed. Ben looked noncommittal. "If that's what Carlos says, I'm not going to disagree," he said. "Carlos has always been right on the money in the past. Anyway, I've made a few quick trips into that time-period during the last few days to get some idea of where the timeline is headed now. The Green movement continues to spread from Europe to America during the first two decades of the century, and after 2020 it becomes a major political issue in the U.S. In the Third World, disease and famine continue to worsen, putting great stress on established political and economic structures on three continents. Then the entire globe goes through a crisis in financial markets, and what results are flashpoints for war and revolution in a dozen or more places around the world."

"So what do we do, Sarah?" Miles asked.

"For now, we need to continue to collect data. All six of us will relocate to that time-period, working in three teams of two. Denise and Ben, we need you to measure the aftereffects in the linchpin's future, so your assignment is 2029, five years after the moment of maximum stress. Jason and I will take 2019, five years prior to the linchpin, to collect baseline data leading up to the event. Miles, the 2024 assignment will be similar to what you and Jack were doing in 2007, so I want you and Ruthie to collect data during the days closest to the linchpin itself.

"This is going to be a recon in force," she continued. "We will probably stay on station for several weeks, if not months, so find yourself some long-term housing and get settled in. I'm going to set up a rendezvous schedule that we will adhere to strictly. Every seventy-two hours, we meet back here at the safehouse to review our findings. No one takes any overt action that might affect the timeline until we've discussed it thoroughly and I've had a chance to clear it with Carlos. Tomorrow, the entire team will get indoctrination briefings on the destination years led by Ben, and then we'll jump to start the mission as soon as possible after that. Any questions?"

There weren't any, not yet, and the team members went back to their quarters to start getting together what they would take on the mission. Ruthie was just relieved to have been assigned to work with Miles, and she said as much to him as soon as they were alone.

"Sarah wouldn't separate us, not for a period of possibly months," Miles said. "Denise and Ben got to be assigned together as well, you notice."

"Do you believe what she said — about Carlos predicting that we would need to shift the timeline at this particular linchpin to save the world?"

"I take it you don't."

Ruthie didn't answer aloud. She wasn't sure if this room was free of listening devices — perhaps it wasn't bugged, but she still thought it was wise not to speak her treason aloud. "I don't know," was all she said. "I suppose that's what we'll be finding out."

"Look, Ruthie," Miles said, "this is what we do. I know it all still seems so very far-fetched, that six ordinary people can affect the fate of the human race, but when you think about it, how could it be otherwise? The timebands give us the power to see beyond the horizon, to know what's coming up, and where and when we have to be to stop it. It doesn't take thousands of people to stop the march of history — sometimes it just takes the right person in the right place with a little foreknowledge. In fact, that's usually all it takes."

"No, I get that. Really. I just wish I knew more about Carlos. You've never met him?"

"No."

"And yet you follow his orders blindly?" Ruthie asked. "What's wrong with this picture?"

"Yes, I'll admit that I've wondered about Carlos in the past. Why is he so secretive, why doesn't he show himself? I don't know the answer. But I believe in the work we're doing. I have to believe we're doing some good. Let's go see what's happening in 2024. We can see with our own eyes if mankind's on the right path, or if we need to take some action to set it right."

Ruthie nodded. She wanted to believe that Miles was right, that the team's purpose was to help humanity, not doom it. But she had met Caesar, and Miles hadn't. She found it much easier to believe that kind, thoughtful gentleman than some unseen figure hiding in the shadows.

Chapter 14

Miles and Ruthie arrived in 2024 Chicago on what was for them late the next day. From their indoctrination session earlier that day, they had come to expect a world not much different from what Ruthie remembered from 2007, and not nearly as alien as the Chicago she had glimpsed in 2088. But there would still be some major differences. The country had been through some bad economic times in the twenty-teens, and there was widespread unemployment across most of the United States. Prices also had skyrocketed, and many working people were having a hard time making ends meet.

Also, there had been several years of major petroleum shortages, which meant there were far fewer motor vehicles on the road. In cities like Chicago, most people walked or took bicycles when they could. Some suburbs were in danger of becoming ghost towns, since they were not designed to be lived in by residents who couldn't regularly find gasoline for their cars. Ruthie and Miles visited one such location on their second day in 2024, a suburb thirty miles outside of Chicago called Bolingbrook. They saw street after street with large beautiful homes, but nearly every home was empty. Front yards were overgrown with weeds, and each yard had a "for sale" sign inviting buyers that never came.

"Five years ago, this town had a population of over sixty thousand." Miles told Ruthie, reading a summary he found on the Internet. "Less than a tenth of that live here now. You can't live here if you can't put gas in your car — these suburbs were laid out to be dependent on cars for transportation. Nothing's within walking distance. Once the gasoline supply became unreliable, people quickly moved out."

"What about alternative fuel vehicles?" Ruthie asked.

Miles hunted around the web on his smartphone for information. "They exist, but with the economic hard times, most people can't afford them. For the average person, the best solution was to live close enough to walk to their workplace — if they work, that is — and be able to buy groceries from a market in their neighborhood."

"I'm glad we don't have to get jobs." Money would not be a problem for them. The team had long ago — both in subjective and historical time — set aside a fortune in gold in various Swiss banks, and the accounts had survived despite numerous reality waves which had transformed nearly everything else in Western civilization. Miles and Ruthie could draw from nearly unlimited funds, which meant they would not have to look for work in 2024, unlike many others who lived in that year. Their first priority would be to find a place to live, and then establish a routine where they could monitor the events of the year.

Deciding that the suburbs would not be the best place to situate themselves, they decided to find an apartment in the city of Chicago, someplace where it would be easy to walk to all the necessities of life. Ruthie suggested a neighborhood not far from where she had lived in the years before they met.

"Will we be spending our mornings reading papers in a diner?" Ruthie asked him playfully, as they walked down a city street shortly after their arrival. It was strange — this ought to be one of the busier streets in Chicago, but there were few cars on the road. Many cars were parked on the street, but most looked as if they hadn't been moved in weeks.

"Possibly," Miles said, smiling as he remembered the place where they first met. "As a tribute to Jack if nothing else."

Ruthie hesitated, then brought up the subject she had been avoiding during the time they were in the safehouse together. "I have a meeting tomorrow. In August 1930. I'm going to meet Ellie and Tonya."

Miles nodded. She had already told him this, a week ago in the woods outside the compound, and he remembered.

"I'd like you to come with me," Ruthie continued. "They asked me to bring you — they'd like a chance to try to convince you."

He frowned. "I don't think that's a good idea."

"Why? Are you afraid to find out that you've been wrong all these years?"

"Maybe. Maybe I just want to be able to do my job here, and not have to worry about which side is right and which side is wrong. You see, before I became a Traveler, I was in the military. In the C.S. Air Force we were taught to follow orders, not question them. You're asking me to do something that goes against all my training."

"So you're just going to be a good soldier and let a madman destroy all of humanity?"

"I don't know he's a madman," Miles persisted. "All I do know is that he knows a great deal more about alternate timelines than I do, and if he thinks it's important to jump-start Variation Seven in 2024, I'll do what I can to make it happen."

Ruthie stared at him in wide-eyed anger. "How does that make you any different from those Nazis we saw running the country after the reality wave?"

Miles looked stung. "I'm not a Nazi," he insisted. "All I'm saying is that you take on a huge responsibility when you wear a timeband, and I don't want to make a mistake. Before I disobey Carlos and Sarah I want to be sure — absolutely sure — that following them is wrong. But Ruthie, I want you to do everything you can to prove me wrong. Meet with Ellie and Tonya tomorrow. Let Caesar know what Carlos is having us do. If he can come up with proof that we're on the wrong course, I'll be willing to listen to it. Until then, I'll do what I have to do, but I want you to do what you have to do. Agreed?"

Ruthie was somewhat mollified by this, but she still wished that Miles would have been more willing to join her right away.

They spent the night in a downtown hotel, and in the morning Ruthie headed out to make the jump to 1930. She left Miles in the room watching television, taking notes as he switched from one cable news show to the next. Walking several city blocks to get to the Water Tower, still standing in this time-period, she looked for a secluded alley where she could disappear unobserved. Once she was out of sight of unwelcome observers, she made the jump back eighty-four years to meet Ellie and Tonya.

She appeared on a warm, overcast day in the summer of 1930. She had chosen plain, nondescript clothing that would not look out of place in either 2024 or 1930, so that when she stepped out of the alleyway no one would find her appearance odd. It was exactly noon when she appeared, and she immediately saw Ellie and Tonya waiting for her, on the street corner not far from the structure. However, they were out of synch with her by three minutes, so she was still in their future and invisible to them — and by extension, everyone in range of them. So she stepped back into the alleyway, slid ahead in time three minutes, and returned to the street corner to greet them.

"Told you she'd be here," Tonya said upon seeing Ruthie. The two women embraced Ruthie like long-lost friends.

"Where's Miles?" Ellie asked.

"He wouldn't come," Ruthie explained. "I told him everything, but he's not convinced." Seeing the concern on Ellie's face, Ruthie added, "Miles won't betray me. He needs proof that he's been helping the wrong side, but he'll keep his silence for now. You can trust him."

"You can," Ellie said pointedly. "I can't. Hold on!"

Without warning, Ruthie felt herself shifted through time. Once again, Ellie had taken control of her timeband and given it a psychic command. Ruthie didn't think Ellie would be able to do that a second time, but Ellie accomplished the forced takeover of Ruthie's timeband with apparent ease. In an instant, every motorized vehicle had vanished from the street, replaced by nearly as many horse-drawn carriages — and the smell of horses and their byproducts in the air. A check of the date confirmed what Ruthie had already guessed. Ellie had taken the three of them back to the 1890's — April 27, 1892, to be exact.

"Why did you do that?" Ruthie asked with alarm. She looked around to see if anyone noticed their sudden appearance. Apparently no one did. There was a fail-safe built into the timeband to keep a Traveler from materializing inside a solid object, like a pedestrian, but nothing prevented someone from seeing a Traveler suddenly appear where there had been no one there an instant earlier. However, Ruthie had been told that the chances of this happening were extremely slight. Human brains seem to have trouble processing things like paradoxes in time, and usually people tend not to notice the sudden appearances of Travelers unless it happens right in front of them.

"Did you tell Miles when we were meeting?" Ellie asked.

"Um, yes. But he wouldn't do anything. Really, he wouldn't." Ruthie wondered if everyone involved in this time-traveling business became paranoid

"Look at this, Ruthie," Ellie held up her left arm, letting her shirt cuff fall back from her wrist. The fine mesh of the timeband glinted in the sun. "This is the most powerful device in creation, able to defy the basic physical laws of the universe. There are only twelve of them. Whichever side has more timebands can control the world's history. I'm glad you think your boyfriend is too kindhearted to track us down and kill us for our timebands, but I don't know that for a fact. Until I do, I'm going to make it very hard for him or anyone else to find us. Now just in case he's got a way to track us back to 1892, let's get off the street and out of the open."

Tonya just looked sympathetically at Ruthie, but she didn't dare contradict Ellie. The three women quickly made their way down the street and into a small cafe. Customers looked at them strangely, seeing how they were dressed, but no one made any comment. They sat at a table away from the window, and Ellie ordered coffee and pastries for them.

"We know Sarah has sent the team into the early twenty-first century," Ellie began, after the waiter had taken the order and left. "Tell us what she's planning."

"How did you know that?" Ruthie asked.

"We told you. There's another person on your team leaking information to us. We just need confirmation from you that the information we're getting is accurate. Tell us what you were told, so we can see if it matches what we already know."

With a bit of hesitation, Ruthie went ahead and told Ellie and Tonya everything that Sarah had told them about the new mission. "The year 2024 is supposed to be the linchpin that will create Variation Seven," she concluded.

Tonya nodded, and Ellie said, "That's what Caesar believes as well. Blocking the rise of an eco-friendly worldwide consciousness in the succeeding years will likely bring about Variation Seven. From there, mankind faces a rapid decline due to vanished energy resources, global plague and famine, and rampant regional strife and revolutions. By the end of the century, the remaining global superpowers are on a path that leads to total war and the extinction of the human race. This is what Carlos and Sarah would have you bring about."

"What should I do?" Ruthie asked. Everything Ellie was telling her was only conforming her worst suspicions.

"As long as your task is just to observe and collect data, there's no problem. Keep doing it, and keep reporting to Sarah what she wants to learn. If you don't, she'll get suspicious, so don't hold anything back. As soon as she wants to take any action that might bring about Variation Seven, that's when we've got to act. Luckily since you and Miles are on station in 2024, she may assign you the task of intervening in history there. If she does, tell us first before you do anything. Understood?"

"Yes." Ruthie did not like how complicated this had all become. Now she was taking orders from both sides, unable to tell for sure whom she should be helping. She felt like a pawn in a great game of chess, except that in this game, she couldn't even see where all the pieces were on the board, or even which side each belonged to.

Before they separated to return to their respective time-periods, Ruthie made plans with Ellie and Tonya to meet again at another prearranged moment in time. Ellie made Ruthie promise to keep the details of this rendezvous secret from Miles, and Ruthie agreed. Ruthie watched her two friends vanish into the future before she did the same, jumping ahead to 2024.

Miles didn't ask her how the meeting went, which was just as Ruthie expected. He already knew far more than he wanted to about Ruthie's activities, so when she returned to the hotel room, he talked instead about how his research had gone while she was away. He had taken extensive notes about what he had learned from watching the news channels, and much of it seemed relevant to the supposed upcoming linchpin.

Ruthie kept quiet about what Ellie had told her about the future awaiting the world in Variation Seven. Until she could present some kind of proof to Miles, he would not be convinced by this sort of conjecture. She even briefly considered jumping far into the future herself, as far as the timeband would take her safely, to see if the dystopia that Ellie had described was actually part of this timeline. Perhaps Miles would go with her, and together they could see who was lying and who was telling the truth. But a blind jump into the future like that seemed to have more than its share of risks, and Ruthie thought it would be better to play it safe until she had no other choice. So for now, she decided to continue following the instructions she was given for this mission, and joined Miles in making observations and collecting data, like she was supposed to.

Two days later, they returned to the safehouse in 1504 for their scheduled rendezvous with the rest of the team. Everyone seemed genuinely happy to see each other again, even though it had only been three days since they had gone off to their separate assignments, and they spent quite a few minutes chatting away about what they had seen and what they had done in the intervening time before Sarah finally asked them to quiet down and get to business. Only Ruthie seemed more subdued than the rest, still bothered by the knowledge that some of her supposed friends in this group were really the enemy.

For the next two hours, each team reported in turn what they had witnessed in their assigned time-periods. It was remarkable what dramatic changes would take place over a ten-year period in one American city. Sarah and Jason reported on a crisis that was looming on the horizon but hadn't yet struck in full force. Financial markets abroad were in trouble, but the stock market here in America still seemed strong, and the American dollar was doing well in relation to most foreign currency. But worldwide production of oil was failing to keep up with demand, and Americans found they had to deal with not only a rapid increase in gas prices, but also the occasional gas shortages. Yet in 2019, most people tried to cling to their old patterns of gasoline consumption.

Five years later, Miles and Ruthie could see America in the grip of a true crisis. The unemployment figures had hit their highest marks in decades, and the uncertainty whether gasoline could be found to be bought at any price had begun to lead to widespread changes in the way people were living. The suburbs were hit hardest of all, since people could not afford to live in areas where the necessities of life were not to be found within walking distance of their homes. But more than just personal means of travel was affected. Interstate trucking of goods became extremely difficult, and many goods, once available everywhere, became scarce in various regions of the country. A black market was flourishing, as a wide variety of items soon became available only if you were willing to pay exorbitant prices for them.

By 2029, Ben and Denise were seeing a very different America from the one that the other teams were observing. There was great civil unrest everywhere, as the dwindling supply of goods and resources came under the control of a variety of criminal organizations, which varied in size from street gangs to crime families to illegal private armies. Traditional police and other law enforcement agencies could only maintain control in areas where strict martial law was enforced, usually in municipalities where some strongman had managed to seize and hold power. Both the Democratic and Republican parties had ceased to exist as effective political organizations, as established political entities splintered into newer, more radical factions, usually occupying the extremes of the political spectrum.

Strangely, though, even as the civilized society slid farther into anarchy, technology by 2029 had continued to make incredible advances. The information revolution of the 1990's and early 2000's had not slowed at all as the century approached its fourth decade. Instant communication and access to information was freely available to everyone on the planet. The processors that ran computers had been shrunk to a size that could fit inside practically any object, at a cost of practically zero to the consumer, so every citizen of the world was now part of a worldwide wireless network, and no one was ever alone again. Whether this did anything to mitigate the suffering as civilization collapsed was debatable; perhaps it only made it worse. For one thing, it did make the global political situation more volatile; a new movement could arise in some corner of the world and spread across the globe in days, or even hours, only to be supplanted almost immediately by the next shift of the ideological winds.

"It seems clear to me," Ben said. "The country that Denise and I are seeing is already past its tipping point. If change must take place, it has to happen earlier. Perhaps in 2024, perhaps earlier than that."

Everyone around the briefing table nodded. The mood in the room, once festive when the team was first reunited, had now turned solemn and sober as Ben and Denise finished their report.

"Agreed," Sarah said. "But we're still far from being able to reach a decision on what is to be done. Each team is to continue to gather relevant data. We'll meet again in three days to discuss what new information you've uncovered."

The meeting concluded, the six teammates spent the next hour saying their good-byes to one another, as friends always do when they know they have to separate but would rather not. Sarah and Jason vanished first, returning to their assignment in 2019. Then a new round of good-byes commenced, and it was another twenty minutes before Denise and Ben hugged Ruthie and Miles one last time, and each pair jumped into the future to take up their posts in their assigned years.

Later that night, as Miles was in the bathroom of their hotel room, preparing for bed, Ruthie took the slip of paper out of her jacket pocket that she had found there earlier in the evening. She hadn't looked at it then, though she knew she had not put it there herself. She also didn't know how it got there, but that wasn't a great mystery in a room full of Travelers who could stop time with their timebands. Now that Miles was out of the room, she opened the note and read it.

"*Ruthie, have courage,*" the note read. The handwriting was done in carefully-made block letters, so that any resemblance to the writer's normal handwriting was hidden. "*You are not alone. Sarah and Carlos will not succeed in achieving their mad dreams. When the time comes, I will stand with you to stop them. Be patient, and be ready.*"

Ruthie destroyed the note immediately and did not tell Miles about it. Over the next few days, the two of them settled into their routine. They rented a furnished apartment in a quiet neighborhood, using assumed names, and Ruthie began recording their observations of societal trends that they could report back to the full team. At first it was fun, setting up housekeeping with Miles, and Ruthie spent as much time shopping for items for their apartment and themselves as she did joining Miles in their research.

But she couldn't shake the feeling that this mission was really a fraud, that her true mission should be to expose Sarah and her possible murderous accomplices to Miles and the rest of the group. She tried to explain this to Miles, but he had difficulty agreeing with her.

"So you think Carlos is wrong?" Miles asked her one night, while they were alone in their new apartment. "If we follow his directions and change history, we will actually make things worse for the world?"

"I think so," Ruthie admitted. "How do we know if Carlos is being truthful? We're not even allowed to meet him, for God's sake. Caesar thinks that Carlos is psychotic. What if he is?"

"Ruthie, look at the world outside. Have you seen how bad the world is getting? I had to pay seventy-five dollars this morning to buy a bunch of bananas. That's a nine-dollar banana you'll be putting on your cereal tomorrow morning. Things are going from bad to worse, and it's obvious that someone's going to have to do some major intervention in this timeline to keep the country from descending into chaos."

Ruthie nodded. Miles had a powerful argument, but he hadn't met and talked with Caesar. She had, and she couldn't believe that Caesar was trying to deceive her in any way. "I don't know. Maybe this is just a bad time, but things get better on their own in the future. Maybe if we intervene, things really do get so bad that the world never recovers. We just don't know, and I'm not so sure I can follow orders from Carlos and Sarah any more."

"Are you going to tell Sarah that?"

"No, of course not. If I'm right, I'd be putting my life in danger. So I'll cooperate with the mission, keep on collecting data like I'm supposed to, but eventually, I'm going to have to make a choice and choose sides. And so will you."

"And if we don't choose the same side?"

Ruthie looked at Miles, but she had no answer for that. She didn't want to lose Miles, but could she possibly be a party to the destruction of the human race? That was too big to contemplate, and she fell into an uneasy silence for the rest of the evening. Miles returned to his research, also unwilling to return to this topic of discussion.

Ruthie continued to slip away at regular intervals to meet Ellie and Tonya at prearranged meeting places in the past. She kept them informed of her team's progress, but they could do little to help her except offer her words of encouragement. She always hated to part from them when it was time to go, and every time the thought crossed her mind that she should simply go back with them, defect from Sarah's team once and for all, and let Caesar and his people protect her. But that would probably mean losing Miles for good, and this she could not bear to do.

Chapter 15

"Miles, I'm bored." It was fifteen days into their mission to 2024, about eight in the evening. Miles was at the kitchen table, with two laptop computers in front of him. Ruthie was in the next room, watching on television reruns of a comedy from the 1960's. Even a couple of reality waves hadn't altered *Gilligan's Island.*

"Sorry, did you say something?"

"I said I'm bored!" Ruthie was up now, walking into the kitchen. "I don't know how you can do this, day after day, night after night! When I got this timeband and joined the team, I thought we'd be doing more — changing history, fighting bad guys, whatever. That's what all that training was for, right? I didn't imagine we'd be cooped up in this apartment, surfing the Internet night and day!"

"Sorry, Ruthie. I guess a Traveler's life isn't as glamorous as that. You know most of what we do is studying the timeline, researching where a possible linchpin might be…"

"I know that! I just can't do it twenty-four seven, okay? I need to get out of this apartment, I need to have some fun, or I'm going to go crazy in here!"

Miles looked up at her. "So go out. I'm not stopping you. If you need to get out of the apartment, by all means, go."

"Come with me, Miles," she begged. "There's a nightclub just a few blocks from here. We'll listen to music, go dancing — it will be fun!"

He smiled. "We'll do it soon. But I can't tonight. I think I've tracked down an important cause-effect cycle in these online journals — I want to get it all put together before tomorrow's briefing with the team. I've got several hours of work ahead of me here. But you go out without me. Please. The last thing I want is for you to go stir crazy while I'm trying to work."

Ruthie really wanted Miles to go out with her that night, but she realized she was fighting a losing battle. When Miles started concentrating on a task, he could shut out all distractions and work on that one thing for hours. That ability to focus and persevere was a facet of his personality that she loved about him, and Ruthie would not want to see Miles change just to please her. So while she couldn't stand the thought of another evening spent looking at blogs and news sites, she knew that if she was going out on the town that night, she was going alone.

She changed into one of her favorite dresses, told Miles she wouldn't be too late, and left the apartment.

It was raining that evening. As Ruthie was walking the seven blocks that took her to a section of the neighborhood with some of her favorite night spots, a bus splashed her with water from a puddle in the street while she was waiting at the curb for the light to change. She was drenched, and her dress was spotted with big blotches of wet mud here and there. This, however, was no problem for a Traveler. She jumped back half a minute to just before the incident, and then stepped back from the curb. Once again the bus roared through the puddle, but this time Ruthie was far enough away from the spray of water. She had become accustomed to doing small edits to her life almost automatically, and she hardly gave the incident another thought as she continued on to the nightclub.

There was a live band that night, playing a type of music that Ruthie wasn't familiar with. Compared to the rock music she had grown up with, this version of it sounded tuneless and repetitious — mostly nonsense syllables repeated over and over to the beat of the bass and drums. The keyboard player was playing something that wasn't quite in the same key as the guitarists, and the dissonance seemed jarring to Ruthie's ears. Yet the crowd that night seemed to enjoy the sound the band was making — you couldn't quite call it music — and after a few hours of this, Ruthie just got used to it.

It was disconcerting to think that her tastes in music were now two decades out of date. Ruthie wasn't that old — actually she was about the same age as most of the other patrons of the club — but she felt like she belonged to a different generation. Maybe this is how people of her mother's generation thought about the music she listened to when she was growing up.

She had a couple of glasses of wine, something she almost never did. Ruthie had seen what drinking had done to her mother, and she never wanted to end up like that. Alcoholism ran in her family, and she'd seen enough of it to know that it was something she did not plan to fall victim to. Yet she was feeling down enough to want a second glass of wine tonight, though she told herself it would be her last one before she left.

Coming here was a bad idea, she admitted to herself. She had thought that a night on the town would cheer her up, but she felt more depressed than ever. The sight of crowds of people, all having a good time, only made her feel even more sorry for herself. She felt trapped, doing monotonous tasks in a city of strangers, following the orders of someone who might just be the most dangerous person in history.

This was not the life she had hoped for when she had joined the team and had been allowed to keep the timeband! At least there was Miles. Ruthie had never known anyone like Miles, and she had come to depend on his quiet strength and unshakeable calm. And Miles loved her as well, which made it all the more wonderful. That should be enough, shouldn't it? Why should she find herself hoping for more?

Lost as she was in her own dark thoughts, she almost didn't hear the voice beside her ask, "Can I buy you a drink?" She turned her head and saw a tall, blonde-haired guy with tattoos on his arm.

"No, thanks," she replied. She held up the wine glass in her hand, still almost full. "This is my limit tonight."

"Nice bracelet," he said.

This confused her, because she wasn't wearing any bracelets. Then Ruthie realized he must mean the timeband. It was usually nearly invisible on her arm, but in this light the tiny lights in its mesh were easy to see, flashing almost in time with the music. "Thanks," she said.

"You here alone?"

Ruthie began to feel even more uncomfortable. She understood what this was leading up to, and while under other circumstances she might not mind this person's company, this was not what she was interested in tonight. "Uh-huh. Look, I'm just here tonight to listen to the music. My boyfriend had to work tonight, and…"

"That's okay. I wasn't trying to pick you up or anything." Ruthie didn't believe that for a moment. "What do you think of the band?"

"I — I think they're pretty awful." That was certainly the truth.

"Yeah, so do I. My name's Todd," he said.

"Ruthie."

Long pause, filled by the noise of more nonsense syllables in rhythm from the vocalist. Todd looked toward the dance floor, where a crowd of people was moving in synch to the drummer's insistent beat. "Do you want to, uh, dance?" he asked.

Ruthie shook her head emphatically. "No, not really."

Another pause. "You really do want to be left alone, don't you?" Todd ventured.

"I guess I do," Ruthie agreed.

Todd scanned the crowd, looking for other prospects. "See you around," he said, and wandered off.

What am I doing here? Ruthie wondered. This wasn't what she wanted to be doing. She wanted to be home with Miles, not out clubbing with strangers. Without finishing her drink, she headed for the door and headed for home.

It was just after midnight when Ruthie returned to their apartment building. Climbing the two flights of stairs to their floor, she realized how tired she felt. Maybe it was the two glasses of wine, but she wanted nothing more now than to crawl into bed and stay there until sometime in the next afternoon. She found her keys in her purse and opened the door as quietly as she could, not knowing if Miles had gone to bed yet or not.

But the living room light was still on, so Miles wasn't in bed yet. "Miles?" she called. She could hear the sound of the television from the next room, but Miles didn't answer. Confused, she set her purse on the kitchen counter and continued on into the living room.

The couch was turned away from the entranceway to the kitchen, so Ruthie could see the back of his head — Miles was sitting on the couch, facing the TV, which was showing a broadcast of some old movie from the 1990's. Confused, Ruthie called his name again, and then she simultaneously realized two things.

First, she remembered the reason why Miles would not, could not answer her. Her timeband was trying to tell her that there was a synchronicity deviation of thirty seconds. That was the amount of time Ruthie had jumped back to avoid being splashed by the bus going through the rain puddle. She had never corrected for that small edit, and now she was out of synch with Miles for that amount of time. Even though it was less than a minute, she was still coming from his future, and looking back on his past. This image of Miles was not yet aware that Ruthie had entered the apartment, and neither was the person on the couch with Miles.

For the second thing Ruthie realized was that Miles was not alone. Miles had his arms around another woman, embracing her tightly. As shock and rage overwhelmed Ruthie, the two parted slightly, and Ruthie could see that the other woman was Denise. She was speaking something softly into Miles's ear that Ruthie could not hear, but Ruthie didn't need to hear any of it to understand the situation.

Almost involuntarily, Ruthie slid ahead thirty seconds to get in synch with Miles and Denise. Their positions had not changed significantly in that amount of time, and they both looked up in surprise when she appeared in the room with them, her face already contorted with pain and tears. "Ruthie!" Miles exclaimed. "Wait, I —" he tried to say, but Ruthie wasn't waiting to hear the rest of it. She leaped randomly into the past, trying to get as far away from this sorry situation as she could.

She ended up in June 1857, and she spent the night crying in a stable. The following day she wandered the streets of early Chicago, not caring how strange she looked to the citizens of that town. She felt betrayed, and she wished to have nothing to do with Travelers or missions or anything of any world-saving significance. She wanted to go back to her life before she put on the timeband, but that life was gone for good.

The next night, after the owner of the stable had found her and thrown her out, she spent part of the night huddled in the doorway of a bank building as a cold rain came down. She fell asleep there, but ended up being rudely shaken awake.

"Miss? You can't stay here." Ruthie opened her eyes to see the figure of a man standing over her. He was wearing a constable's badge.

"Sorry," she said. She didn't even bothering worrying about how she must look to this nineteenth-century man, wearing a twenty-first century dress. "I'll go somewhere else." She got up to go.

The constable grabbed her by the arm. "Do you have a home to go to?"

Ruthie admitted she hadn't.

"What's your name?"

"Ruthie McDonald."

"Well, Ruthie McDonald, there are laws in Chicago against vagrancy. Come along with me. I've got a warm bed where you can spend the night — in jail."

The constable led Ruthie to the city jail, where she was asked various questions about address and date of birth that she could not give coherent answers to. Frustrated, they locked her in a jail cell and left her there until the morning.

Ruthie had no intention of staying locked up in any jail. It reminded her too much of the Nazi police station, on her first day with the timeband, when she was nearly brutalized by the thugs wearing police uniforms there.

She sat down on the small cot that was the sole piece of furniture in the cell, which was no more than a cage with iron bars all around. Then she started speeding up the time flow. To her eyes, everything around her started to move at high speed, like a video tape on fast forward. Anyone watching her would have seen her go into slow motion, if she had been moving at all, which she was not. Ruthie just sat on the cot, waiting for someone to open the cell door.

Her chance came about an hour later of real time, which seemed like just minutes to her. A guard opened the cell door to bring her an extra moth-eaten blanket, since the night was getting cold. As soon as the door to the cell was unlocked, Ruthie froze the rate of time-flow at zero. The guard stood frozen as a statue, the blanket in his outstretched hand. She sidestepped around the hand holding the blanket, exited the cell, and walked out of the jail building.

After that she was more careful about where she spent her nights. She still wanted the solitude of the distant past for now, but she didn't want to be taken away to jail, either. But there were always shadowy places to hide in this growing city on the western frontier. The choir loft of a church one night, a box car on a railroad spur the next — it didn't matter to Ruthie. She was feeling miserable, and she just wanted to be left alone for a while.

Several more despondent days passed. By now Ruthie realized that she had not only missed the scheduled briefing with the rest of the team, but she hadn't kept her appointment to see Ellie and Tonya. Both teams of Travelers must be aware of her disappearance now, but she really didn't care. She was hurting, and on a clear night under a full moon, she sat at the edge of Lake Michigan looking out across the water.

The thought occurred to her that she should walk into the lake and not come out again. But as sorry as she felt for herself, she couldn't bring herself to self-destruction. No, she knew what she had really come to the water's edge to do.

She touched the lights on the timeband in a certain sequence, and it popped open. It felt like a part of herself was suddenly lost from her when the device deactivated, and the sudden sense of loss almost made her reconsider what she had resolved to do. But no, she had made up her mind, and now she was going to follow through on what she had planned. Ruthie slipped the timeband from her arm and prepared to heave it into the lake, as far as she could throw.

"Don't do that," a familiar voice said from behind her. "I'd just have to swim after it, and the lake's too cold for swimming."

Ruthie turned, feeling rather foolish. There was Ben, dressed in casual twenty-first century clothes. He stepped down the gravelly shore and sat down beside her.

"Hi," she said. "How did you find me?"

He took the timeband from her and held it in his hands. "I do historical research, remember? I'm working in an age where every piece of information ever in print is part of one gigantic database. Here, take a look."

Ben took a folded piece of paper from his jacket pocket. It was a reproduction of the July 30, 1857 edition of a Chicago newspaper. He had circled in red a news item that was buried near the bottom of the front page. "Mysterious Disappearance from City Jail," read the headline. The story told about how one Ruth McDonald, address unknown, had been arrested for vagrancy and escaped from custody. The local jailers had been reprimanded for their failure to do their duty properly.

"Once I turned this up, it wasn't hard to track you down. Do you mind telling me why you ran off like this? Everyone's worried about you."

"I know. I had to get away. I — I saw something I shouldn't have, and I had to get out there…"

"I know what you saw," Ben said. "Miles told me. So did Denise. If you had stuck around, you would have found out that what you thought you saw wasn't it at all. Nothing's going on between Miles and Denise. Nothing at all."

"Then what…?"

"Denise and I had a fight," he explained. "She got mad at me for something — and I deserved it — and she stormed out of the house and jumped back to find you. You were the one she wanted to talk to, but you weren't home. She was still pretty upset when Miles found her, and he talked to her and tried to comfort her, which is when you popped in on them. Then you jumped into the past before they could explain why she was in his arms."

"That's all?" She knew she should be happy, but she wasn't. Her eyes were still filling up with tears, and she was trying to keep herself from sobbing aloud.

"Hey, what's wrong? I told you, everything's okay. Miles wants you to come back — we all do — is something else the matter?"

"Everything's the matter," Ruthie confessed. She knew she shouldn't say anything more, but she wanted to trust Ben. He had been a good friend to her, and she admired his intelligence and his steady confidence. She was too emotional to hold her tongue now, and she felt she could tell him everything. "I've learned things I shouldn't know. Caesar's not the enemy. Carlos is the one trying to end the human race, not Caesar. Sarah's been lying to us, and Miles doesn't believe me. The person who killed Jack is one of us, and I don't know who…"

The words stuck in Ruthie's throat as she looked in Ben's eyes, and she saw his face turn hard and cold. "You know all that, do you? I'm sorry, Ruthie. Really, I am."

Ruthie got up quickly and backed away from Ben. Suddenly it was all clear to her — who Jack's killer had to be. Ben was the only one who understood the timeline well enough so that he could commit murder, then jump back to set off a reality wave that would erase all traces of the crime. In panic she willed herself back to an earlier time, any time that Ben would not be able to trace her to.

Nothing happened. She looked down at her left arm, but it was bare. Ben still had her timeband.

She started to run. She had been a high school athlete, and she still kept herself in good physical shape, especially now that she had been trained by Jason. She knew she could outrun Ben, who was not very athletic or fit. She ran as fast as she could away from him.

Except it really didn't matter how fast she ran. She covered a distance of about a hundred yards, and then he was right there in front of her, popping back into the normal time flow after walking to catch up to her while she, for him, had been frozen in a single moment of time.

He reached out to grab her, but in her rage she tackled him, knocking him down to the ground. Her timeband fell from his grasp and fluttered with the lake breeze away from them.

Ruthie knew that with a thought, Ben could freeze her in time again and slip away from her. She didn't plan to give him the chance to do that. She smashed her fist hard into his face as they rolled on the ground tangled together. Her fist hurt, but she drew it back and hit him again. This time, her fist passed through empty air. Ben had disappeared again.

"Is this what you want?" he said from several feet away, holding the timeband up like a piece of meat he might tease a dog with. "Come and get it." His face was red and swollen where she had hit him, but he paid no attention to the pain as he tormented her with the timeband he had taken from her.

Ruthie got up on one knee, tired and sore. She knew it would be a futile gesture — there was no way that she could reach him as long as he wore a timeband and she didn't. Yet she lunged at him anyway, stretching out her arms to close on where he was standing.

Once again, he wasn't there — he had stopped the timeflow and walked away while she was held trapped in a single moment of time. But this time he had left something behind with her. She looked down at the sudden sharp pain, and she found a knife between her ribs. Her torn dress was red and drenched with blood around the wound.

"You're really pathetic, do you know that?" Ben said, now regarding her from a little farther away. "Take away your timeband and you're nothing but a sad little waitress. We've been given the power of gods, and all you can think about is whether your boyfriend still wants to hang around with you."

Blood was dripping now down her side, and she was starting to feel faint. She thought she might stand a chance of survival in a modern medical facility, but nothing like that was available here in this nineteenth-century town. She felt her knees get wobbly, unable to hold her weight. Ruthie dropped down to her hands and knees, but still she struggled to stay conscious.

"Why?" she whispered. "Why did you kill Jack?"

"You know why. We were on the verge of achieving Variation Seven. Carlos would have succeeded in stopping the human race from spreading its contagion to the stars, but Jack turned against us. He said he would ruin everything that we hoped to achieve. Carlos ordered his execution — I carried it out."

With a supreme effort born of hate, Ruthie rose back to her feet. Ben laughed at her as she started to stagger across the ten yards that separated them, a knife still protruding from her side. Even though she knew each time she tried to attack him, he would simply freeze time and walk away, she had to make the attempt. She couldn't simply lie down and die. Summoning the last of her strength, she broke into a run.

Ruthie aimed herself at the smug expression on Ben's face. Any second now, she knew, he would appear to vanish, only to reappear again somewhere just out of her reach. He'd keep this up until she blacked out from loss of blood.

But he didn't. His expression changed to one of shock and panic. Somehow, Ruthie realized, Ben wasn't able to control his timeband. He was as powerless as she was. She threw herself on him, and they both crashed to the ground, even as Ben was still struggling to take control of his own timeband. Ruthie grabbed Ben's head with both hands, raised it up and then smashed it down hard on the rocky shoreline.

The side of Ben's head was now bloody where it had hit the rocks, but the blow wasn't sufficient to kill him, or even to knock him out. Ben pushed hard on Ruthie with both hands, shoving her away from him. Ruthie's strength was gone from the exertion and the loss of blood. She could do little more than lie on the ground after that, barely able to stay conscious.

Ben staggered to his feet, still dazed by Ruthie's last attack. He didn't understand why his timeband stopped functioning, but it was time to finish the fight once and for all. There was a heavy rock on the ground, about the size of a football. He grabbed it and lifted it up with both hands. Ruthie lay just a few steps away, unable to defend herself.

With blurry vision, Ruthie could see an object lying on the ground just out of reach. It was her own timeband, right where Ben had dropped it. If only she could crawl the short distance to get to it, she could save herself. But with a cry of anguish she realized she could not even do that — she was too weak to do anything but die here, inches from the one thing that could save her life.

Ben was right over her now, the rock in his hands. "Goodbye, Ruthie," he said, and Ruthie knew in the next instant the rock would come crashing down on her head, and that would be the end of her.

That instant never came.

She saw his head come apart first — a large chunk of his forehead flew away, accompanied by a spray of blood and brains. Then, as the sound from the gunshot arrived a split-second later, she heard the weapon being fired, and then running footsteps. What was left of Ben crashed to the ground, the rock dropping with him and missing Ruthie by inches.

The footsteps stopped as hands reached for her. "Don't move, Ruthie, you're going to be all right," a female voice said. She was seeing to her wound, applying emergency first aid with the skill of a combat medic. Ruthie was a little surprised to recognize the voice as belonging to Ellie.

Another pair of hands was replacing the timeband to her arm — she felt the pleasant prickly feeling as the device resumed its cybernetic connection to her. "I'm linking your timeband to mine," this person said. Ruthie knew at once who he was.

"I'm sorry — so sorry," Ruthie told him, her voice a strangled whisper.

"Don't speak. Everything's all right," Miles said.

Next came the familiar sensation of jumping through time. Ruthie tried to focus on the mental indicators of destination date and time, but unconsciousness took her before she could determine when they were taking her.

Chapter 16

Ruthie awoke in an unfamiliar bed. Her side still hurt, but it was a dull pain, not sharp like it had been just after being stabbed. She felt more dopey than anything — drugged, she guessed. There was an IV drip in her arm, and nearby were electronic monitors keeping track of heartbeat and breathing. Her timeband was on her left arm, as it should be, and she was dressed in a hospital gown. But the room was absolutely quiet, too quiet even for a hospital. "Where am I?" she asked, her voice a ragged croak. She knew when she was — September 23, 2088, at eleven in the morning.

"Someplace safe," a voice, deep but softened with age, said from nearby. Ruthie turned to see Caesar sitting at her bedside.

"Hi," she said weakly. "Am I on your island?"

"That's right. You gave us all quite a scare, but we found you. You're going to be all right. If you're up to it, there's some people who have been waiting to see you."

He walked over to the door, and it slid open. "She's awake now," Caesar said. Miles was through the door first, followed by Ellie, Denise, and Tonya.

"I'm so sorry," Ruthie said, but Miles bent down and kissed her.

"It's forgotten," he said. "All that matters is that you're safe."

"I remember fighting Ben," Ruthie said, trying to piece together what had happened. "Then Ben got shot, and you came, and I must have passed out then. What happened?"

"When you didn't show up to meet Tonya and me," Ellie said, "we decided to go looking for you. We looked for you in 2024, but you weren't there. We did find Miles and Denise, though, who were waiting for you to come back."

"When you had seen us together," Denise interrupted, "I had just found out the truth about Ben — that he was the one who had murdered Jack. I was upset, and I jumped back to warn you and Miles. But you saw us together and misunderstood."

"If you haven't figured it out," Caesar added, "it was Denise who was our other source of information on your team. She was the one who leaked to us the details of your trips to the 1940's."

"I left the note for you, at a time when it looked like you needed some encouragement," she said.

"By this time I was more than convinced that everything you had told me about Sarah and Carlos had been the truth," Miles said. "I'm sorry for having ever doubted you. Ellie showed me how she could track your jump back into the past. That's a clever trick; I'll need to learn how to do that. But you had jumped too far, and it took time for us to pick up enough of the trail to find you in the 1850's. We finally found you while you were fighting Ben. But when we arrived, we were out of synch with the two of you. We could hear what he was saying — we saw him stab you — but we couldn't stop him. We had to jump ahead to get in synch with you, and then it was almost too late."

"I slaved his timeband to mine," Ellie added, "and Miles shot him. Just in time."

"Yes," Ruthie agreed. A sudden thought occurred to her. "If Ben is dead — did you get his timeband?"

"No," Miles admitted. "Our first thought was to take care of you. You were losing a lot of blood by that point, and every second counted. We got you to a hospital emergency room in the twentieth century, and soon as I knew you were out of danger, I jumped back to collect Ben's timeband. Unfortunately, when I arrived, I saw Jason was already there to collect it. We were out of synch, so there was nothing I could do to stop him. He removed Ben's body with the timeband still hanging unlocked on his arm, and then he jumped out of there to some unknown year. I don't know how he arrived on the scene so soon after Ben's death — maybe Ben had left word with him about when you could be found. I don't know. But Ben's timeband is back in Sarah's hands. She and Carlos have four, but we have eight."

"Will Jason stay loyal to Sarah?" Ruthie asked. "Or can he be convinced to join us, too?"

"I don't know. I'd like to talk to him. He's a good man to have on your side. In any event, Sarah's operation is severely crippled. It will be much harder for her to bring about Variation Seven with no one to help her except possibly Jason and whoever wears Ben's timeband. Unless Carlos comes out of hiding."

"He won't," Caesar said. "He can't — he's totally psychotic, beyond hope of recovery."

"So what happens now?" Ruthie asked.

"Now," Miles told her, "you stay put and get better. When you're well enough to get out of that bed, we'll talk about plans for the future."

Ruthie healed quickly, thanks in part to the futuristic medical science available to Caesar's team, and in part to the constant attention given her by her newly united circle of friends. In just a few days she was pronounced fit enough to be on her feet again, as long as she didn't overly exert herself.

By this time Miles and Denise had finished moving their things, along with Ruthie's, into the large island house that Caesar's team used as a base. Miles had even made several trips back to Wrigley Field to recover personal items. This wasn't difficult, since he deliberately chose to appear there at moments when he was out of synch with the remaining residents. He could see past images of both Sarah and Jason as he removed items from the safehouse, but they were unable to perceive him or keep him from completing his tasks.

On the last one of these trips back to their former stronghold, Miles left a note where he knew Jason would find it without Sarah seeing it. It was a request to meet, face to face, at Buckingham Fountain in Chicago at midnight on December 31, 1999. Jason would know, from this choice of a very public venue, that Miles had no intention of ambushing him or trapping him. If Jason showed up, he would know that it would just be for the opportunity to talk, nothing more.

Miles told Ruthie what he had done, and she agreed that it was a good idea. "Except I'm going with you."

"No, you're not."

"Oh, yes, I am. I'm well enough to go, and I'm going. We're partners. When I forgot that, I almost got myself killed. But this way, we'll watch each other's backs. If he wants to start something, he'll have to start it with both of us. It's settled."

Miles found he couldn't argue. Tonya took them back to Chicago in the space plane, and later that day, at a moment that Miles had specified in the note when they would be in synch with

Jason, the two of them jumped back to the last moments of the 1900's.

Jason was standing by the edge of the fountain, dressed in a woolen jacket. He was already in synch with them, and he nodded in acknowledgment as Miles and Ruthie pushed through the New Year's Eve crowd to join him.

"Got your note," he said laconically. "So you've defected to the other side? Both of you?"

"Yes," Miles answered. "Denise as well."

"Thought so. It was awfully lonesome at the last briefing, just Sarah and myself. You know, that was a mean thing to do, killing Ben like that."

Ruthie stepped forward. "Jason, he killed Jack!"

"Yeah," Jason said, fidgeting nervously, as he usually did. "I heard him say that. I saw it all, too, out of synch with you. By the time I was caught up and in synch, everything was all over, and it was just poor Ben lying dead on the ground. I scooped up what was left of him and brought him back to the safehouse for a proper burial."

"We want you to join us, Jason," Miles said, putting his hand on Jason's arm. "Sarah's been lying to us since the beginning. Caesar isn't evil. His team has been trying to save humanity, not destroy it. We need you on our side, not working against us."

"I know. But I don't think there's only two sides to this question. Maybe you're right, maybe Sarah's right — or maybe no one is. Maybe none of us is wise enough to decide what's the right path for history to be set on. After everything that's happened, maybe I don't feel I can support Sarah any more. But I'm not sure I can support you, either."

There was a long pause as no one spoke. Ruthie broke the silence. "Jason, what will you do?"

"Go someplace to think things over. A cabin in the woods somewhere, far from the effects of any reality wave. I may be there for months, maybe years. You'll be hearing from me once I know what to do."

"Are you sure?" Miles asked.

"Yeah. And by the way, Sarah doesn't have Ben's timeband. I never delivered it to her. It's safely hidden in a time and place that only I know about. When the time is right, I'll decide what to do with it. But until then, I'll keep it hidden."

There seemed to be nothing more to say, so Ruthie hugged Jason and kissed him good-bye. Jason and Miles embraced each other like brothers. Then Jason took a step back and prepared to jump to another time. "Say good-bye to Denise for me," he said, then vanished.

Later, after they had returned to the island and 2088, Ruthie and Miles joined the other six members of their new team around a large conference table in Caesar's house. In a way it felt almost like it used to, back in the common room at the old safehouse, the house they would never return to. But it felt different, too, sitting with their former opponents now as one united team. Ruthie wondered if it felt as strange to everyone else as it did to her.

"I think we can take Jason at his word," Miles said after finishing his report about the meeting in Chicago. "Sarah and Carlos only have their own two timebands. Two more are off the board, for now, and we have the other eight."

"Now that we have the advantage of numbers, as well as the secret location of her stronghold," Stan suggested, "I say we take the opportunity to strike at Sarah. We know where and when she lives; let's go get her."

"She won't be there," Miles told him. "Now that the safehouse has been compromised, she'll abandon it. We won't find her that easily, or Carlos either."

"I suggest we stop worrying about Sarah," Caesar said. "She has been used to working through intermediaries for a very long time now. It's been a while since she took it upon herself to interfere personally with the timeline. I doubt if she'll be a factor with whom to concern ourselves for the foreseeable future."

"Then what do you want us to do, Caesar?" Ellie asked.

"Relax. Take a vacation. Find some exotic location, some exciting or restful time-period, and enjoy some time off. You've earned it. The timeline seems stable enough for the next few centuries; mankind will achieve its bright future without any further help from us for now. So take a few weeks and enjoy yourselves. When you come back, we'll get back to work fixing what problems are left in the timeline. But worry about that later — have fun now, while you can."

Ruthie looked to Miles and smiled. She didn't need to be asked twice.

Chapter 17

Ruthie and Miles sat on the deck of the ocean liner, watching the sun set behind the distant city, with the Statue of Liberty in the foreground. They had taken Caesar's advice and taken a vacation, but with the end of this ocean cruise, their vacation was coming to a close, and soon they would need to return to 2088 to get back to their real work, fixing and improving the timeline where it needed it.

"Penny for your thoughts, Mr. Terwilliger," Ruthie said after one particularly long stretch of silence.

"Just thinking. There's a lot of people on this ship who don't realize by rights they should be dead. They should be thankful for a second chance at life, and they don't even know it."

"Did we do the right thing? By changing history, we didn't start another reality wave, or jump the entire timeline into a different Variation, did we?"

"I doubt it. The timeline is a mighty resilient thing. If someone was really supposed to die during this week in 1912, and we managed to keep them from drowning, odds are that when they get off the boat in New York City, they'll be hit by a streetcar or something like that."

"That's horrible!"

Miles laughed. "But, most people's lives don't have any really significant effect on history. It really wouldn't hurt the timeline any for it to let a few hundred or so lives slip through the cracks, and keep living when they should have died. I doubt we'll be reading about over a thousand streetcar accidents in the paper next week."

"Good," Ruthie said. "I'd hate to think we did the wrong thing, when we warned the captain about the iceberg."

"Right. And don't forget the most significant consequence of that action."

"What's that?"

"If we hadn't asked Captain Smith to steer around the iceberg," Miles explained, "then he wouldn't have lived to perform the marriage ceremony at sea. And that would have had a major effect on our own personal futures — correct, Mrs. Terwilliger?"

Ruthie Terwilliger — now that would take some getting used to. "Not quite. You would have found the timeline most resilient in that case, too. I would have simply married you somewhere else instead — no escaping that particular destiny."

"True."

They grew silent once again, watching the sunset. After a while Ruthie spoke again. "Do you think we'll see her again? Sarah, I mean?"

"Not for a long time, I hope. I'm sure she's looking for us, but the world's a big place, especially when you've got to comb through all of modern history as well. A needle in a mighty big haystack. She may figure out where we've been — especially if we keep doing minor fixes in the timeline like this — but it will be hard to get in synch with us and figure out where and when we are."

A thought struck Ruthie. "Do you mean she could be right here with us, out of synch, listening to what we say?"

"Get used to it," Miles said. "As long as we've got timebands, and she's got a timeband, there's nothing we can do about it. She would be coming back from a point in our future, when we've already left, but she'll still be seeing our afterimages, hearing our words." He lifted his teacup and addressed the air. "So, Sarah, if you're here listening to us, here's to you. You gave us a home when we needed one, but we were lucky to get out when we did. Give our regards to your crazy friend Carlos, and leave us the hell alone."

"Amen," Ruthie added.

They became silent again, and some minutes later Ruthie asked, "So what's next?"

Miles looked at her and smiled. "There'll be time to figure that out later. Plenty of time."

They embraced as the last rays of the sun disappeared behind the horizon, and the good ship *Titanic* docked in New York City at last.

Mike Manolakes is an author of science fiction, alternate history, and historical fiction. He is also an American Civil War reenactor, actor, director, and retired classroom teacher. He lives in Illinois with his wife Rae and their dogs and cats.

The Traveler Series by Mike Manolakes

Book 1: *Variation Seven*
Book 2: *Strange Times*
Book 3: *Living in the Future**
Book 4: *Dying in the Past**
Book 5: *Travelers' Tales**
Book 6: *Past and Future Tense**
Book 7: *Future Imperfect**
Book 8: *Final Variation**

*coming soon